# A BROTHER'S PEACE

Sunstone books may be purchased for educational, business, or sales promotional use.
For information please write: Special Markets Department, Sunstone Press,
P.O. Box 2321, Santa Fe, New Mexico 87504-2321.
Printed on acid-free paper
∞
eBook 978-1-61139-683-6

Library of Congress Cataloging-in-Publication Data

Names: Linn, Jan, author.
Title: A brother's peace : a novel of relationships / Jan G. Linn.
Description: Santa Fe : Sunstone Press, [2022] | Summary: "A debut novel by
  a well-known author, teacher, and pastor"-- Provided by publisher.
Identifiers: LCCN 2022038538 | ISBN 9781632933874 (paperback ; acid-free
  paper) | ISBN 9781611396836 (epub)
Subjects: LCSH: Families--Fiction. | LCGFT: Christian fiction. | Novels.
Classification: LCC PS3612.I55464 B76 2022 | DDC 813/.6--dc23/eng/20220920

LC record available at https://lccn.loc.gov/2022038538

WWW.SUNSTONEPRESS.COM
SUNSTONE PRESS / POST OFFICE BOX 2321 / SANTA FE, NM 87504-2321 /USA
(505) 988-4418

# A BROTHER'S PEACE

## *A Novel of Relationships*

## JAN G. LINN

SANTA FE

*In families there are no crimes beyond forgiveness.*
—Pat Conroy, *The Prince of Tides*

# ACKNOWLEDGMENTS

My thanks to Rollie and Becky Bible, Carole Kerl, Mary Linn, Judith Roark, Gay Crawford, Louise and Don Ragland for their insights and encouragement as early readers of the book. Special kudos to Darrell Laurant, journalist and author in his own right, whose sense of story helped me to tighten up the one this book tells.

My close friend, Bill Blackwell, who played an integral role in proofreading and copy editing several of my previous non-fiction books, was the obvious person to whom I turned once again for this, my debut novel. His numerous corrections and suggestions measurably improved the book, and for that I am exceedingly grateful.

Beyond being the love of my life, no words can capture what the support and patience of my wife, Joy, have meant to me during the process of bringing this book to life. Looking back on the number of times she read the same section or entire chapter again and again makes me realize I pushed the limits of her patience further than any sensible person should have. Yet she stayed with it and with me. That says more about who she is than the book, as well as reflecting a devotion she has to helping me write better books than I ever could on my own.

I have known the satisfaction of having a non-fiction book published on more than one occasion, but having a novel published is an experience like no other. The folks at Sunstone Press made it all possible. More than that, the enthusiasm they have shown for the book from the beginning has made this a special experience.

Finally, I am grateful to my parents for their example of the power of unconditional love that transcends and even redeems family struggles, and to my brothers without whom I would have never experienced the mystery of the bond that siblings are privileged to share.

# PREFACE

There is a story about a child-prodigy who was invited to perform a piano solo before a world-renowned pianist began his concert. The nine-year-old played flawlessly and the packed music hall attendees gave him a standing ovation. When the boy came back stage, the master put his hand on his shoulder, smiled at him, and said, "Young man, you play the piano beautifully, and someday you will make music."

That story is a metaphor for my writing life. I have spent years "playing the piano," all of it enjoyable and satisfying, and perhaps on occasion contributing to the field of study in which I was writing. In the end, though, the measure of my writing was competence, as if I were playing the piano. Non-fiction writing normally involves researching a subject and then doing your best to put together a well-reasoned and well-written argument that your reading audience will find credible, informative, and depending on the subject, personally helpful. Sometimes non-fiction writing is beautiful, even inspiring, but it is finally judged by knowledge of the subject and skill in presenting it, not unlike a young pianist being judged by the skill demonstrated in playing "Bach's Prelude No. 1 in C."

Fiction writing allows words to become music as it creates characters born of the writer's imagination, weaving their individual stories into a meta-narrative about human existence in all its wonderful, wild, and weird manifestations. There is nothing like a novel to stir the human spirit as readers see themselves and people they know in the characters they read about and the struggles they encounter. Sometimes the story captivates their minds and steals their hearts.

The imaginative possibilities a novel offers was a driving force during the nearly two years I spent writing *A Brother's Peace*. It is a story about a family not very different from yours or mine. In this instance, it is a family of brothers, but could have just as well been one of sisters. The experiences of the various members of the Strange family may resonate with your own.

It would not be surprising if you find yourself understanding exactly why they say and do what they say and do, especially as each responds to one of them losing his way.

I think the secret of the universal appeal of a novel lies in the fact that it is a fictionalized story arising from real life experiences writers themselves have had or people they know have had. What is more, one of the serendipities novelists experience is when characters they create say or do what could not have been planned or even imagined before they appear in the story. That is the joy of making music with words. You control the story, and at the same time you don't. That happens more than once with and to the Strange family. Yet, what remains constant throughout is their resilience that reflects the interplay of human frailties and strengths that fill their days with laughter and tears, joy and sorrow, despair and hope. In the process their story becomes a mirror into which any of us can look to see ourselves.

Because life is never lived in a vacuum, the Strange family's story includes life in their small North Carolina town that reflects the customs, practices, and prejudices common to life in any southern town of the day. As such, the Strange family not only has to struggle to hold itself together when circumstances are trying to tear them apart, but at different times different members find themselves having to choose which side of history they will be on when the old ways of Castle Cove conflict with changing social and racial realities. In those moments, even as town and family life diverge, they are at the same time inextricably interwoven so that the story of one cannot be told without telling the other.

I loved writing every word you will read in these pages and take great satisfaction in being able to share this family saga with you. Despite the twists and turns, ups and downs weaving through every chapter, from beginning to end I had one simple goal, to tell a story that holds your attention and when you are finished makes you feel like the time it took to read it was worth every minute. I can only hope that will be true for you.

# 1

Griffin Hughes got the reputation for being one of the best orthopedic surgeons in North Carolina the old-fashioned way. He earned it one patient at a time. But the injury he was now trying to fix was testing all the skills he had developed over the last twenty-five years. He thought he had seen every kind of broken bone possible, but this one was by far the worst. The fifteen-year-old son of a friend lay on the operating table with an uncertain future because of a compound fracture of the right fibula and a badly shattered tibia.

It wasn't a matter of life and death. Barring an unexpected infection, Sonny Strange would survive his ordeal. The question in the mind of his family was whether or not he would ever play football again. Griffin's concern was whether he would walk without a permanent impairment.

This was not how Griffin was expecting to spend his weekend. Then Sam Strange, a friend he has known since high school, called and his plans quickly changed.

"Griffin, this is Sam. You told me you were coming to town for a family gathering. Thank God you're still here. I'm so sorry to bother you, but my son, Sonny, broke his leg in a football game just a little while ago and the doctor here at the Castle Cove ER says it's very serious. Can you come and take a look at him?"

There was a pause, then Sam responded, "Thank you, Griffin. You don't know how much I appreciate this. See you in a few minutes."

That's how Griffin ended up where he was, trying to save a boy from limping into manhood. Once he had thoroughly examined Sonny, he emerged from the ER cubicle and walked straight to Sam and his wife, Sarah, who were sitting on a bench in the hallway while their other two sons, Harrison and Sydney, stood nearby. "I'll be honest with you," Griffin told them. "This is a very serious injury, very serious. Two bones in Sonny's right leg are broken, one of which is a compound fracture, meaning the bone has protruded through the skin. I can't tell you much more than that until I get him into surgery, but I can promise you I will do everything I can to get his leg back to normal."

"Do what you need to do, Griffin," Sam said.

More than three hours later Griffin came into the waiting room and sat down across from Sonny's family, his scrub cap in hand.

"Well, the surgery went well. The leg was as bad as I thought it was, but everything came together nicely. I'm afraid Sonny is in for a long recovery."

"What does that mean, specifically?" Sam asked. "Weeks, months?"

"At least a year." His words stunned all four of them. "A lot will depend on him, of course, and how fast his body heals, but in situations like this he could be in a cast for about six months, and then he will need to have a special brace he will wear for probably another six months."

No one responded immediately, then Sam asked, "No football anytime soon, then, is that what you're saying?"

"If at all, Sam. It's possible he will play again, but it is also possible he won't. I'm sorry to be so blunt. He has a good chance he will be able to play, but there's no guarantee. To be honest, it is even possible that Sonny could come through all of this with a slight limp. Right now, though, let's focus on getting him back on his feet. This is going to be as painful as it will be long. It's important for Sonny and all of you to understand that. I'll check back tomorrow and then later in the week. The doctors here will keep me updated on his condition."

"You'll be his doctor, though?" Sam asked, "especially after he gets out of the hospital."

"Yes, of course. As you know, I am not here daily so the docs who are will let me know if anything changes in-between my visits. When he gets home, he will come to my office in Halifax for check-ups."

"Thank you, Griffin," Sarah said to him. "Having you here means everything."

"I'm just glad I was in town and could help, Sarah."

Everything about that day was unusual. The game, the circumstances, the accident itself, the news at the hospital about the extent of Sonny's injury. Sydney had managed to get down onto the field from the stands in the midst of mass confusion. When he saw Sonny lying on the ground completely motionless, he thought he was dead. Later when he told Sonny that was his first thought, Sonny responded that he may as well have been. One minute he was a rising star on the gridiron, potentially the best-ever running back to come out of western North Carolina, according to the Halifax Gazette, the biggest newspaper in Allegheny County. The next minute he was a teenager suffering the worst luck any kid could have, a freak accident that would change the course of his life.

The day had begun in great anticipation that the entire town of Castle Cove was going to see the freshman phenom play against his own high school varsity football team. The Strange name was well known in Castle Cove for several reasons, football exploits being one. Sonny was the middle one of the three brothers. Harrison, the oldest, had been an outstanding wide receiver for Castle Cove in his own right. Tall and muscular like his father, he played a key role in Castle Cove winning back-to-back district championships. Harrison was named to the all-state first team his senior year, which helped him get a scholarship to Greenwich College, a small liberal arts school in eastern Carolina that was a powerhouse in football. Sydney, the youngest, had all the makings of becoming a star quarterback in his own right. Already tall and lanky, he made the freshman team as a seventh grader because of an arm stronger than any upper-class quarterback on the team, but what happened to Sonny would change all those dreams and expectations for him as well as his brother. He later wished for the impossible, that someone would have foreseen the impact that fateful day was going to have and stopped it before it happened.

The shortened junior varsity season of seven games because of North Carolina High School League rules was enough to prove to J. V. coach Sam Hill and varsity coach Bob Saunders that they had someone special in Sonny Strange. They were already anticipating next year when as a sophomore he would be the starting running back for the varsity. Coach Saunders even allowed himself to think about three straight state championships with a talent like that running behind an offensive line that was going to be second to none.

Average size for a fifteen-year-old at five feet nine and a hundred and fifty-five pounds, Sonny looked quite ordinary as a football player until he got the ball in his hands. Speed and toughness are what set him apart from the pack. He could run around most defenders, and when necessary, he would try and usually succeed in running over them. Gifted with natural talents you can't teach, he knew exactly when to slow down or speed up, when to cut or go straight. Sonny had it all. He was fun to watch. The usual small crowds that gathered on Saturday mornings to watch J. V. games played on the varsity practice field had grown large and boisterous because of Sonny Strange. When the whistle blew to end the last game of the season—Sonny had run for a sixty-five-yard touchdown and had his fifth straight hundred yards plus game—the crowd started chanting his name. Then they shocked Coach Hill when they changed their chant to, "We want more, we want more, we want more."

They weren't going to get it, or so it seemed, for at least a year, until Coach Hill pitched the idea to Coach Saunders for a varsity/junior varsity game to cap off the season.

"With Sonny Strange I think we can give you a good game, Bob," Coach Hill said. "And I know the Castle Cove fans would love it. It would add some excitement to the end of an average varsity season by letting them see what is coming next year. I can't see a downside to it at all. Besides, I know you'd like to get an early glimpse of what Sonny can do against varsity level competition."

"You actually think your boys could stay on the field with us?" asked Coach Saunders.

"With Sonny Strange, no doubt about it."

"Okay, I'll run it by Principal Haynes and if he agrees we'll make the announcement together to both teams and then the student body at the next Assembly."

Everybody signed on to the idea. Game on. Within a week every ticket had been sold. It doesn't take a lot to bring excitement to small towns. News of the "big game" was the biggest thing to happen in Castle Cove since a former governor held a campaign event in town ten years earlier. The varsity/junior varsity game was all anybody talked about. Kids were making bets on who was going to win. Sydney decided to bet his bicycle with a guy he knew whose brother played varsity. With Sonny playing Sydney thought the J.V. would win hands down. Once he made the bet, though, he immediately regretted it. Who was he kidding? he thought to himself. Of course, the varsity was going to win. That's why it's the varsity.

As excited as everyone was about the game, Sonny was strangely nonchalant. He could have been accused of being downright uninterested.

"It's just a game, Sydney," he said when Sydney asked him if he was excited to play. "Just a game. Besides, who cares who wins? It's not like it makes any difference. It won't have much effect on who plays varsity next year and who stays on junior varsity."

"But it could become something they do every year." Expressing his unspoken hope that one day he might get to play in a game like that.

"It's out of my hands, Sydney, out of my hands," Sonny said as he mimicked washing his hands.

It didn't matter that Sydney was more excited about the game than Sonny was. Everybody else was, too. Even Harrison said he would come home from Greenwich to attend. On game day the weather was perfect. A little rain on Friday night. Sun shining on Saturday afternoon with cool temperatures around fifty-five degrees. Perfect football weather. The field at City Stadium looked in good shape. The teams went through their warm-up drills with the junior varsity wearing away game jerseys and the varsity wearing home. Sonny looked relaxed, paying no attention to the varsity players as if they weren't even on the field. It was a game to him, nothing else. He would do his best along with every other player and see what happens. Take your licks, give as many as you can, and leave the rest to chance.

Football is a violent game to everybody except the players. To them it is a battle. Winning is the goal, but playing is the heart of the sport. The first hit you take or give is the best one in the game because it unleashes the adrenalin you need to do the job your team is counting on you to do. Violence is the juice players need to keep them going; not mayhem but controlled by rules of fair play. Most fans won't admit it, but they come to see the violence. They don't want to see a flag football game. They are there for the contact. Even to hear it. Because it's a violent game, though, playing against your own teammates is not an easy thing to do. That's what varsity and junior varsity player were, teammates, friends who sat beside each other in class and ate together in the cafeteria. Hitting a teammate is a lot harder than hitting a stranger. You still hit as hard as you can, but you don't want to do anything more than that to somebody you know and like.

That's why when Jamie Sturgis and Josh Landry hit Sonny at the exact same time crushing his right leg, they both had tears in their eyes as they watched him lay on the ground. He was their rival in the game, but off the field he was one of them, one of their own. They were also smart enough to know his potential as a future star, someone who would likely take them to a championship before they graduated. Nobody wants to end someone's career. That's why when they saw the bone sticking out of Sonny's shin, they felt sick. Josh later said he thought he was going to faint.

Coach Hill was on the field before they had hardly gotten to their feet. As soon as he looked at Sonny he yelled, "Call the rescue squad." Kneeling to see the extent of the injury up close he turned his head and this time screamed at the top of his voice, "Somebody call the rescue squad." Sydney had climbed over the railings and was on the field and could see and hear everything. By the time he saw Sonny he was laying on the ground motionless and eerily quiet. He was stunned by what he saw, to the point of having to fight back tears. Coach Saunders arrived and started telling the players, "Nobody needs to see this, guys. Form a circle, get on one knee, join your arms, but try not to look at Sonny."

Sarah and Sam Strange were stunned by what they were witnessing with their son. Sarah had hold of Sam's arm as if she couldn't stand on her own. The sound of the siren became louder and louder as it got closer to the stadium. The rescue squad entered behind the press box, crossed the cinder track and jumped the curb onto the field.

"He's in shock," one EMT said to the other as soon as he got to Sonny. "Cover him with a blanket and get oxygen on him." They wasted no time putting him on the gurney and loading him inside the van.

"Come on, Sydney," his father called out from the bleachers. "We need to get to the hospital."

By the time they walked into the ER Sonny was behind curtains. After what seemed like an eternity a doctor final appeared and came to where they all were sitting.

"Your son needs immediate surgery," said the doctor looking at Sam and Sarah, "I will have the orthopedic surgeon who's on call contacted immediately."

"No, don't do that," Sam answered. "Let me make a call before you call anyone else."

The last thing Griffin Hughes did before leaving the hospital was to talk to Sam and Sarah once more, telling them he was confident Sonny would be fine. Sadly, he was wrong. The trouble started almost immediately when they filled Sonny with doses of morphine for two solid weeks to give him relief from the intense pain he was experiencing. The day Sonny was to be released Griffin examined Sonny and read over his chart, then he asked Sam and Sarah to step outside into the hall. He told them he was concerned that Sonny was becoming dependent on all the morphine they had been giving him. Sam did not react well.

"I don't understand, Griffin," Sam said testily. "How can he be addicted to a drug the hospital's been giving him?"

"I know it's confusing and sounds bad," Griffin answered. "First, Sonny is not addicted to morphine. He is only showing signs that dependency could become a problem. You have to understand, this was a terrible injury. The pain was excruciating for Sonny, forcing us to give him high doses of morphine just to keep him calm. That is almost always not a problem, but Sonny has been asking for more as we have begun to lower his dosage. That's what alerted the nurses to a potential problem. We know his pain levels have declined because he's been sleeping through the night without any problem, something he couldn't do initially. But he keeps asking for morphine when he doesn't need it. It's more a psychological need than a physical one. That's what makes it borderline dependency. At this point there is no chemical dependency involved, which is why we're not talking about an addiction. But we don't want to take any chances, so I've decided to take him off morphine completely and use a non-narcotic pain reliever until he gets used to that. That means keeping him here a few more days. They could be a little rough, but he'll get through it."

"You think that will work?" asked Sarah.

"Yes, I do. Eventually he will get used to not having any morphine in his system. That's when he can go home."

Sonny was in a cast for a full six months as Griffin Hughes said he would be, and then he wore a handmade leather and metal brace for another six months. The metal brace was attached to each side of his shoe and to a leather covering that wrapped around his lower leg from his ankle to just below his knee with laces in the front. He didn't seem to mind the brace after he got the cast off. Griffin told Sonny and his parents that his progress was very good. It didn't matter, though, at least not for football. He had missed the entire season of his sophomore year healing.

Once he was able to walk on his own without the brace, the truth was in plain sight. Sonny had the slight limp Griffin feared was possible. Still, he pushed himself to play ball again against great odds. He started to jog as soon as he was given the medical okay. Within a few weeks he was running at a slow speed and then he began to pick-up the pace. Two months later he was running at full speed, not bad compared to others, but nothing close to the speed he had before he broke his leg. When football season started Sonny's junior year, he was on the junior varsity again. That was the second worst hit he had taken as a player, his leg being the first. It meant varsity Coach Saunders had moved on without him. Sonny was devastated, but pretended like he wasn't. He had recovered better than the worst scenarios he had run through his head, but not enough to be the football player he had been and certainly not the player everybody thought he would become.

His senior year Saunders did bring him up to varsity, but played him only on defense. Sonny's toughness made him an above average defensive cornerback. But nothing could change the fact that in what he knew was his last chance to play football he was tackling people instead of being the one everyone else was trying to tackle. He did it better than most—and hated every minute of it.

# 2

When Sydney decided to quit football, he was the only one who could understand why, only he didn't either. All he knew was that what had happened to Sonny took the life out of the game for him. That's how he knew he wanted to quit. Passion for the game you play is the foundation for playing it, and certainly for playing it well. If you don't love the game you've played since you were six years old, you can't play it well. That was his thinking anyway, so he decided to walk away from it.

Deep down he thought he might get over the way he felt, but when sign-up for spring sports arrived he hadn't. That was the test that made him realize that what was going on with him was not an overreaction to Sonny's injury. Castle Cove football coaches looked at spring sports as a sign of how committed you were to staying sharp and in shape. High school rules prevented coaches from holding spring football practice as colleges did, but they could and did expect players to participate in a spring sport rather than sitting around doing nothing. Football players had only two choices, running track or playing baseball.

Sydney never liked baseball. He said watching it was like watching paint dry. Playing it was better, but not enough to make him want to. He had run track in the spring of his eighth-grade year. Ninth grade was different. Playing baseball or running meant you had a chance to play varsity football team in the fall as a sophomore. That happened only to a handful of talented players, but the chance to be one of them was enough incentive to make guys try to impress Coach Saunders. Locker room gossip had it that he had his eye on Sydney. The day Sydney showed up to try out for tennis sent a shock wave through the athletic department.

A friend of his named Jeff Grayson had suggested Sydney play tennis. They had been playing tennis off and on for a couple of years, but Sydney had never given any thought to being on the school team. Jeff wasn't the best player, but he was very good, especially at doubles. When Sydney told him he was thinking about quitting football, Jeff suggested he try tennis. He was sure Sydney would like playing with the guys on the team. Sydney decided to take Jeff's suggestion. Tennis wasn't a popular sport at Castle Cove. Only enough people to have a varsity squad were interested in playing. Sydney made the team by virtue of trying out, but the game came easy to him, and he worked hard to gain a spot in the singles rotation. Before the team had its first match Sydney had secured the number one singles spot.

To win in team tennis you must win four singles matches and three doubles. When they finish their matches each player or doubles team goes to cheer on teammates still playing. Number one singles matches were almost always the hardest, the last ones to finish, and usually went three sets. Sydney loved the fact that at every competition his teammates came to his court to cheer him on after they finished their matches. Near the end of the season he told Jeff as they walked off the courts from practice that he felt like the team support was the main reason he was still undefeated and made him feel like he definitely made the right to decision to quit football.

Two days before he was to play his final match, he got a message in his school mailbox that Coach Saunders wanted to see him. Anxious to know why, Sydney went to his office after school that afternoon. Saunders told him to come in and sit down, that he wanted to talk football with him.

"How are you, Sydney?" he asked.

"Fine, sir."

"Good. Good. And how's your brother doing? Terrible thing what happened to Sonny --tragic, in fact. He would have been some kind of running back."

"Yes, sir. He would have. Maybe the best ever to play for Castle Cove."

"He might have been. We certainly had high hopes for him. It was such a freak break. Almost unbelievable."

Sydney didn't respond, letting silence hang in the air.

"Did I hear right that you're playing tennis?" Saunders finally asked.

"Yes, sir, I am," he answered.

"You know the two spring sports for football players are track and baseball."

"Yes, sir, I know that. I ran track last year."

"I remember that. Thought you would again. But tennis, that's a problem for football. It's virtually a year-round sport that doesn't leave much room for football. I had you slotted as back-up to Grady Wilson with a chance to compete for the starting quarterback position next fall. You would be one of only three sophomores on the varsity. So I'm wondering why you're playing tennis. What's going on, Sydney? Don't you want to be on the varsity next year?"

"No, I don't," he answered and realized that wasn't what he meant. "I mean, yes, I would want to be on the varsity if I played next fall, but that's just it, I'm not planning to play. I've decided to give up football and play tennis. Just don't have it in me to keep playing."

"I don't understand, Sydney," Coach responded. "You have a great future ahead of you."

"I can't explain it, Coach. It's just that my desire to play has disappeared. I've been struggling with this decision for a long time, but in that time how I feel about football hasn't changed. I just don't want to play."

"Is this about Sonny?" he asked.

"No, Coach, this is about me, about my future, not Sonny's. I don't know what else to say. I might not have been sure about my decision had I not played tennis this spring, but now I have no hesitation about what I'm doing."

"Well," he responded, "I'm disappointed, and I think you're making a mistake, but if you don't want to play, you don't want to play. I hope you will continue to think this through in the coming months, and if you change your mind before the fall, come talk to me."

"I will."


Sydney didn't know when he would tell Sonny about his talk with Coach Saunders, but when Sonny walked by his bedroom a few days afterwards he called out for him to come into his room. Sydney was sitting at his desk. Sonny sat down on one of the twin beds.

"What's up?" Sonny asked.

"I need to tell you something," Sydney replied. "I talked to Coach Saunders a few days ago at school and told him I was not planning to play football next fall."

"You did what?" Sonny said in a raised voice and a look of shock on his face that let Sydney know right away the conversation wasn't going to go well. "Are you crazy? You might be the starting quarterback next year as a sophomore. You can't quit."

He raised up from the bed and got closer to Sydney and continued, "Listen to me, you don't get to quit. I can't play. My injury took that away from me so I'm done. I would give anything to have the chance you do, so you are not going to throw it away."

He sat back down on the bed.

"Sonny, I can't. I just can't. I don't want to play and you know what that means. Besides, you're the reason I don't want to in the first place."

"What do you mean by that?"

"I still see the disappointment in your eyes. I know what they did to you holding you back and taking away any chance you might have had to be a starting running back. I hate them for it."

"That's not what happened. Sydney. Breaking my leg is what happened. It wouldn't have mattered had they put me on the varsity. My speed is gone. Once I started working out again I could tell I couldn't run and cut like I once did. I told myself it would all come back, but it didn't take long for me to know it wasn't going to happen. Worse, every time I ran the ball practicing with the other guys I couldn't stop thinking about my leg when I made a cut or suddenly stopped. My leg is permanently damaged. But you, you can play. In fact, you can play for both of us now."

It was at that moment that Sydney saw how much pain his brother was carrying. It was eating away at him. Sonny's football injury had done more than break his leg. It had broken his spirit, his "never-say-die" attitude, his lack of fear, his willingness to take on any dare. Sydney could tell from what he was saying that he wanted to live his dreams through him. Just the thought of that overwhelmed him.

"Listen, Sonny, I was wrong about what happened to you being the reason I want to quit. It bothers me a lot what happened and even more how you were treated, but the truth is, I love playing tennis. I know football and tennis are played at different times of the year, but there's no way I can play football and become as good as I want to be in tennis. You've never seen me play so you don't know how natural I am at it. The competition is fierce, more demanding in fact than football because you're on your own. It's great. We have team play, but when you're on the court everything depends on you and nothing else. I love that feeling."

Neither of them said anything for a minute or two, then Sydney said, "Look, I'm sorry to disappoint you. I sort of get what you mean about playing for both of us, but it's not something that is real. You know that. But tennis is real. It's real for me and it's what I want to do more than anything else."

At that Sonny stood up and walked out of the room without saying anything else. Sydney was very upset by Sonny's reaction. He was as surprised by it every bit as much as Sonny was by what Sydney had told him. Two down, he thought, and one to go. Sonny and Coach Saunders didn't make his decision any easier. Telling his father would probably be the same. Figuring he may as well get it over with, he decided to walk down to the mill right then instead of driving. That way he could clear Sonny out of his head and think about what to say to his father.

No one was in the office when he arrived. He spotted Mrs. Smith, his father's secretary, in a huge room to the side of the office that had a lot of small equipment spread around.

"Is father in?" he asked, startling Mrs. Smith who had a note pad in her hand and seemed lost in thought.

"I'm sorry," said Sydney, "didn't mean to startle you."

"Oh, that's okay, sweetie, how are you anyway? You doing okay?"

"Yes, okay, I guess."

"Something wrong, Sydney?"

"No, nothing's wrong, but I need to talk to father. Is he here?"

"For you he is. You go on into his office."

His father's office was large, but messy, papers and drawings stacked on the floor, small tables and hundreds of orders on his desk. He was on the phone when Sydney opened the door. He motioned for him to sit in the chair in front of his desk. After several more minutes his father finally hung up.

"Sorry about that, Sydney, a perpetually unhappy customer I have to deal with more than I should have to, but never mind about that. What brings you to the mill?"

Usually Sydney found it easy to talk to his father. Sam had a good way with people, didn't go overboard with friendliness, but enough to make you feel at ease. He worked hard and ran the company well. The sawmill didn't make the Strange family rich, but it provided them with a very comfortable living, due in no small part to Sam's competent management.

"Well, I need to talk to you about something."

"Okay, but couldn't this have waited 'till tonight?"

"Yeah, I guess it could've," Sydney candidly admitted, "but I just talked to Sonny and it didn't go well, so I decided I may as well come talk to you and get it over with."

"Hmm," Sam said, "this sounds serious."

"Yeah, I guess it is, at least a little, though not anything involving life and death."

"Well, that's a relief," he said with a smile as he lit up a cigarette. Sam was a chain smoker, which the doctor said was ruining his health. He promised to quit several times, but never did.

"Father, I want to play tennis."

"I know that Sydney. You're playing on the team right now. I'm sorry, by the way, that I haven't gotten to any of your games. Seems like every time I get ready to something comes up here and I can't get away."

"Matches, they're called matches, not games," said Sydney, immediately feeling childish for correcting his father like that.

"Yes, matches, sorry again. But what's the problem? If you want to play, keep playing."

"Well, that's what I plan to do, and I'm pretty good at it. My coach says I can be more than good, that I have the potential of being a top player in the state, if I work at it. I want to do that, but it would mean concentrating on tennis and nothing else."

"When you say, 'nothing else'," his father responded, "do you mean no other sport at all, like football?"

"Yes. I can't spend all the time football takes up and work on getting better in tennis the way I would have to. I need private lessons for tennis. There's a pro at a club in Halifax who is supposed to be very good. Coach Hailey knows him and has already asked him if he would take me on. He's willing to."

"How much will that cost?" Sam asked. "Sounds like a lot, if he's giving you private lessons."

"I'm not actually sure, probably a lot, as you say. I was hoping you would help me pay for the lessons. I've never asked you to help me before."

"Sydney, let's slow down a minute. You need to think this through. Coach Saunders told me at the last Lion's Club meeting that he was planning on bringing you up to the varsity in the fall. He also told me that he wouldn't be surprised if you ended up as the starting quarterback by mid-season. If so, you would be the first sophomore at Castle Cove ever to be the starter."

"But I don't want to play football, Father. I like tennis. It's just that simple, and if I improve as much as Coach Hailey thinks I can, I have a chance to play in college, maybe even get a scholarship."

"Trading a football career for tennis. I just don't understand, Sydney. You've never acted like you didn't want to play football, just the opposite in fact. You love the game. What's going on here? What's making you want to do this?"

Sydney chose not to respond so his father continued.

"You've even talked about playing pro ball one day. You just may be that good. Coach Saunders thinks so. Harrison has said he thought you had that kind of talent. Now you want to just quit, throw it all away. I'm having a hard time understanding what this is all about. Help me here, Sydney. You've never been impulsive like this."

"I don't know what else to say, Father. I want to play tennis instead of football."

"Okay," his father said. "I believe you. But will you think about what I've just said before you make up your mind for sure?"

"Okay," Sydney replied, "as long as you don't expect me to change my mind, that you're just hoping I will."

"All I can do is hope you will. Nothing more. We can talk again. See you at supper tonight?"

"Yeah, I'll be there."

"Good. See you then, son."

Sydney exited his father's office and said good-bye to Mrs. Smith as he was leaving.

"Nice to see you, Sydney. Don't be so long coming back."

# 3

Sydney felt a cool breeze as he stepped out the door of the sawmill office onto the wooden porch four feet above the ground, feeling relieved that he told Sonny and his father he was quitting football. He stopped long enough to take in the beauty of the mountains he spent so many hours playing in as a kid and where he was hoping his father would let him work next summer as a member of one of the lumberjack crews. The Appalachian Mountains stood on the east side of Castle Cove with the Blue Ridge Mountains in the distance looking west. The Blue Ridge earned their name with a blue hue that looks like it was painted on the top of the ridges. The Appalachians don't have the majestic beauty of the Blue Ridge, but they do possess the nation's most famous walking trail that runs from Maine to Georgia.

From the outside looking in, small town life can seem, well, small, but when you're a kid living in one it feels as big as it needs to be. Your neighborhood is where you spend most of your time. The rest of the town is mostly outside your experience so it may as well be a thousand miles away as right across town. Stories abound of kids who can't wait to get away from the small town they grew up in. The lesser-known stories are ones about those who come back when they find out that getting away wasn't what they thought it would be.

Saw Mill was Castle Cove's original name because of the sawmill business Sydney's great grandfather Strange had established that employed almost everybody in the area who wasn't a farmer. After his great grandfather died, some of the town council members began speculating about changing the town's name, something they had kept to themselves until he was gone. They saw a town growing into a city as the population increased with new job opportunities and more and more people discovering the beauty of the area. Saw Mill didn't strike the town leaders as a name for the future.

Still afraid of offending the area's biggest employer and tax revenue source, the council sent a couple of its members to talk to grandfather Strange to see how he would react to changing the town's name. He shocked both of them when he said that he never liked the name Saw Mill for the town in the first place and changing it suited him just fine. In the fall a referendum was approved by an overwhelming majority of residents who voted to rename Saw Mill "Castle Cove" because of the Castle River that flows out of the cove where the two mountain ranges come together as if they are reaching down to hug. There were a few people who didn't think Castle Cove was much of a step-up from Saw Mill, but it's been Castle Cove ever since.

Growing up Sydney and his brothers enjoyed no special favors because of their name being Strange. They were kids just like all the others in Castle Cove. But their home was a popular hangout. It was big compared to most. Since great grandfather Strange first built it each generation had added to it. Grandfather Strange added two additional bedrooms on the back. After Sydney was born his father had some of his sawmill guys build a master bedroom on the Blue Ridge Mountain side of the main level and a wrap-around porch that started in the front and went all the way round to the Appalachian side. It was some twenty feet wide and quickly became the place where the Strange brothers spent the most time with their friends.

Harrison and Sonny had more than they could count, certainly more than Sydney had. He was pretty much of a loner, with only two people he could say were real friends, which to him meant having a relationship where nothing or no one could ever get between them. That's the way it was with Sydney, Bailey Farmer and Reggie Morrison.

Bailey was tall, almost as tall as Sydney and he was tall for his age. She was also very slim. Rude kids in her fifth-grade class called her skinny to her face. She had long brown hair, wore glasses, had braces on both legs from the knees down and walked on crutches. At recess the first day she showed up at school she sat down beside Sydney, pointed to his arm in a sling and asked him what happened. He told her he chipped his elbow playing sandlot football. He then asked her why she had braces and crutches and immediately felt bad for bringing it up. With no hesitation she said she had had polio when she was five that left her unable to walk without help.

Bailey was very smart. She knew the answer to every question her teacher asked her and answers to the questions she asked the whole class that no one else knew. Bailey was the reason Sydney learned to love to read.

She said she liked reading because she could imagine what places she had never been to looked like, and also because she wanted to become a writer herself someday. Together they read The Adventures of Tom Sawyer and The Adventures of Huckleberry Finn, and two he had never heard of, The Celebrated Jumping Frog of Calaveras County and Pudd'nhead Wilson. Sydney told her he liked Jack London's White Fang. She told him she liked a book named Anne of Green Gables. They agreed to read each other's. He liked hers, but she didn't like White Fang at all.

Reggie was small for his age. A few months older than Sydney, he was a head shorter and weighed a lot less. Both had blond hair the summer sun turned almost yellow. Reggie's family obviously didn't have much money. He wore the same long-sleeved white shirt and farmer's overalls every day, had holes in the soles of his shoes that had broken laces, and wore socks with the heels ripped out. Soon after he and Reggie became friends, Sydney's parents gathered a bunch of clothes that belonged to him and his brothers, boxed them up, and left them on the porch of the rundown shack Reggie's family was renting. They didn't want the Morrisons to know who left them, especially Reggie. The next day Reggie had on one of Sydney's plaid shirts that looked nice on him and a pair of Sonny's white buck shoes that were very popular. Sydney couldn't tell whose socks he had on, just that they didn't have holes in them.

A quiet kid, Reggie looked like he had a smile on his face all the time. He could run faster than any boy at school and loved playing ball of any kind. He was not a good student, probably because he didn't have any of the books he needed. When Sydney found out he gave him his. Sonny had used the same ones when he was in the fifth grade so Sydney dug them out of the closet to use for himself. There was nothing special about Reggie, but he was about the most likeable kid you could ever know. Nice doesn't come close to describing him. The fact that he wanted to be friends meant a lot to Sydney.

Sydney felt like the luckiest kid in Castle Cove having Bailey and Reggie as his friends. Then one day they disappeared and he never saw them again. Reggie disappeared first. They were in fourth grade together and then in the fall of their fifth-grade year Reggie was gone. Sydney's mother told him that some families moved a lot from one neighborhood to another and even one town to another because the father would lose his job and they would have to go where he found work. She said that may have been why Reggie left so abruptly. All Sydney knew was that one of his two best friends didn't come back to school after Thanksgiving break.

Bailey's disappearance was even more hurtful. Sydney felt like his heart was going to break when she was gone. Her father worked for the company paving gravel roads in Allegheny County. He drove a road grader and was the best his company had, which was why they moved a lot. He was the grader they wanted on big jobs. Sometimes his work lasted long enough that her family got to stay longer in one place than in others. She didn't think the Castle Cove job was one of them. Even though having to go to different schools was hard, she said she got to see more of the world than she would see any other way, so it wasn't as bad as Sydney probably thought.

The summer after their fifth-grade year they spent nearly every day together, mostly hiking the mountains around Castle Cove. Sometimes they would pack a lunch and go down to the Castle Cove river at the beginning of the gorge where the mountains seemed to meet. There was a huge rock near the water's edge they would sit on eating their lunches while they watched the swift current taking stuff downstream. The water was too cold to swim in and Sydney's mother said it was also dangerous because of sink holes at the bottom of the riverbed. Sometimes he explored the area around the rock looking for Indian arrowheads and other types of rocks and brought them back to Bailey who would lay them out on the big rock and arrange them in different types of formation. They would keep the ones they liked the best for the rock collection they had and throw the others into the river.

The second week of August the Strange family always rented the same cottage at North Carolina's Emerald Isle Beach. Sydney didn't want to go this year because of Bailey, but once he got there he had as much fun as ever. His father fished off nearby Morehead City pier while the rest of the family spent their days at Emerald Isle near the cottage enjoying the ocean. That's where all the boys learned to body surf. One day when Sydney went fishing with his father a man caught a stingray. It looked huge, but Sam told him it was too small to be an adult ray that can be as big as six feet long and five feet wide. The tail on the one the man caught wasn't long, but still dangerous. A ray's tail can cut like a razor blade and its poison can even kill you. A man nearby managed to get his foot on the small ray's tail while the man who caught it used plyers to work the hook loose. As soon as it was free it flopped around furiously and got close enough to the edge of the pier to allow the two men to push it off the dock back into the ocean.

Even though he was having fun, Sydney still wanted the week to go by fast so he could get back to Bailey. He couldn't wait to tell her about the stingray. As soon as they got home and unloaded the car on Saturday afternoon, he jumped on his bike and rode over to her house. It was empty when he got there. Not empty like she and her family had gone somewhere. Empty as in no furniture at all in it. He felt confused and thought he was at the wrong place. A neighbor came out of her house and headed to her car parked on the street. Sydney stopped her and asked if she knew where the Farmer family was.

"They moved, sweetie," she said. "Dorothy, Mrs. Farmer, told me Mr. Farmer's work on the highway was done here in Castle Cove so his company was sending him on to Greensboro or thereabouts. The truck came on Thursday to get their furniture and they followed after it."

Sydney was stunned. Devastated. He thanked her, got on his bike and peddled home as fast as he could, ran into the house, shut the door of his room, laid down on the bed and buried his face in his pillow hoping no one would hear him crying. His mother opened the door anyway and came in, sat on the bed, pulled Sydney up and wrapped him in her arms.

"I know what happened, Sydney. The neighbor who told you about Bailey moving called me because she thought you looked upset by what she said. I am so sorry. I know it hurts."

Like nothing he had felt before. He didn't think the pain would ever stop. To his surprise, though, it did, and life went on without Bailey or Reggie even though he didn't want it to. Families like Reggie's were invisible, forgotten when they moved before they could be remembered. Kids like Bailey were called "cripples," a description she once told him hurt her because it made her feel different from everyone else in a way she couldn't change. The three of them had experiences he would never forget, like the day they walked into Miller's Drugstore to get a milkshake and heard Mr. Miller telling some black kids sitting at the lunch counter to get out of his store. He sounded very mad. He must have scared those kids to death because he scared the three of them. The kids he ran out were doing what Sydney, Bailey, and Reggie did all the time, but Mr. Miller told them the lunch counter was for whites only. Sydney knew the water fountains around town and in the Castle Coves city parks had signs that said the same thing, but until that day at the drugstore he hadn't thought much about them.

Months after Bailey disappeared and the distance between him and his two friends got bigger, on occasion what had happened at Miller's Drug would still flash in his mind. It happened often enough that he finally decided to talk to his mother about it, and also about the "whites only" signs all around town. She had fixed lunch for him and Harrison and Sonny on the side porch of their house that faced the Appalachian Mountains. She had planned to let the boys eat by themselves while she went to the grocery store, but changed her mind and sat down to eat with them. It's not often that she had the three of them together to herself as she did now.

"Mother, I want to tell you something that happened a long time ago when Bailey and Reggie still lived here," Sydney said as they were finishing lunch.

He then proceeded to tell her the story of Mr. Miller running the black kids out of his drugstore when they were doing what he, Bailey, and Reggie had done many times. Sydney's story was not how Sarah was expecting the conversation with her boys to go, but she decided it was an opportunity to talk to them about the reality of race relations in Castle Cove, which they would only become more aware of as they got older.

"It's called 'segregation', Sydney, the word for whites and blacks living in the same town without mixing together. That's the best thing to be said about it. Years ago white people passed laws that still prevent black people from having the freedom whites do. The Civil War ended slavery, but it didn't change the way whites looked at blacks. That's why Mr. Miller told those boys to get out of his store. It's also why the "whites only" signs are at the water fountains around town. Your father and I don't think the laws or the way black people are treated is right, but most white people do."

"I don't understand," Sydney responded. "It doesn't make any sense."

"It doesn't have to," Harrison chimed in. "It's how things are. Nothing you or anybody else can do about it."

"I'm not so sure, Harrison," his mother said correcting him. "In fact, I think the day may be coming sooner rather than later when segregation laws in Carolina will be eliminated. There are lawsuits right now intending to do just that, and one big one that has already been decided. Have your teachers talked about the decision the United States Supreme Court made a few years ago that said keeping the races separate in public schools was not right—unconstitutional is how they put it?"

"Not yet," Harrison said.

"Well, they will eventually because what the Supreme Court said means that the schools in Castle Cove and everywhere else will have to stop separating white and black kids based on the color of their skin. It's coming. Maybe not tomorrow, but it's coming. You boys will live to see it."

Sarah stood up and started gathering the dishes to take in when Sydney asked, "How will it happen? The change in schools you said was coming."

"Let me take these in and get some more lemonade, then I will tell you."

"Come on, Sydney," Sonny whispered as their mother went inside. "It's not important so stop asking so many questions. There's a pick-up baseball game at City Park and I want to play, but I'll be late if you keep on."

Sarah came out again and poured the boys more lemonade and sat down before Sonny could finish.

"I know you want to leave, Sonny," his mother said. "It's okay, but I want you to hear this part before you do. The change will come gradually, but in real ways. Take the neighborhood divide that exists now here in Castle Cove. It's existed forever it seems, but Saw Mill Lane has made it more obvious than it was before it was built. To be honest, your father is responsible for the road being there.

"How?" Harrison asked, Sonny glaring at him when he did.

"Well, he convinced the county to build it because of a conflict he was having with several Main Street business owners who constantly complained about sawmill trucks coming through the middle of town. They considered them a nuisance and a hazard. Your father is a practical man who tries to work out problems. He believed the conflict was bad for everybody's business so he came up with the idea of there being a road that would run parallel to Main Street and give trucks access to the sawmill without using Main at all. He convinced the Castle Cove town council to put up half the money to entice the county to build it. He even had an architect draw up a blueprint of what it would look like that included new businesses on either side of the new road that would become a fresh source of tax revenues for Castle Cove and the county."

"Pretty smart, if you ask me," Sonny said, shocking Harrison and Sydney and shrugging his shoulders when they both turned to look at him.

"Your father is smart, Sonny, but an unintended consequence of the new road was that Saw Mill Lane became the dividing line that identified where people lived based on the color of their skin. Whites now live on one side. Blacks live on the other. It's the way segregation works. There doesn't always have to be a law to keep the races apart. Attitudes do, too. Castle Cove doesn't have a law saying black people can't live south of Saw Mill Lane. They just don't because they know they aren't welcomed in white neighbors."

"What would happen if a black family did anyway?" Harrison asked.

"Right now they can't because nobody white will rent or sell them a house. But if that did happen I'm sure there would a lot of trouble, maybe even violence. White prejudice against blacks is very strong. That's what you saw that day at Miller's Drug, Sydney. There was no reason those boys couldn't have gotten milkshakes or ice cream cones. It was Mr. Miller's attitude toward black people that was the problem."

A few weeks after the porch talk Sydney heard words reflecting the same attitude Mr. Miller had, only this time they came from his own grandfather. It was quite by accident that he did. During the summer he would sometimes sit on the outside steps of the sawmill offices waiting for his father to get off from work so they could walk home together, a time when they would talk about anything and everything. This particular evening as soon as Sydney opened the office door he heard his father and grandfather talking, so loud it sounded like they were arguing. He quietly shut the door and sat down on the steps to wait for his father, but he could still hear what they were saying.

"You shouldn't have done it. Niggers don't cut trees," his grandfather said loud enough that Sydney had no trouble hearing from the office steps. It was the first time Sydney had ever heard anyone in the family use the "n" word.

"They sweep the sawdust and clean the machinery and the offices," his grandfather said.

"Not anymore," his father answered with a stern tone. "I took Abe Jordan with me the other week to clear some trees that had gotten cross ways when the men felled them. There was no one else around to ask. Turned out he could use a chain saw as good as I could. I asked him if he would be interested in doing some logging. He said he would and I offered him the job on the spot. He asked if Ezra Smith could be his second man and I agreed. They have already shown they are as good as any crew we have and their skin color has nothing to do with it."

"That's not the point," his grandfather snapped back. "You're gonna lose those white crews if you keep those niggers, you wait and see. "It ain't right having niggers doing white man's work."

"There's no right or wrong about it," Sydney's father fired back defiantly. "It's about being able to do a job or not doing it. Abe and Ezra can and that's what matters to me. If any of the white workers don't like it, they can quit."

"There's gonna be trouble, son, you mark my word. There's gonna be trouble."

Sydney's grandfather was right. A week after he heard the argument somebody tried to set the mill on fire. The night watchman told his father that he had dozed off after checking the yard earlier when he heard a truck drive into the lumber yard. He jumped up from his chair in time to see somebody in the truck throw a bottle with a rag sticking out of it that was on fire. The truck sped out of the yard blowing up so much dust the watchman didn't see who was in it or get the license tag number. He ran out of the office door with a fire extinguisher. The burning bottle had landed on a stack of half-cut plywood and broken open, but the top sheet was scorched more than actually being on fire. The watchman doused it and made sure there were no sparks anywhere around the wood. He then hurried back inside and called Sam who was there in a matter of minutes. They both checked the area again and were satisfied everything was okay.

The next day Sam gathered the loggers and mill workers in the yard. "We all know what happened last night," he said. "We're not going to pretend we don't know why. This mill has been here as long as there's been a town and we're not going anywhere anytime soon, if I have anything to do with it. I hired all of you, and I mean all of you, because I thought you could do the work. In return I would pay you a fair wage. I think you've tried to do that and I hope you think I've held up my end of the bargain. So let me say plain as I can. I hired Abe Jordan and Ezra Smith to lumber jack for the same reason. They can do the work and I'm paying them no more or no less than anybody else. A fair wage for a day's labor. If anybody here has a problem with that, I hope you're man enough to tell me straight up. I'll pay you what I owe you and you can take your leave."

Sam paused, then asked, "Any takers?" No one stepped forward. "Good, then," he said. "I was hoping that would be the case. You're good men and I'm glad to have you working for me. Now here's what we're going to do. Instead of doing what we normally do, today we're going to fence in the entire lumber yard and tool sheds so no one can drive close to them again. The fencing will be six feet tall and have a strip of barbwire on top of it in case some fool wants to try to climb over it. Just so you know, there will also be a couple of German Shepherds running the yard at night. I would appreciate it if you would work hard today to get the fencing in place so we can get back to normal tomorrow. Now let's get to work."

# 4

Working at the sawmill was what the men in the Strange family did because it's what they've always done. The story goes that by the time he was fifteen years old Sam Strange was as good a lumberjack as anybody ever saw in western Carolina. His father was, too. Every man in the family worked in the woods first before there was any chance of getting into management. Sam told his sons that you had to know a business if you wanted to run it.

Of the three brothers, Sonny was the one who didn't like working at the sawmill when they were young. He seemed allergic to hard work. Trying to get him to do whatever job his father gave him became such a hassle that when he turned fourteen and could drive with a learner's permit, Sam made him the company "gofer." He delivered pick-up truck size loads of lumber to construction sites and then picked up supplies Sam had ordered from businesses in town.

Sydney first started working at the sawmill when he was in the sixth grade doing mostly clean-up in the shop area. He was fascinated by the skill of the workers who cut and trimmed the logs into different types of boards. By the time he was an eighth grader, he was working in the woods just as Harrison had done. Ironically, his favorite crew was Abe and Ezra. Neither of the men was physically imposing. Abe was average height, lean and muscular. Ezra was taller and carried more weight than Abe, but didn't seem to be hampered in the least by the extra pounds. They knew how to cut trees and seemed to have boundless energy doing the work. They had Sydney doing the clean-up cutting on small stuff while they handled the rest. Everybody knew they were the best lumberjack crew around.

A month into the summer after his junior year, Abe told Sydney he had something special for them to do as they loaded the equipment. They hiked maybe a mile into the woods from the truck when Abe stopped at a white oak tree some four feet in circumference and so tall you could hardly see its top.

"You ready to do real man's work, Sydney?" Abe asked with a sly smile on his face.

"You mean cut that down?" Sydney asked.

"Well, it ain't coming down any other way, but if you don't think you're up to it..."

"No, no," he interrupted, "I'm ready. I've been waiting a long time for this day to come."

Abe took the four-inch rope he had with him and tied it up the trunk of the massive oak as far up as he could reach, then started walking away from the base slightly uphill. He wrapped the rope around a tree about thirty feet away and slightly above the one Sydney was to cut. He turned and went down-hill to another tree about the same thirty feet away and wrapped the rope a couple of times around it and then around one of his arms and held it with both hands.

"Okay, Sydney, start cutting."

Sydney knew exactly what to do. He stood on the side facing the first tree Abe roped and made a level cut about ten inches. Then he made another cut at an angle that would meet the back of the first cut he made. He used the butt end of the saw to knock the notched piece of wood from the tree. He immediately went to the backside of the tree and started cutting slightly above the notch on the opposite side. Everything was stable until he reached the point where the tree started leaning toward the notch ever so slightly. That's when he knew he had it. He ran the chainsaw full out until that huge oak began falling in exactly the direction he wanted it to and came crashing down on the forest floor. It was a thing of beauty.

"Good job, Sydney," Abe yelled. "You cut it like you knew what you were doing."

"Hey, Abe," Sydney yelled back, "I did know what I was doing. Don't forget, I was taught by the best." He could see Abe get a big smile on his face. "I simply did what I've seen you do many times."

Abe didn't say anything. He just wound the rope as he walked toward the trees he had circled and then toward Sydney.

"Let's head up the hill a little," Abe said. "Ezra will finish trimming this one."

They went up a couple hundred yards and got ready to repeat the process they had just finished, when an emergency call came over the walkie-talkie all crews carried. A couple of loggers were in trouble. The tree they were cutting had jack-knifed. A gust of wind caught the top just before the cut was all the way through the trunk, tilting it back where it split right at the base. The force of the tree was too fast and strong for the logger holding the rope to let go, seriously burning his hands when the rope cut through his gloves. The guy who was cutting at the tree base had it much worse. He tried to get out of the way but fell backwards. Lucky for him the bark at the base where he had been cutting tore down but didn't tear free of the trunk. That held up the end of the trunk so the full weight didn't hit the ground. It pinned his legs but didn't crush them. Making matters worse, he was lying on the hillside below the tree where it could roll over him if the bark tore free.

Abe and Sydney heard the call that went to everybody, left Ezra to finish up, and headed up the mountain, getting there before the first-aid crew did. Abe took one look and said the guy on the ground was ready to go into shock, giving them no time to waste to keep his internal organs from shutting down. Sydney put his jacket over him and tucked it under his sides and then put his hard hat on him. Abe then told him to bury the cant hook into the trunk near the base and position it to get leverage once he cut the other end. A cant hook has a long handle with a crescent shaped steel hook on one end with a flat base on the other. Once the hook is locked-in, pulling back on the handle secures the flat base providing leverage that could easily move the trunk or hold it tightly in place.

The man was lying head-first down the hill, but the cant hook would keep the trunk from rolling. With Sydney holding the handle, Abe cut off a good size limb twenty feet from where the man was and then cut two pieces from it. He put them on the hillside against the trunk, moved to the other side of where the man was and started cutting. His chain was razor sharp and worked quickly, stopping just short of going all the way through. Abe braced himself against the trunk and finished cutting. The trunk moved slightly once it was free and the man yelled in pain, but nothing moved again. Abe asked Sydney if the cant hook was secure. He replied yes. Abe slowly moved from where he had been kneeling and got below the man's shoulders while Sydney pulled uphill on the cant hook creating just enough space for Abe to pull the man free.

He quickly dragged him around the tree base to the higher side and leaned the man against a smaller tree close by. Sydney gave the man some water and kept him wrapped up. Shock makes the body feel cold even in hot temperatures like it was that day, some eighty degrees with high humidity. Abe asked the man if he could feel his legs. He touched his legs and said he could feel his hands on them. Abe said that was good because it meant he still had circulation in them. Just then the medics showed up. Sydney couldn't believe the equipment those three guys carried, including a cool fold-up stretcher made for mountain rescues. They got the man on the stretcher and wrapped him in a blanket. Then one of them put salve on the other guy's burned hands and all of them headed down the mountain. They were gone in a matter of minutes. Abe and Sydney stayed behind to pack up their gear and what belonged to the other crew.

"That was close, too close, if you ask me," Sydney said to Abe.

"It was, Sydney, but I've seen worse. It was good he still had feeling in his legs. Accidents happen when you do this kind of work. Your father trusts you a lot to let you be in the woods. Not many kids your age are responsible enough to see the dangers."

"I try to pay attention to you and Ezra to make sure I learn what I need to know," said Sydney. "The first thing I've learned is that safety is not just for me, but for everyone around me. I mess up and somebody else can pay the price."

"You're more than smart, Sydney Strange, you're mature, and that is the most important qualification for someone young working in these woods. I'll work with you anytime."

"Thanks, Abe. That means a lot for you to say that."

Sydney meant it. Abe was the best at what he did and to know he thought Sydney should be in the woods like everybody else made him feel good about himself. He thought about what his grandfather had said about Abe years before. The memory hurt, and at the same time made him mad. It also made him feel even more proud of his father.

# 5

Sonny called it "the stare," the intense glare that felt like an x-ray penetrating your brain his father always gave him and his brothers when he wanted their undivided attention. It seemed like he could hold it for an eternity. Exactly two years after Sonny broke his leg and one year after he was solidifying his reputation as the life of any party, Sonny was about to experience "the stare" like he never had before.

Mrs. Smith told Sonny his father was expecting him, but he had to run out to the yard for a minute. He could wait in his father's office. Sonny sat down in the chair facing the desk. Ten minutes felt like an hour. He nervously put his right leg on his left knee and jiggled his foot and then switched position. He had never been comfortable in the office area of the sawmill. Finally, Sam walked in, went to his file cabinet to put some papers in and then sat down at his desk. He picked up the phone and punched in Mrs. Smith.

"Rachel, hold my calls for a few minutes."

"Will do, Mr. Strange," she replied. At that he put the phone back on its rack, leaned back in his chair and gave Sonny "the stare" he was expecting.

"How old are you, Sonny?" he finally asked his middle son, catching him off guard.

"What?" Sonny asked as if he didn't understand the question. "You know how old I am."

"Yes, I do, son. But I want to know if you do, so how old are you?"

"Seventeen, soon to be eighteen in November."

"Where do you work?" his father asked pushing him harder.

"Here, of course. You know that, too. Part-time during school and full-time in the summer."

Do you make enough money to support yourself, buy your own food, clothes, car, pay rent?"

"You know I don't, Dad," Sonny replied. "You're the one who pays me. But if you want to pay me more that will be fine."

"Pay you more?" That brought a smile to Sam's face. "Instead of paying you more, what if I fired you?"

"What?" Sonny responded.

"That's right, fired you," answered his father. "Why shouldn't I? If I treated you the way I treat all the other workers I would. In fact, you'd already be gone. And here's why. I don't pay workers to drink on the job, especially summer workers, but I know letting you go wouldn't do anything to help you."

"What are you talking about?" Sonny said as if he didn't know.

"You came back from lunch yesterday, Sonny, smelling of alcohol. Several of the men confirmed it so don't deny it."

"I had a beer at lunch, no big deal."

"You had more than one beer and you know it, so don't make matters worse by lying. But one is too many when you're working here. That Sullivan kid you're hanging out with is nineteen years old and can buy beer. You and he were sitting in the parking lot outside The Market in his car drinking. People know me in this town, Sonny, and Bill Owens who owns the convenience store called me because he thought I'd want to know what you were doing in the middle of the day. How do you expect me to let you make deliveries when you're drinking?"

Sonny didn't say anything.

"You're seventeen years old, Sonny. You're not old enough to drink in North Carolina, and sure as hell not old enough to drink and drive. But you are apparently stupid enough to think you can. What you're obviously not thinking about is that you are putting the sawmill at risk by drinking on the job. I'll lose customers eventually. Worse, what if you had an accident, not just with truck, but with a load of wood? Suppose you miss a strap that holds it on the truck because your drinking made you careless? What if you turn a corner, especially with how fast I know you drive, and wood comes flying off and hits another car or, God forbid, somebody getting ready to cross the street? I'm sure you think it will never happen, but that's exactly why they are called accidents. No one expects them to happen until they do, and then it's too late. I can't take that chance."

Sam paused and Sonny sat still.

"Are you listening to me, Sonny?"

Sonny looked up and said, "Yeah, I'm listening."

"Well, you better listen good," Sam shot back. "Here's what's going to happen. I can't stop you from drinking even if it's worrying me and your mother day and night. If we could do something to help you we would, but what I won't do is let you work here while you're drinking. Mike Lambert is going to check you into the yard before you take one of the trucks. If he smells even a hint of alcohol on you, you're finished here, and I mean finished.

His father stopped, waited for everything he had said to sink in and then asked, "Do you understand what I'm telling you, Sonny?"

"I get it," Sonny responded instantly. "I hear you loud and clear."

"I hope you do, son. More than anything I hope you'll stop what you're doing. Your mother and I want nothing but the best for you, but you need to know that I won't pay for you to throw your life away."

"Message received," Sonny said in mild sarcasm. He was tempted to add a salute to his words, but had presence of mind not to. Instead he leaped to his feet and was gone before his father could say anything else.

Predictably, what Sonny's father said to him fell on deaf ears. Sonny managed to finish high school and spent a year at the community college in-between going to parties. One day out of the blue he announced that he had joined the National Guard and was headed to boot camp at Fort Gordon in Augusta, Georgia for six weeks. He would be on reserve duty for four years after that. His mother wasn't happy about his decision, but his father was, thinking the service might help Sonny grow up. Nothing else had. Maybe the discipline of military service would.

The timing of Sonny's decision to join the National Guard could not have been more fortuitous. He left for basic training a week before Harrison got out of the army. In spite of becoming a starter his sophomore year at Greenwich, Harrison said playing didn't make up for his dislike of his classes, all of them. His grades were okay, but he hated school. He dropped out and enlisted in the army, knowing that he would likely be drafted if he didn't. The Viet Nam War had not become the hot war it eventually would, but the draft had heated up and was grabbing anybody who didn't have a deferment. As fate would have it, Harrison ended up spending his entire tour of active duty stateside. His parents were hoping that once he got out he would go back to school, but instead he chose to work with his father at the sawmill. Within a year he and Maryanne McCarthy got married. They had grown-up together, started dating the summer after his senior year and had been together ever since.

It didn't take long for Sam to see that Harrison had a head for business and also knew how to supervise workers. He was pleased that Harrison seemed to enjoy being out in the plant and even in the woods with the lumberjacks. They knew he was the "boss man," but he made them feel like he was one of them. Harrison was at ease with people and could give as good as he got when he and the other workers were kidding around. At the same time, he seemed to have no trouble maintaining enough administrative distance that no one forgot Harrison was the one who was ultimately in charge.

That first year Harrison came into the mill as the heir apparent proved critical in building trust among the workers that when time came for Sam to step down the mill would be in good hands. Not that Sam and Harrison didn't have their moments as they worked through the differences between being father and son and partners running a business. Not totally unexpected, Sonny was the cause of their first conflict. For reasons known only to him, without talking to Harrison, Sam offered Sonny a job at the sawmill after his six weeks of basic training were over. When he heard about it Harrison went to Sam and objected strenuously. Sam listened as Harrison made his case against it, but stuck by his decision. He told Harrison he was confident the military had helped Sonny mature the way he had hoped it would. Harrison told his dad rather bluntly that he was making a big mistake. It wasn't like he didn't want Sonny at the mill, only that he knew his brother well enough to know working there was never going to be a good fit.

Six months later Sonny quit. Harrison chose not to tell his father "I told you so." but he didn't have to. Sam told Harrison a few days after Sonny was gone that he had been right all along. He even admitted he wasn't surprised Sonny quit, that he thought that having him there was one way he could stay in regular touch with Sonny in the hope that being around family might get him to change his behavior.

While that family drama was unfolding at the mill, Sydney was focused solely on his last season of tennis. His goal was to win a college scholarship. He thought it unlikely that would happen with a Division I school, but a Division II scholarship seemed within reach. He went undefeated again, making it two years in a row, leading Castle Cove to a conference championship and a spot in the state tournament. Just before state got started Western University in Kenwood, North Carolina, less than an hour from Castle Cove, offered him a full ride. That inspired him to play his best tennis since taking up the game. Even though Castle Cove finished second in the team competition, Sydney won all his singles matches. A week later he took the singles individual state championship, the first ever for the Castle Cove tennis program.

Feeling like he needed a break from tennis, Sydney decided to work at the sawmill the summer after graduation. He competed in a few weekend tournaments and won two out of three, but he mostly followed his instructor's advice to focus on practicing rather than playing tournaments in order to be ready to play at Western. His primary concern, though, was spending as much time as possible with his girlfriend, McKenzie Langston. He had first seen her the day she delivered a message from the principal's office to his freshman social studies teacher. He often told her that when she left the room his heart went with her. It was love at first sight for him, he would say later, but it took her a few "sightings" to feel the same way. She was beautiful, maybe five foot four, very petite, perfectly proportioned, with blonde, shoulder length hair. At six-two, a hundred and eighty pounds, he towered over her the first time he stopped her in the school cafeteria to ask her for a date.

Two years older than him, McKenzie had skipped third grade and was three years ahead of Sydney in school. He was afraid their relationship wouldn't survive when she left to attend Smith College in Raleigh, but it did. In the fall, though, he would be moving to Kenwood to attend Western while she finished her senior year at Smith. That would be even harder than the last three years, but the big question was what came after that. McKenzie's parents wanted her to come home to Castle Cove to teach once she graduated, but that was not an option for her or Sydney. They were planning a future together and her moving back home didn't fit into them. Teaching in or near Kenwood was what made sense to them. Her major college professor happened to know the superintendent of Boone County schools in which Kenwood was located. He told McKenzie that if in the spring she wanted to apply there he would be glad to make a call on her behalf. He did and that led to a job interview at Matthew Pugh High School in Parkville teaching junior English. Parkville was the largest city in the county, and only a twenty-minute drive from Kenwood.

Not unexpectedly she got it and by early June she had rented a place in Kenwood that made the commute to Pugh High an easy one.

The change McKenzie graduating brought was a welcomed relief to her and Sydney, given how difficult her senior year and his freshman year had been for them. Their schedules had forced them to see each other primarily on holidays. Her moving to Kenwood was like Christmas for both of them. Instead of taking his stuff home for the summer, he moved most of it to her apartment and spent the summer in Kenwood. In the fall they decided that because of Sydney's scholarship he would keep a dorm room just as he had done his freshman year. Not surprisingly, though, he spent most of his time at McKenzie's.

A Strange family friend who was an attorney had mentioned to Sydney the summer before he left for Western that English was an excellent undergraduate major for students who were thinking about a career in law. Not that becoming a lawyer was something Sydney hoped to do, but he was interested in English as a major for the unconventional reason that he actually loved grammar. It was the logic of it that fascinated him. Besides that, his freshman English professor managed to make grammar fun. Then in the spring he had enjoyed a course reading Chaucer's The Canterbury's Tales in old English. By the end of that first year at Western, he decided to make English his major.

His sophomore year got off to an even better start than his first year had. The Western tennis coach, Taylor Green, told him during fall workouts that he would be playing second singles when the season started in March. During spring pre-season drills coach informed Sydney that he was going to alternate him with Barry Moore who was slated to play number one singles. Both of them had a winning record through six matches, though Sydney thought coach was putting him against the toughest competition. He didn't mind at all, especially when he finished the season with only one loss against a senior at Davidson College who had been named as a second team Division II All American.

Life that year was good for Sydney and McKenzie. They delighted in being together. After five years they were still very much in love. They didn't have a lot of money, but enough to go to a few movies and get tickets to the musical, The Fantastics, being performed by a local theater group at the City Park outdoor venue. They even managed to spend a long weekend at Emerald Isle beach where the Strange family used to go every summer when Sydney was young. By the time fall arrived and he was beginning his junior year at Western, Sydney felt like he and McKenzie were living the dream. Then the wheels came off.

# 6

You don't choose ministry. It chooses you.

That's what Sydney once heard Gerald Connolly, his hometown parish priest, say in a sermon. He didn't remember it until he began feeling that was happening to him. He didn't like the feeling, upsetting him unlike anything he had ever experienced. "Why me?" was all he could think about. He wasn't getting an answer, just the persistent feeling that becoming a minister was what he was supposed to do with his life.

It hit him suddenly, unexpectedly, shockingly. He was taking a class in oral interpretive reading as a required course for Speech Communications after he had decided to do a double major with English. A month into the class he was scheduled to do his first interpretative reading assignment. Struggling to find a suitable reading, McKenzie suggested 1 Corinthians 13 in the Bible. It's a beautiful poem she told him. She was thinking about assigning it to her students when they got to the poetry section of their English literature class. Sydney wasn't familiar with it, so she pulled out a copy of it from her pile of papers and read it to him. When she finished Sydney couldn't say anything. It was as if he had been dumbstruck by what he had heard. Only he hadn't. Confused more than awed. He sat there without saying a word. He finally managed to tell her he needed to practice reading it out loud before deciding whether or not to use it.

McKenzie handed him the paper and he went into the bedroom, sat down on the bed and stared into space. He felt calm and nervous all at the same time, quiet and ready to jump out of his skin. His mind was flooded with a strange, even bizarre, thought—that he should become a minister. He didn't know what to make of it. Absurd as it was it was right there in his head. He didn't even go to church. Occasionally on Christmas or Easter like most Episcopalians, nothing more than that. He had been raised to go to church. His mother had taken him and his brothers every Sunday until they were old enough to say they didn't want to go anymore. Sydney would still go with her once in a while.

Stories he heard about church members getting mad at their priest didn't make ministry appealing either. At lunch one Sunday after church his own mother told a story about Jacob Adams, a prominent member of Saint Patrick parish, being upset with Reverend Connolly because he thought the morning's sermon was too political. Reverend Connolly came right back at him.

"'Well, Jacob,'" she said she heard Reverend Connolly say, 'the gospel is political. When Jesus said to render to Caesar what is Caesar's and to God what is God's, he was being very political, and as one of his ministers I have no choice but to do the same. If I ever become partisan, I hope you will call me on it, but when I am being political, that is, engaging the issues of our lives, I hope you will recognize that I am preaching the gospel.'"

"I bet Jacob didn't like that," said Sam. "He's always been a bit of a bully. If I had been there, I would have told the Reverend good for him."

"Everybody could tell Jacob didn't like that," Sarah added. "I asked Reverend Connolly if he was all right. He said he was, not to worry. Jacob would get over being upset. It wasn't the first time the two of them had clashed. And then he told me with a smile on his face, 'If he doesn't, I suppose I will have to explain the difference between being political and being partisan to him all over again.'"

"I knew I liked Reverend Connolly," Sam responded enthusiastically.

"I'll be glad to remind you of your own words when the time comes," Sarah quipped.

Stories like that certainly didn't make ministry any more appealing to Sydney. He thought his becoming a minister was as strange as some people thought his name was. And as much as he liked Reverend Connolly, he didn't much like the idea of being like him. Ministers had to be good, not that being good was a bad thing. Sydney was sure it was a good thing, just not something he wanted to spend time thinking about. He figured being a decent person who tried to be nice to people and get along with everybody was enough.

A few days went by without Sydney being able to shake thoughts about ministry. They came to mind at the strangest times, in-between sets in a tennis match, sitting in the coffee shop on campus reading a book, or watching TV with McKenzie. Finally, one night, unable to stand it any longer, he turned off the television and told McKenzie he had something he needed to talk to her about.

"That sounds scary," she said. "You're not going to tell me you've changed your mind about us because if you have I will be really mad at you for making me believe you loved me as much as I love you and I cannot imagine having to tell my family we've split up when I've told them you are the person I want to marry."

"McKenzie, stop!" Sydney insisted. "It's not about our relationship. It's not even about us, at least not at the moment. It's about me."

"You're not gay, are you," she blurted out.

"Would you stop it," he said firmly. "Give me a chance to tell you."

"Okay, I'm sorry. You're just scarring me."

"You don't need to be scared about anything; we're fine, it's nothing like that. It's serious, but it might be a good serious. It started when you read the love poem from the Bible. Almost from the moment you did I've have had a confusing, inexplicable feeling that I can't get rid of."

He paused, causing her to say, "Well, are you going to tell me what it is?"

"I'm not sure you will like it," said Sydney.

"Now you stop it, Sydney. Just tell me what it is."

"It's this unrelenting thought that I should become a minister."

She looked dumbstruck, like Sydney had just said something harsh to her.

"Crazy, isn't it? Me, a minister," Sydney said in a low voice as if he were saying it to himself.

McKenzie still didn't say a word. She just sat there staring into space. After a while her silence began to make Sydney anxious.

"McKenzie, you've got to say something, anything. Don't leave me hanging like this."

"I don't know what to say, Sydney. What'd you expect me to say? That I think it's great? If you do, I can't say that. I don't know whether it's great or not. I don't even know what you're talking about. My family hardly ever goes to church and now you're saying I'm going to have to spend the rest of my life in church if I'm with you."

"I didn't say that," he said trying to put her at ease. "I only said I felt like I was being called to be a minster. I haven't said I was going to do it."

She stood up without saying anything and walked toward the kitchen, turned and said, "I need to think about this before I say something I shouldn't say. You've knocked me for a loop, Sydney. You've got to know that. I think you should go back to the dorm tonight. I need to be alone to process what this means for us."

"No, no, McKenzie. I don't want to leave. Let's talk this through."

"Sydney, I need to think, not talk. If you're here you'll do what you're doing now, push me to talk. So please leave. We can talk tomorrow."

"Okay, I'll leave, but I don't want to. I think I should stay."

She didn't respond, just looked at him very sternly. Sydney got the message and left.

To say that didn't go well was an understatement. The only way it could have been worse is if McKenzie had told him to leave and not come back. Sydney didn't know what to do. He didn't see or talk to McKenzie the next day, or the next. When he called she sounded okay, but it was as if she were being careful with what she said. He asked her if he should stay at the dorm. She thought that was still a good idea. He then asked about Thanksgiving, if she was still planning to go to Castle Cove to be with their families like they had done the last two years. She said yes, of course.

By the time he picked her up the Wednesday before Thanksgiving, he was calmer about everything than he had been the week before. He realized he didn't have to make any decisions about what he was feeling about ministry. No one even knew about it except McKenzie. He wasn't ready to bring it up with her again. He had always been able to talk to his mother whenever anything was on his mind. She was as wise as anyone he knew. Maybe he would talk to her sometime during Thanksgiving.

Early Friday morning after a nice Thanksgiving Day with both families, one for lunch, the other at supper, Sydney found his mother sitting in the wooden swing on the side porch facing the Appalachian Mountains. She loved the mountains. Raised on a farm, Sarah had always felt more at home close to the mountains than the fields she plowed as a girl. She loved to tease Sam by telling him that if he had been a farmer instead of a mountain man she wouldn't have married him. He would remind her that he wasn't a mountain man, he was a man of the city who happened to need the trees on the mountains to keep his business growing. She would then remind him that when he was a boy Castle Cove wasn't big enough to be called anything other than a wide-spot in the road.

Sydney sat down with his mother, coffee cup in hand. As usual she was drinking tea.

"Sydney, I hope you know it's so good to have you home."

"It's good to be home, Mother. I miss Castle Cove, something I never thought I would say. It often felt small to me, but the older I get the bigger it seems to be."

"Yes, well maybe you're whose gotten bigger, in your heart, and now you see it with more maturity. It's still small, for sure, but I've always thought that how you think about where you live has more to do with you than where you live."

"I'm sure you're right about that, Mother."

"And how are you and McKenzie?"

It was like she was reading his mind.

"We're fine, at least we were, but something has come up that might be between us, something I wanted to talk to you about."

She looked at her son intently, inviting him with her eyes to say more.

"McKenzie," he continued, "has been having a good second year at the same school where she taught last year. My classes are going fine. I like my professors and it looks like we're going to have a pretty good tennis team. I like my teammates a lot. Everything is good right now, excellent, in fact, and then I messed things up. At least, that's how I feel about it."

"Okay, tell me what's going on," said Sarah in her gentle, but firm way.

"Well, what I'm about to tell you may surprise you, even shock you. It did me, surprise and shock, I mean. A couple of weeks ago a thought or feeling, I don't know which, came to me that I haven't been able to shake, and to be honest it has been eating at me ever since. In fact, it hit me like a sledge hammer because it seems so crazy to me and I have been in turmoil since."

"Sydney, what are you trying to say. Just say it, sweetheart."

"I feel like I am being called to be a minister, Mother." He paused, and then said, "Don't you think that is crazy?"

Sarah sat for a minute, looking down at the ground and then lifting her eyes to his as she smiled and said, "Of course, I don't think it's crazy, Sydney. Just the opposite. I think it's wonderful. I can't think of anyone who would make a better minister than you. You're smart, but you also have a tender heart, you're strong, physically and morally. So, no, I don't think it's crazy at all."

He sat quietly thinking about what she just said. She finally spoke again, "Tell me about the experience you describe as a call to be a minister. I want to hear all about it."

"It's hard to explain, in fact, I can't explain it. I just have to tell you what happened."

Sydney told her everything, his looking for something to read for his class, McKenzie's suggesting he read 1 Corinthians 13, the persistent thought after she read it to him out loud that he should become a minister, about the anguish he has had ever since. When he stopped talking and lifted his eyes from the porch floor and looked at her she had tears streaming down her face.

"What's wrong?" Sydney asked his mother.

"Nothing," she answered softly. "Nothing at all. What you just told me was beautiful and it sort of overwhelmed me. I am so proud of you, Sydney, who you are, the young man you've become. No matter what you decide to do, I always will be."

Sydney smiled as he placed his hand on top of hers.

"But I want you to listen to me," she said to him in a tone of voice that only mothers have. "I don't know anything about how minsters get 'called,' or whatever it is that leads them to enter the ministry. But I do know the world needs somebody like you to be a leader in calling people to live right, do right, and be right. If God wants you to be one of those people, I suppose there's nothing you can do about it but accept the invitation. He must see something in you to help the world. Besides, I've heard Father Connolly say more than once that when God gets hold of someone, that person is "gotten."

"Yes, I've heard him say that, too, just never thought about me being one of those 'gotten' people before now."

"And I'm guessing this is what is between you and McKenzie," said Sarah.

Sydney nodded yes and then said, "It didn't go well."

"What do you mean?"

"Essentially, she said she wasn't sure she wanted to spend her life in the church, but that being with me meant she would have to. We haven't talked about it since."

"Well, Sydney, it's a lot for her to take in, just as it is for you. Give her some time. I'm sure y'all can work things out."

"I hope you're right, Mother. I can't image choosing between McKenzie and ministry."

"That's not going to happen, Sydney," said Sarah firmly. "You love each other too much for that to happen, but I do think you should be honest with yourself"

"What do you mean?"

"I think you know what you want to do about this feeling you have. You want to explore it more to see how real it is, and I suspect that's what McKenzie knows, too, which is why she reacted so strongly to it. She knows you want to pursue it, but she doesn't know what it means for her, and for your future together."

Sydney pondered what his mother had just said as he took another sip of coffee.

"I knew I needed to talk to you," he told her. "I just needed to hear someone else say what I have known deep down, that as strange as this feeling is, it's also intriguing and exciting and I'm at least ready to follow it to see where it leads me."

"Then do it," Sarah replied, "but not before you talk with McKenzie. She may surprise you in a good way about how she actually feels now that she's had some time to think."

Sydney gave his mother a hug.

"I love you, Mother."

"I love you, too, sweetheart."

The day after Thanksgiving McKenzie and Sydney drove back to Kenwood. Several times he was ready to talk with her again about ministry, but quickly lost his nerve. He knew it was silly to act that way. McKenzie was his best friend, and he believed their relationship was strong and solid, but was it enough that his becoming a minister wouldn't put it at risk? He was half-way expecting she might tell him he should stay at the dorm when they got back, but she didn't.

The weekend was quiet. They went shopping on Saturday for a while, grabbed a bite to eat at a hamburger place near the strip mall, went home and the next day watched some football. Monday morning he went to classes and she went to school. As the weather turned cooler Sydney started playing indoor tennis exclusively to try to keep his game sharp. McKenzie got busy with student papers and upcoming exams. Before Thanksgiving they had been treating themselves to one night a month at a nice restaurant, a kind of "dating" night. Sydney suggested they do so again and McKenzie agreed. They had read about "The Best of Italian," a new upscale restaurant that was getting good reviews.

McKenzie had a workday on Friday and Sydney's two Friday classes were meeting, so they decided to go to the new restaurant on Thursday evening. He ordered baked rigatoni and she ordered chicken alfredo. Not much for wine, they both accepted the complimentary glass of a Napa Valley red wine being offered because of the grand opening.

"How are things at school with the semester coming to an end?" Sydney asked.

"Good, actually," McKenzie answered. "It's been a good fall and I love my students, especially my seniors. They've been reading Romeo and Juliet and have shown some real maturity in the discussions we've been having. I was afraid they would make fun of it as a silly romantic story, but thus far they have been willing to focus on the nature of tragic literature the play represents and the social comment it makes that is still relevant."

"That's amazing," he responded. "Impressive, actually."

"Well, I'll find out how much they actually learned after their exam."

They paused to eat a bit and then McKenzie shared that she was getting to know a couple of new teachers she thought Sydney would like. A woman who also taught English and was married and a single man who taught history. She wondered about inviting the three of them over sometime.

"Three? I thought you said there were two."

"Susan's husband, Sydney. I can't very well leave him out. You can keep up better than that."

"Oh, right," he said. "Little slow on the uptake on that one, wasn't I? Guess my mind was somewhere else."

McKenzie looked at him, smiled, and said, "It happens to the best of us."

They finished a delicious meal and Sydney suggested they order some tiramisu and coffee. She wanted tea. They split a single order of the tiramisu. He told her to take the last bite. He held his coffee between his hands as she did, but didn't say anything, just stared into space.

"What's with you, tonight, Sydney. Your mind is obviously somewhere else or on something else. What's going on?"

He decided to come clean.

"We need to talk, McKenzie, and I'm pretty sure you know what I'm talking about."

"Yes, Sydney, I do, and I agree. It's time to talk."

She put down her fork, tapped her lips with her napkin and looked straight into his eyes. The minute she did he wished he hadn't brought the subject up.

"But let me begin," McKenzie said, surprising him. "I've done a lot of thinking about what you told me before Thanksgiving about being a minister. I know my reaction upset you, but you have to understand, I don't know anything about church or ministry or what being a minister's wife would involve. All of it is out of my realm of experience. Church is not something I've thought about one way or the other. The bottom line is that I'm very unsettled about what you want to do, but I don't want to stand in your way. Maybe the best thing would be for us to take a break from each other for a while."

Sydney was stunned. Tears welled up in his eyes. Seeing his reaction, McKenzie quickly leaned over and put her hand on his.

"Oh, Sydney, I am so sorry for saying that. I was trying to be funny to lighten things up. I didn't realize I would upset you like this, but I should have known the subject was too serious for me to kid about it. I feel terrible for upsetting you."

He wiped his eyes with his handkerchief and took a sip of water. She moved closer to him and took both his hands into hers and said, "I want you to listen to me, Sydney, because I am being serious now. I love you with all my heart. Surely you know that by now. It was a spur of the moment joke that wasn't funny. Can you forgive me for being insensitive?"

"Yes, yes, of course. It's okay. I'm okay. Just got caught a little off guard. I thought you were dead serious."

"Actually, Sydney, I am dead serious, only not in a negative way. The truth is, I could make that stupid joke because I am all in on what you feel called to do, a hundred percent. I don't understand much about it or even what it is, so you'll have to help me. But what matters, and I want you to hear this clearly, is that we will be together. I cannot imagine my life without you. Don't even want to think about it. This is something we are going to do together."

That choked him up again.

"I don't know what is wrong with me tonight," he managed to say. "I can't keep myself together. I guess hearing you say that released all the emotions I've been holding tight since I started feeling the way I do. I wouldn't do anything if it meant losing you. You saying you are with me in this is all I need to know. Everything else will work out as long as we're okay."

"We are okay, Sydney, we are, but I do have one condition before we move ahead."

"Anything."

"You have to make an honest woman out of me and marry me."

A month later the college chaplain married them in a private ceremony in the college chapel.

# 7

The Sullivans of Halifax were a prominent family, but hadn't lost their sense of self and never took their good fortune for granted. Carrie was the youngest of three daughters. A delight to be around as the Strange family discovered when Sonny brought her to his mother's sixtieth birthday dinner. He had met her at a party soon after he got back from basic training. She was educated, thoughtful, and, in contrast to Sonny, relatively quiet. By the time dinner was over everyone was taken with her and delighted that Sonny had met someone of such quality.

Carrie and Sonny dated for a couple of years and then in the fall announced that they had gotten married at the county courthouse and had rented an apartment in Castle Cove. That caught his and her families completely off guard, especially since Sonny had been bouncing around from one job to another after quitting the sawmill. Stable was not a word to describe him, but the additional surprise in their announcement was that Sonny had been hired by Julian Hogan, a guy he grew up with who had opened The Men's Corner clothing store. Good news, of course, but no one could be blamed for wondering how long that would last. The gossip around town was that Julian's first business mistake was making his store exclusively for men. The second was hiring Sonny Strange.

Turns out people were wrong on both counts. Julian knew Sonny had a drinking problem because he had spent more than a little time of his own in Castle Cove bars. The difference between them was that he left that life behind when his father put up the money to open the store. He was betting on Sonny being the natural salesman he thought he was and initially that bet was paying off in spades. Sales soared immediately, mainly due to Sonny. Within a year Julian and his dad were talking about the possibility of opening another store across town. Eventually Julian made Sonny the store manager so he could devote more of his time to the new venture.

When The Men's Corner added a line of shoes, Sonny came into his own. He could sell a pair of shoes to a horse. More than that, he knew which shoes would sell and which wouldn't. As soon as a delivery arrived Sonny would tell him which ones would sell out fast and which ones wouldn't sell at all. He was right every time. Eventually Julian realized he was the wrong person to be going to the shoe buyer's show in Atlanta, that Sonny should go instead. His decision proved itself to be the right one. Every line of shoes Sonny bought would sell, so much so that shoe sales began to rival the store's clothing line.

Carrie got pregnant a year after Sonny began at The Men's Corner and had a baby girl they named Annie. Eighteen months later she had Anthony. Sydney's mother told him on the phone one day that she believed the family had finally gotten through some very tough times with Sonny and that he was finally settling down to adulthood. He wanted to believe she was right and had no real reason not to, yet he couldn't rid himself of the worry that it was all temporary. The first hint that he was right came when Carrie took a job with Allegheny County District Schools as assistant personnel director. Sonny was making a good salary and Carrie had never expressed any desire to go back to work. A few months later she confided to Sarah that she had taken the job to stabilize her finances because Sonny was drinking again, and she didn't know how bad it would get or how it would eventually affect his job.

"And we all thought he was doing fine," Sydney told his mother when she related the conversation she had had with Carrie.

"I suppose we believed what we wanted to," she responded. "Carrie is such an amazing young woman. She said Sonny went to Atlanta to a shoe show as usual and the day after he was supposed to come back she got a call from Julian Hogan, who asked her if she had heard from Sonny. He was expecting him back the day before, but he didn't show. Apparently, Sonny had called Carrie and said there was some kind of problem in shoe orders that would keep him in Atlanta at least another day. He said he would call once he knew when he would be coming home. He never did. She told Julian she would tell Sonny to call him the next time she heard from him.

"Carrie said he showed up three days later as if nothing had happened. She said a cab let him out at the house and he walked in without saying a word, went upstairs and came down after he had shaved and showered ready to go to work. She was sitting at the counter drinking coffee when he poured himself one and whispered in her ear that he was sorry. She said it was the last straw and she let him have it."

"Did she tell you what she said?"

"Yes she did. I have never heard Carrie so upset. She said she had to keep from screaming when she asked him what he was sorry for. Making her lose her mind in worry, having to lie to Annie and Anthony about where their father was, for not knowing if he was dead or alive, for drinking his life away and destroying their family in the process?"

"Poor Carrie," said Sydney, then asked, "Did he lose his job?"

"No, Julian just said he would if it ever happened again, but that's why Carrie went back to work. She said she couldn't continue to live in fear of having no income at all."

Sydney was frustrated and angry when he and his mother ended the call. He felt helpless. Sonny's life was becoming a soap opera that was pulling everyone in the family into it, and there was nothing they could do about it. He tried not to think about it but didn't have much success. Then a few days later his cell rang. It was Sonny.

"Sydney, she's gone."

"Who is gone, Sonny?"

"Carrie. Carrie's gone."

"What do you mean, 'she's gone?'"

"Just what I said. She left a note saying she was picking up the children after school, and going to her parents in Halifax, and would decide later what to do about school for the kids. Said right now she needed space."

Sydney didn't respond.

"Guess I really messed up going to Atlanta," Sonny continued. "I know better. I know I can't handle a trip like that, but Julian wanted me to do it. I can do the job. I know shoes, what will sell and what won't, but I can't go off on trips."

"Did he fire you?" Sydney asked.

"Should have, but he didn't. I went to the store as usual the day after I got back and he let me work all day. I went in to see him after the others left for the day. He said he realized sending me was a mistake, that he would keep me in the store and go himself next time. I apologized and thanked him for keeping me on. When I got home that night I tried to tell Carrie what he said, but she wasn't interested in hearing it. Said she didn't want to hear anything anymore, that changing my behavior was the only thing that would make any difference to her. I thought that meant she would give me another chance."

"Sounds to me like she is giving you another chance, Sonny, only she's not going to stay at home waiting to see how it turns out. She's smart enough to know a few days or even a week or so is not a reliable sign that you're different. I guess she wants enough time to pass before she can believe you've changed. About the only place she had to go was to her parents'."

"That's certainly not going to help me, Sydney. You know Jackson hates me."

"He doesn't hate you, Sonny. He hates what you're doing to his daughter, to his grandchildren. And to be honest, I can't blame him."

"Spoken like a true brother," Sonny said sharply.

"Oh, come on Sonny." Sydney said, raising his voice. "You know what I'm talking about. You've got no right to be upset that Carrie, the kids, and her parents are upset with you because of your drinking. It's not easy to watch what you're doing to yourself. I've gotten so I dread it when the phone rings because I fear it is somebody calling to tell me you died in a car accident or that you killed somebody else. Your drinking doesn't just affect you. It affects everybody around you. Spare me the self-pity."

The silence that followed couldn't have been louder, but Sydney waited to see how Sonny would respond.

"I guess I'm just not as good as you, Sydney. You're the good son, I'm the black sheep."

"Oh, for God's sake, Sonny, don't go down that road again."

"No, it's true and you know it is. You're mom's dream son, the minister she always hoped one of us would become."

"That's crap and you know it. The truth is, you're mother's favorite. Not that you're the good son. It's because you're the prodigal and prodigals get the most attention in every family. She worries about you all the time, she and father both. That's all they talk about when I see them, so drop the 'you're the good son' line. You're just trying to lay the blame for your messed-up life on me."

Sydney heard a click and knew Sonny had hung up. Just as well. He had said enough, more than he ever had before, but it didn't make him feel any better. Sonny was in trouble but he refused to believe it. Sydney had a haunting dread that his life was not going to end well.

Then hope appeared out of nowhere. Two months after that conversation Sonny showed up in Kenwood. When Sydney got home from playing basketball in a college intra-mural league, he saw Sonny's car parked across the street as he pulled up in front of their apartment. Sonny and McKenzie were sitting in the small living room drinking coffee when Sydney walked in. She immediately stood up, kissed him on the cheek, and said, "Look who showed up at the door while you were gone."

Sonny sat there smiling like the Cheshire Cat that just ate the canary. Sydney sat down and waited for him to say something. He didn't so Sydney asked him what had happened.

"Nothing," he said in an unusually quiet voice. "Just the opposite. I'm talking to everyone in the family to make amends for everything I've done over the last few years. I joined AA right after Carrie took the children and went to her parents, and I have been to a meeting every day since. Thirty meetings in thirty days is what they call it, only I've extended it. Making amends is the ninth step of the program. I told Carrie I was sorry for it all, all of it, and more, that I would do better. I heard what you said on the phone, Sydney, I really did. I know I act like I'm not listening, but I am. You can only kid yourself so many times and then it hits you between the eyes."

"Have you talked to mother and father?"

"Yes, I have. They were the first ones I went to after Carrie. Then Harrison and Maryanne, now you and McKenzie. I also need to see Carrie's parents, but I guess I'm avoiding Jackson as long as possible. Savannah might be civil, but I'm not sure he will be."

"Don't expect much sympathy from them would be my advice," Sydney told him.

"No, I won't. I'm just hoping they will at least give me a chance to talk to them. This is not for them anyway, it's for me. How they react is their business. Telling them I'm sorry is mine."

"You really have learned some things," Sydney responded.

"A lot more than that. You know when I've told you I was living the life I wanted to live?" Sydney nodded yes. "Well, it was a lie. I hate my life, if you want to know the truth. Always have. It often feels like something has control of me and I can't make it let go. That's what alcohol does to me. It controls my mind completely. It's hard for anybody who is not addicted to understand that. People think all you need to do is stop, and that's actually true, but you don't feel like you are in control enough to do it. I never thought I would end up like this. I never wanted to. I let my broken leg become an excuse to drink after it happened, and it has been downhill ever since. The worst thing is that I know I am a good shoe buyer. I've been told I could be making twice as much money as I am right now if I stayed sober. The whole time I was in Atlanta drinking I keep telling myself that and at the same time I kept on drinking. It sounds crazy because it is. Insane is what AA calls it. It all makes sense because it makes no sense at all."

"So you lash out at me and everyone else to hide the truth?"

"Exactly. That's the worst part, the hurt I've caused, especially to Carrie and the kids. Annie and Anthony deserve a better father and Carrie certainly deserves a better husband. I guess I'm here to say I think you deserve a better brother."

"That means a lot, Sonny. It really does."

They looked at each other for a moment and then Sydney asked if he wanted to spend the night. He said no, that he needed to get back to go to work in the morning. They stood and Sydney started to give him a hug when Sonny stuck out his hand to shake instead. Typical of Sonny. McKenzie would have none of that. She hugged him before he could refuse.

He probably should have left it alone, but Sydney called Sonny a couple of days later to see if he had talked to Jackson and Savanah. They were nice people and wanted the best for Carrie and the children. Savanah is from a prominent Atlanta family that is generations deep in Georgia heritage. Blonde, medium height, shorter than Carrie, but similarly slim, attractive for her age, with a soft-spoken southern drawl typical of anyone from Georgia. Jackson is originally from New Jersey, attended Georgia Tech where he met Savanah at a fraternity party. They got married and when Jackson finished school a Georgia Tech a friend who was three years ahead of him asked if he would consider becoming a partner in a small start-up architectural firm in Halifax. They struggled for a couple of years and then business started growing. The firm is now quite successful with clients all over the southeast.

"Yeah, I talked to them," Sonny told Sydney. "They were okay, actually, no yelling, no big chill. They listened and at the end said this was news they had been praying for and wished me the best."

"Did they say anything about Carrie?"

"No, her name never came up. I wondered if she had forewarned them about what I was going to do, but, if she did, she didn't tell me and they didn't say anything either."

"Sounds like you've done all you can do and now it's time to move on. Take care of yourself, Sonny, and I mean that."

"Thanks, Sydney, I will, and I mean that."

# 8

Sydney knew less about seminary than he did about the church. A few people in the churches he and McKenzie attended in Kenwood and Parkville seemed concerned that seminary might cause him to lose his faith. He had no idea what they were talking about. The only thing he was sure of was that he believed in God. The rest of his faith he described as "under construction," so he didn't see that there was much he could lose. He had taken only two required courses in religion at Western for his liberal arts degree. He would have taken more, but once he became a double major he had no electives outside his two fields to spare. He did read the Episcopal Prayer Book to familiarize himself with the statements of faith the church used in worship, including the creeds. Other than that, he was coming at everything as the novice he was.

Knowing as little as he did about seminaries, Sydney thought choosing where to do his theological studies was a crap shoot. He mentioned Virginia Theological Seminary in Alexandria to McKenzie as one possibility. She decided to contact a college classmate who was teaching high school history in the Fairfax County Virginia school system, supposedly one of the best systems in the country. She told McKenzie a position teaching tenth grade English composition was opening at her school in the fall and suggested she apply. McKenzie told Sydney she thought she should send in an application. If she got the job he could apply to the seminary there. Several weeks later the Fairfax County assistant superintendent called to say that he had received her application and based on her teaching experience and her strong recommendations, the job was hers if she wanted it. She accepted it on the spot. Sydney received his letter of acceptance from VTS soon thereafter and they began to focus on getting ready to move,

The first order of business was to find a place to live. After several days of looking they settled on a two-bedroom apartment in a community called Reston they thought would make both of their commutes easy. Once they moved they discovered that there was no such thing as an "easy" commute in Northern Virginia. Washington, DC rush hour traffic stretched far into the suburbs and had no real time boundaries. You could move at a snail's pace all hours of the day and night. But they managed to adjust and by early fall began to feel settled into their new metropolitan life.

Sydney didn't know what to expect from seminary. His first surprise after being in classes for a month was realizing that he actually liked the Bible. He had tried reading it in years past, but had never gotten very far. Studying it turned out to be much more interesting, even fascinating. He also discovered that theological education is as much about life as it is preparing for ministry. Sydney had never spent so much time reading, discussing, and thinking about the meaning and purpose of human existence. He loved every minute of it. Had he known the kind of education ministers receive, he thought accepting his call to become a minister might not have been the struggle it was.

By the time the Thanksgiving holidays approached Sydney and McKenzie both felt settled and grateful that the move had worked out so well. They enjoyed a Thanksgiving Day meal with no one but themselves for the first time in their lives and were surprised at how much they enjoyed it. Once December arrived, however, their families began insisting they make plans to come home for Christmas. They hadn't been to Castle Cove since moving to Virginia. Being with family at Christmas sounded nice, and that is how it turned out. Each of them had fun being with both families and also running into a few of their high school friends at their favorite Castle Cove coffee shop. McKenzie told Sydney on the drive back to Reston that she had not realized how much she missed everyone until seeing them again. He responded that he felt the same way.

The spring school term for both of them got off to a good start. The weather was warming and azalea bushes around their respective schools started blooming. For reasons neither of them could explain, spring semester always seemed shorter than fall. Sydney finished the middle of May so McKenzie's semester was a month longer than his. He decided to use the time he had to himself to resurrect his tennis game. He had played only a few times since he and McKenzie had moved. He started hitting against the backboards at some well-maintained courts at a nearby community college. One day as he arrived at the courts he saw a guy who looked to be his age hitting balls against one of the boards. Sydney introduced himself and asked him if he wanted to hit together. That was the beginning of Sydney and Charles Townsend becoming tennis friends and playing together at least once a week.

Sydney quickly realized that Charles was a recreational player and could not compete at his level, but their tennis temperaments made playing each other fun. Charles knew what Sydney knew, that his skills were nowhere near as good as those Sydney possessed. One afternoon after a match he told Sydney about the annual summer tournaments sponsored by area cities that would be starting soon. Charles thought Sydney would enjoy the level of competition. Sydney took his advice and called the Silver City recreation department, a town some ten miles from Reston, to request an entry form as soon as he saw the ad for its tournament in the paper.

He found out very quickly that his game needed a lot more work than he thought it did. He didn't make it into Silver City's round of sixteen. Losing didn't bother him. Everyone loses in tennis, although he hadn't lost a lot over the years and never liked it when he did. What really bothered him, though, was how poorly he played, maybe the worst ever. He was very frustrated with himself. Two-weeks later he signed up for another tournament, this was in Herndon. He didn't do any better in terms of matches won, but the score of the games was much closer than last time. Better, he hit a lot of good shots, his serve that had always been his strength was smooth and easy, and afterwards he felt like his game was showing signs of coming around. That was confirmed when he made it to the quarter finals in the Oakton Open, and then the second weekend in August he reached the semi-finals at a large tournament in Vienna. He lost in a tight match to the number one singles player at George Washington University, taking him to a tie-breaker in the third and final set.

He took a few weeks off from tournaments and limited himself to playing Charles in their weekly match. It was a needed rest. Feeling fully recharged, he was among the first entries for the last tournament of the season, the Alexandria Labor Day Classic. He told Charles he thought he had a decent chance to win it even with several top amateur players around the region also playing. The brackets were such that he realized if he did well he would have a rematch with the George Washington singles player who had beaten him a few weeks earlier. Turned out not to be as the kid was unexpectedly beaten in the semi-finals and Sydney ending up facing his opponent in the finals. He surprised himself with how well he played.

It was like he couldn't miss a shot. He won in straight sets to claim the champion's trophy.

"Congratulations, Mr. Strange," McKenzie said as he came out of the gates of the tennis court, "or should I say congratulations to the not yet Reverend Strange?"

"The way I feel right now," he said, "either one is music to my ears. Nothing compares to the feeling of playing a tennis match where every shot seems to go exactly the way you hit it. That's how it was today."

"Oh, I saw it all," she responded. "You really did play well. In fact, I'm certainly no tennis critic, as you know, but it looked like a perfect match to me."

Sydney smiled at her and said, "Thanks, Kenz. It means more than you know to hear you say that."

"Well, my Strange man, you mean a lot to me." She stood in front of him and gave him a kiss. "I'm glad you've gotten back into tennis. I know you love the game."

"I really do," Sydney replied. "This has been a very good summer."

Finding out he still had some game made Sydney wonder, if only briefly, whether he should have given the pro-circuit a try after he had finished Western. His coach had told him he had the shots to play professionally, that the learning curve would be the mental side of the game, choosing the right shots at the right time and having the maturity to stay calm when a match wasn't going well. As tempting as it had been to give it a try, though, his first year of seminary had removed any doubts about choosing instead to follow his call to ministry.

His second year in school was a mirror of his first. The depth and quality of the lectures his professors gave and the discussions after classes with his classmates were as good as what he experienced in year one. McKenzie was also having a good year and agreed to teach English in the first summer school term when her principal asked her. Once the semester was over Sydney chose not to repeat the intense summer tennis schedule he had last year, content to enjoy playing against Charles again. In late June and again the second week in July he entered a couple of tournaments where he felt satisfied with his play. He made it to the semi-finals both times and was competitive in losing. That was enough to satisfy his tennis thirst.

He began his final year with as much excitement as he remembered having the day he first entered VTS. Nothing he had ever experienced compared to the intellectual challenge theology, biblical studies, and church history presented. Icing on the cake was Dr. Margaret Stanton asking him to be her teaching assistant in church history. Early in the semester she invited him to present a lecture on the Reformation to her first-year class. It went well, very well, in fact, and a week later she told him she would like for him to give another one on the immediate cultural impact of the Protestant Reformation when they get to that point in the semester.

The chance to lecture to Professor Stanton's first-year class was unusual for a senior graduate assistant, but Dr. Stanton recognized that Sydney was no ordinary third-year student. He had a maturity beyond his years and an ability to make complicated issues easily comprehensible. Scheduled to deliver a final lecture at the end of the semester on a subject of his own choosing, Sydney had decided to make Martin Luther's anti-Semitism his focus, a subject of critical importance, but one that in his opinion had not received sufficient attention. He was headed to the library to do more research on the subject when he ran into Jack Simpson, another third-year student and one of Sydney's good friends.

"Hey, Jack," Sydney said as the two stopped to talk. "I haven't seen you for a while. How are you?"

"Hi Sydney. Good. In fact, today more than good. I got a phone call last night from the chair of the search committee at Market Square Episcopal Church in Frederick, Maryland telling me they were going to recommend me to the congregation as their new rector."

"Congratulations, man," Sydney responded. "That is great. They have no idea how good a decision they are making. You'll be the best they've ever had."

"It sounds good even if it's not true," Jack replied, "but thanks for the vote of confidence."

"I'm serious, Jack. You're going to do great."

"Hope so," Jack answered. "But what about you? You got any good prospects right now?"

"No, nothing yet," Sydney said, being honest but not telling Jack the whole story.

"You will," Jack assured Sydney. "You will, but let's talk more later. I'm going to be late for class. We need to catch up."

"Yeah, we do. Talk soon."

What Sydney didn't tell Jack was that he hadn't heard from any churches because his name was not in circulation for a parish. The truth was, he had no idea what he wanted to do once he graduated. He hadn't given the future much thought. Sydney was genuinely happy for Jack being called to a church, but hearing about it unexpectedly unsettled him and for the first time he felt a tinge of panic. Here he was about to get his Master of Divinity degree and he had no clue about what he would do next. Some type of Chaplaincy? Congregational pastor? Working with a non-profit? Getting an advanced degree and teaching?

That night he told McKenzie about his conversation with Jack. He admitted it had made him feel anxious about next year. She reminded him that they had been living on her salary for three years so there was no pressure on him to jump at the first thing that came along. She suggested he think about doing further graduate study. She reminded him that he loved school and it might help him gain some clarity about his future. Besides, she told him, she was enjoying teaching and would be happy to stay on at Herndon High School.

Still unsure about what he wanted to do next, Sydney decided to take McKenzie's advice and apply to the Master of Arts degree program in history at George Washington University. His acceptance came quickly which he thought might be a sign that he was doing the right thing. While his first classes didn't excite him as much as his seminary classes had, he found the connection between secular and church history fascinating. The year sailed by and he chose to write his Master's thesis on the role of the Episcopal Church in North Carolina before, during, and after the Civil War. He had no trouble taking classes and doing the writing. A few weeks after he turned in his thesis his major professor, the esteemed historian Hiram Marshall Becker, offered high praise for the paper. "Work of the highest caliber," was how he put it to Sydney.

His George Washington experience made a career in academics appealing to Sydney, especially with Professor Becker encouraging him to stay at GW and get his PhD in history. Sydney was tempted, but once again he had that feeling he had had when he first felt called to ministry, not toward academics, but parish ministry. Not enough to know for sure that was the path to follow, but he knew it was there. He decided live with the feeling a while just as he had done before to see if he got any more clearness about what to do. A few days later the thought of parish ministry was strong enough that he decided to tell McKenzie what he was feeling.

"We've been down this road before, Sydney," were the first words out of McKenzie's mouth. "You know where it's going to end. You had to pay attention to those feelings inside of you once before and that is what got us here. I am sure you will have to now. Am I wrong?"

"No, no you're not," he said almost begrudgingly. "I think I just needed to hear you say it for me. But what about you, your teaching, our living here? You know if I put my name in for a church, we will probably have to move."

"Yes, I know that, but moving after seminary was always in the picture. We delayed it a year, but it's always been there."

"It has, but whether we actually move or not is up to us," Sydney said. "I'm not sure I want to ask you to give up your job again. You like the school, your colleagues, even your students. That's a big ask."

"Yes, at one level it is, and I also doubt I will find a school system anywhere that compares to Fairfax County. But to be perfectly honest I'm kind of weary of the rush of life living here involves. The traffic alone is wearing me down. Reston, in fact, the whole area, has made me realize that I'm a small-town girl more than I ever thought I was. A small town in Carolina, or at least a smaller place than this area, sounds kind of nice when I think about it."

"You're open to moving, then, if that's what happens?" Sydney asked to make sure he was hearing her correctly.

"I am," McKenzie answered. "Yes, I am."

"Well," he responded, "I will get things rolling with the diocese and see where it leads." He paused, looked into her eyes for a moment and said, "I am a very lucky man, McKenzie. I want you to know I know that," leaning over to kiss her.

After his soft kiss she held his face in her hands and replied, "I think we're both pretty lucky, Sydney, and what matters most wherever we end up is that we're together."

Sydney smiled and said, "It does, Kenz, more than anything else."

# 9

The next day Sydney contacted the diocese of Northern Virginia about becoming a candidate for parish ministry. The secretary told him all he needed to do was to fill out the papers and once his references were in his file they would send his resume wherever he wanted it to go. A few weeks later he got a call from the diocese office that his file was complete and asked where to send his papers. He chose North Carolina and the eastern and central areas of Virginia.

Things moved quickly and two months later Sydney and McKenzie were on their way to Saint Alban Parish, a small Episcopal Church in Marian Beach, North Carolina. Marian Beach is a small town of twenty thousand people whose summer population swells by another ten thousand. The beach itself is pristine white and the ocean water has a beautiful green hue. McKenzie fell in love with the place immediately. She thought of it as the perfect beach town, big enough to have everything you need, but not overcrowded by tourists in the summer. Wanting to get to know their new place first. McKenzie decided not to seek a teaching position right away. In January she discovered she was pregnant, and in September when they were completing their first year in Marian Beach she gave birth to a healthy baby girl they named Leslie Madison. It didn't take McKenzie long to tell Sydney she wanted to be a stay-at-home mom for Leslie's first few years and then she would think about going back to teaching.

Saint Alban Church was a picturesque wooden building a block away from the beach with a sanctuary that faced the ocean. On quiet days you could hear the waves crashing when the sanctuary windows were open. From the moment Leslie was out of diapers McKenzie would bring her to the beach. Leslie took to it immediately. To avoid the weekend crowds, she and Leslie would go only on weekdays. Parking at the church and stopping to see Sydney before or after hitting the beach, it didn't take long for them to find their favorite spot.

One day Sydney decided to join them for lunch since they had not stopped by his office earlier. What happened next earned him the label "the shoeless priest." The day was very hot. He had a pair of jogging shorts and tee shirt at the office for times when he went running to clear his mind on days when he got stuck working on a sermon. He quickly put on the shorts, for some reason didn't take off his clerical collar, and headed to the beach barefooted. When he found McKenzie and Leslie, she looked up from her lounge chair and said, "Are you here to swim or preach?"

He laughed and knelt down and kissed her, whispering, "You have the sexiest body of any priest's wife I've ever seen."

"Oh, yeah," she said smiling at him, "and just how many bikini clad priests' wives have you seen?"

"Oh, ma dame," he said, "I've been to the southern part of France where the women wear...nothing."

"But how many are married to an Episcopal priest?"

"Only you, my sweet, only you," he managed to say just as he heard Leslie calling him to come see the sandcastle she had built."

In the summer wearing shorts and no shoes became a sort of calling card for Sydney. It seemed to open doors for lots of conversations, important ones, in fact, with the large number of young people who were at the beach every day, something that became an unexpectedly permanent part of his ministry in Marian Beach.

The first five years in Marian Beach were as good as that first summer. Fall was approaching when McKenzie and Leslie came by the church once again, this time mid-afternoon having spent several hours on the beach. Sydney knew something was different when McKenzie asked his secretary, Madelyn Craig, if Leslie could sit in her office for a few minutes. Loving Sydney like a son and being just as protective, Madelyn had embraced Leslie as if she were her own granddaughter. Having a chance to spend a few minutes with her was a welcome break from work.

McKenzie came into Sydney's office, closed the door behind her, and sat down saying they needed to talk. That had a familiar ring to it. She told him she had a chance to go back to full-time teaching. Collin Ward, the superintendent of the Marian County schools, had called her to say their junior English teacher had notified him that for personal reasons she needed to take a leave of absence for the fall term that was only a month away.

"I called Bill Taylor," Superintendent Ward had told her, "who as you know is Chair of the Graduate School for Education at UNC Greensboro, asking if he knew of someone he could recommend. Yours was the first name he mentioned, that you had taught for four years in Parkville and then a few years in Virginia, and that he had heard you were in Marian Beach as a stay-at-home mother. He didn't know your interest or availability, but what he said he did know was that I could not do better if you were interested. That was all the recommendation I needed."

"He offered me the job, Sydney, right on the spot. I told him Dr. Taylor was my major professor when I got my master's at UNC while we were in Kenwood and was flattered by his recommendation, but that I would need to think about the offer. He said he understood. I told him I would get back in touch in a day or two. Sydney, I think this is something I might like to do."

"I don't know what to say," he said hesitatingly. "What about Leslie?"

"Well, that was obviously my first thought. I haven't regretted the decision to stay home with Leslie. In fact, I've loved every minute we've had together. But she's starting first grade in the fall and that means life changes for me as well. I called the principal at the high school and told her about the situation. I asked if she would allow Leslie to be dropped off at the high school by one of the school buses as its first stop once it leaves Leslie's school. The two schools are only a couple of blocks apart. She thought that could be arranged and that she would talk to her colleague who is the principle at Mary Ward Elementary. I also asked if it would be possible to make my last class of the day my free period. That would allow Leslie to join me in my classroom until school was over. The principle said she didn't think that would be a problem either. Everything seems to be falling in place for this, Sydney. And the icing on the cake is that I will be able to drop Leslie off at school in the mornings so we will get to ride to and from school together every day."

Sydney listened, but didn't say anything. His silence upset McKenzie, though he told her that was not his intention. He was just thinking about what all of this meant, but she took it as disapproval.

"I can see you don't like the idea," she said.

"No, that's not true. I'm just trying to get my head around it all."

"What 'all' are you talking about, Sydney? There is no 'all' involved that I can see."

"I know, I know," he said, "It's just a big change for us. I've enjoyed you being home and the freedom it gives us. And I guess I have some anxiety about Leslie starting school. It's like she's growing up."

"She is growing up, Sydney. It's what kids do, but that doesn't have anything to do with my going back to teaching, something I enjoy and something I am very good at."

"Of course, you are. I know that. Can you just give me the afternoon to think this through and we can talk tonight?"

At that McKenzie stood up without saying a word, got Leslie and left. Sydney immediately realized he had messed up. His lack of enthusiasm had thrown cold water on her excitement about going back to teaching. He didn't intend it that way. He was caught off guard and too slow to realize what saying nothing sounded like.

Just then Madelyn buzzed in and said Bishop Stewart was on the line. Great, Sydney thought. He just had a conflict with his wife and now his bishop was calling, probably to tell him someone in the church had made a complaint about him.

"Thank you, Madelyn."

He punched in the line.

"Bishop Stewart, what a surprise. How are you, sir?"

"Fine, Sydney, fine, and no need to call me sir."

"Yes, sir, I mean, yes, I understand."

"Sydney, I am calling for a specific reason."

Bishop Stewart was not known for being chatty or writing long letters. He got right to the point whatever it happened to be.

"Saint Patrick in Castle Cove is looking for a parish priest and the vestry has asked me to contact you before I suggest anyone else to see if you would consider coming back home."

Sydney didn't know what to say. He had been in Marian for over five years and his ministry seemed to be going well. The people gave every impression of being satisfied with him as their pastor.

"What do you think, Bishop Stewart. You have more experience than I do in these matters. I have been here a while and things seem to be going well."

"From everything I hear, they are, Sydney, and as you know a happy priest and parish makes for a happy Bishop. It is not usually in anyone's interest, including mine, to break up a good thing. But this is not a usual situation, to be honest with you."

"I trust I am not in trouble about something of which I am unaware," Sydney quickly responded.

"No, no, no, I can assure you that is not the case," the Bishop said. "Just the opposite, in fact. It's the church that is in trouble, or headed in that direction, and your record is why I would like for you to give this possibility some thought. You see, the last priest Castle Cove had, Cyrus Haynes, you might know him, had a bit of a problem, drinking to excess, to be specific."

"Yes, I do know, Cyrus," he said. "I wouldn't say we know each other well, but my parents seem to like him."

"Yes, most people do, in the church and in the town. That said, I received a call from the chair of the vestry several weeks ago to alert me to a problem that turned out to be quite serious. Cyrus, it seems, was spending more time in some of the town bars than he was visiting people in the hospital. He was missing meetings he was expected to attend both at the church and in the town. On one occasion he attended a vestry meeting with the smell of alcohol on his breath. This went on for a while until finally the vestry met with him to confront him about what was going on. Apparently, he didn't deny anything, even thanked them for confronting him because he knew he had a problem. He told them he had already talked to his brother who was a doctor in Halifax about helping him get into a rehab center there. He then said he thought it best for the church and for himself to resign and give health issues as the reason. The vestry agreed and his last Sunday was a week ago. I have arranged for James Redmond who recently retired to go there as interim."

"I'm very sorry to hear all of this," Sydney told Bishop Stewart sincerely.

"Yes, well, I'm afraid Cyrus is an example of a failure on the whole church's part to deal with this sort of thing. Alcoholism is more prevalent in the Episcopal priesthood than most people might think, but we've been very good at pretending it wasn't. It's not easy to know the extent of the problem because clergy and churches try to keep it secret as if alcoholism is a moral failing instead of a disease. At this point the most reliable estimates are that the rate of alcoholism for clergy is close to what it is among doctors, lawyers, and the police, which is two to three times the rate of the general population. In other words, it's a serious problem."

"I confess I didn't know any of this. To be honest, I haven't given it much thought, probably because I don't drink myself. Not for moral reasons, more because of family dynamics."

"Yes, well it is a problem I'm afraid all of us in church leadership are going to have to think about it a lot in the coming years. Most of my Bishop colleagues say it is something they are confronting more and more with their priests. Cyrus is my first one, but I'm sure he won't be the last. But, as I said, I didn't call you to talk about him, but to see if you would allow me to submit your name to Saint Patrick."

"Well," Sydney said to Bishop Stewart, "I can't say one way or the other, to be honest. It's not just me, it's my wife. I need to hear what she thinks of going back. She just had an opportunity to go back into teaching here. We haven't made any decision about that either. This could help with that or complicate it, so I need some time."

"I understand, Sydney. Actually, I told the vestry chair just that, that you would probably need some time to think this through before starting any conversation. Why don't we leave it at that and you give me a call as soon as you've decided. Would a week be enough time?"

"Yes, I think so."

"Okay, then, I will wait to hear from you, Sydney. Good to talk to you, and I appreciate the good work you are doing at Saint Alban."

"Thank you, Bishop Stewart, that means a lot coming from you. As you know, this is my first parish and I am trying to do my very best."

"You obviously are, Sydney. I look forward to hearing from you, and, please know that this is your decision and I am not in any way trying to get you to choose one over the other."

"I understand, thank you, and I will call you in a week."

Sydney left the church with a million thoughts running through his mind. He hadn't thought much about someday serving Saint Patrick. Going home might be nice. His mother had been subtle but clear that his father was not doing as well as he wanted everyone to think. His doctor put him on heart and blood pressure medications to get things under control. Sydney only learned six months ago that his father had suffered heart failure when he and his brothers were in high school. He thought he was out of town on business, and he was, but he had an attack late one night in the hotel and they managed to call nine-one-one and got him to the hospital in time. He stayed four days and was back home without Harrison, Sonny, or Sydney knowing what had actually happened. Sarah had told them he had a stomach problem that delayed him from flying home, but that he was fine, just needed some rest.

It occurred to Sydney that maybe it was time for him to help Harrison carry some of the responsibility for their family. Running the sawmill had worked out well thus far and Harrison would be exactly the person to take over when his dad decided to turn everything over to him for good. Sam wasn't ready to do that yet, but Sydney thought it wouldn't be long. It might be nice to be back with the family again, he thought. With her parents still living in Castle Cove, McKenzie might also think being near her parents as they get older would be a good thing. Nothing but thoughts at the moment, though, since nothing would change without Saint Patrick first calling him as its senior vicar.

At supper Leslie talked about what she and her friend, Molly, did at the beach earlier in the day. Out of the blue she said, "I think I want a goldfish. Molly has one and it is so cute. She showed me what she did to take care of it. I could do the same thing."

McKenzie and Sydney waited for the next sentence asking if she could get one. It didn't come. Finally, Sydney said, "Well, I think that is an idea your mother and I should give serious thought to, you getting a goldfish, I mean."

"Oh, not now, daddy. I don't want one now. Maybe after the summer when I can't go to the beach because I will be in school. My schedule is just too busy at the moment."

Both of them looked at each other dumbfounded.

"Excuse me," he said to Leslie, "did you skip from six to thirteen today or are you still six, because you sound thirteen to me."

"Oh, daddy, don't be silly. I'm still six."

At that she asked if she could be excused and took off for her room without waiting for an answer.

McKenzie smiled at Sydney. They both were quite proud of their little girl who seemed grown-up already. Sydney got up and started preparing to wash the dishes. When he finished he put a cup of the morning's coffee in the microwave to warm, waited for it and then sat down with it in hand at the counter across from McKenzie.

"I feel like we didn't finish our conversation this afternoon," he said taking sip of coffee. "I know I didn't respond the way I should have. And right afterwards I had a phone call I will tell you about that got me sidetracked from this."

"What was the call about?" she asked.

"I can tell you about that later. We first need to talk about your teaching offer."

"No, actually we don't, Sydney. There is nothing to talk about."

"Why would you say that?"

"Because I called Collin Ward late this afternoon and told him I would take the job."

# 10

It was Harrison rather than his mother who called Sydney to tell him his father had been injured at work. When he told McKenzie about what happened, he said he now realized that the day you discover your parents are not going to live forever is when you truly come of age. He had always thought his father was as strong as an ox. Why wouldn't he? Sam Strange grew up cutting trees and hauling lumber when the work was as hard as it gets. He married Sarah Jane Hargis when they were in their early twenties, unusual at a time when most kids got married right out of high school. Sam believed a man had an obligation to provide for his family and was determined to be sure he could before taking the big step.

Feeling himself to be the man he had always been, he decided on a cool fall morning in October to get out of the office and help the men in the woods. One of the loggers had a family emergency and couldn't come to work. Sam decided it would do him good to fill-in. He worked with the others as if he was still doing so every day, but when quitting time came he couldn't get in the truck cab to get back to the office. The workers managed to lift him onto the tailgate, which made him feel embarrassed. When they got back to the lumber yard he stayed in place while they went into the office to get Harrison. Harrison called the emergency squad before even going out to see his father. That made Sam mad, but Harrison expected that. The EMT guys told Sam he needed to go to the ER. He insisted he was fine, but still couldn't move. They loaded him on the gurney and took him to the hospital.

X-rays showed a dislocated disk in his lower back. The doctor said it was probably age, that a person of any age, but certainly in his sixties, could simply move a certain way and dislocate a disk. That made Sam mad all over again. The damage looked minimal, the doctor said, but would require surgery and extended rest. Sam said no he wasn't having surgery. Sarah said he was and they wheeled him away.

Harrison took over managing the mill full-time while his father recovered. When Sam did come back three weeks later he could only work a few hours a day. It was a couple of months before he regained his full strength. In the meantime, Harrison was proving he was quite capable of running the business. Sam handled it better than anyone thought he would. He began to spend more time with Sarah. They went shopping together, something they had never done. They would drive to Halifax and even Charlotte to visit old friends. Sydney called Harrison regularly to see how things were going. He said he thought their parents seemed happier than he had ever seem them.

There was little news about Sonny. Carrie had brought the kids back to Castle Cove six months after she had left because Sonny seemed serious about his recovery. Then Sonny got a chance to work for C & S, a major store in Halifax. He and Carrie decided he should take it and they moved there. Part of their reasoning was that Carrie could transfer to the school district's main office in Halifax. They found a nice two-story Cape Cod in Halifax that was a rent-to-buy deal.

Both families were surprised by it all because they thought Sonny would someday take over full management of The Corner Shoe. He explained that the C & S offer was an opportunity to work for a major chain retailer he couldn't turn down. It helped that his salary virtually doubled as the manager of the men's department in the Halifax store. C & S stores were structured in an unusual way. Each department had managers who also did the ordering for their area, thereby avoiding having to hire mid-management personnel. This organization style gave Sonny a chance to show his skills in buying and selling shoes and clothing. Upper management was impressed with the job he was doing.

Balancing life and ministry was a new challenge for Sydney and McKenzie now that she was teaching again. Before she quit teaching it was just the two of them. Now they had Leslie with all her school activities. Sydney was disappointed he had had to tell Bishop Stewart he couldn't let his name go forward with Saint Patrick, but his ministry at Saint Alban was going extremely well. There was some lingering disappointment about what had happened, or more how it happened, but the fact that all three of them genuinely liked living in Marian Beach was solace enough.

"I'm thinking about driving to Castle Cove today," Sydney told McKenzie at breakfast on a Thursday morning. "I'm having some uneasy feelings about Sonny. He's called me a few times over the last few months that raised concerns about how he was really doing. I can't put my finger on anything in particular, but something doesn't feel quite right. I need to get away from the office and I would like to see how mother and father are doing as well. I should be home by seven."

"That's fine. Tell them hi and that Leslie and I will see them on Thanksgiving."

The drive could not have been more pleasant. The air was cool at the rest area the locals called Murphy's Ridge. He could see the Appalachians and the Blue Ridge in the distance. He took a minute to breathe in the beauty of the view. The scene never got old to him. He drove into Castle Cove earlier than he had expected, so he decided to stop by the sawmill to see Harrison.

"Well, look what the cat drug in," Mrs. Smith said as Sydney walked in the door, making him feel right at home as she got up from her desk and met him at its corner to give him a hug. Squeezing him hard she said, "I'm so proud of you, Sydney, and so is your father, even if he never tells you."

"Oh, I know he is," he replied. "He shows it in his own way. But I'm not here to see him, at least not yet. I'll head over the house soon enough. I'm here to see Harrison, and you, of course."

"Well, you've seen me, but Harrison's out in the yard. I'll call him on his walkie-talkie and tell him he has a visitor."

"Thanks, Mrs. Smith. It's so good to see you."

"I would have been very mad at you if you had come to town and not stopped by to give me a hug," she replied with a smile.

"I would never do that. You can count on it."

Just then Harrison walked in pulling off his gloves.

"So to what do I owe this honor, Reverend," Harrison said as we went into his office. It was next to Sam's office, but a lot more orderly. Sydney sat down in a very comfortable leather chair adjacent to a nice leather couch against the wall. Harrison sat opposite from him in a chair the twin of the one Sydney was in.

"I didn't have any particular reason for coming to town today," Sydney said answering Harrison's earlier question. "I haven't been to Castle Cove in a while and today worked well in my schedule so I decided to drive over. I need to see mother and father. How's he doing, by the way?"

"Okay, I think," Harrison answered. "He's here more than he needs to be, but not as much as he could be. Actually, he just left to go to his Lion's Club officer's meeting before their luncheon. He's slowing down. I can see that. Mom says she does, too. He's letting go of stuff here little by little."

"I'm sure it's not easy for him to do that," said Sydney.

"No, but you know, deep down I think he is ready to. He is doing more things outside work. The Lion's Club, more fishing, and, get this, he's even going to church with mom."

"You're kidding," Sydney responded. "More than his once-a-month routine?"

"Every Sunday."

"No."

"The absolute truth," Harrison said, holding his hand over his heart. "People apparently thought the priest they had, Cyrus Haynes, was a good guy, but then he left kind of suddenly. I heard he had a drinking problem, but that was probably more gossip than anything. Anyway, they have a man filling-in who is older, retired I guess, and he and dad kind of hit it off when the guy showed up for a Lion's Club luncheon. Apparently, he has been pretty active in one over in Raleigh where he lives. Dad has hardly missed a Sunday since he's been here. All of two months, I grant you, but, hey, that's more than he ever attended when we were kids. More than I do now."

"I know mother is pleased about it. She never pushed him to go to church with her, at least as far as I ever knew, but she obviously wanted him to as she did all of us, including you, Harrison."

"Don't remind me, Sydney, but those days are in the past. I figure I paid my dues when I was young. Went every Sunday, president of the Saint Pat's Youth Group, went to church camp every summer for at least three years, and was an altar boy at one point. I think I did my duty so I'm good."

"I don't think that's how it works, Harrison, but I'm not here to talk about that. What I would really like to hear is what you know about Sonny."

"Nothing really, if you want the truth, at least nothing good. I say that, but I guess that's not quite fair. I think he's still got the C & S job. I don't have any direct contact with him at all. He doesn't call me and I don't call him. Anything I know comes from Maryanne. She talks to mom and to Carrie. You know mom, she will hint at things, but avoids saying much openly, at least to me. To her credit, though, she knows I don't want to know anything about him. Maryanne says she can tell from what little mom does say that she is worried about Sonny, which means he must be drinking. Carrie apparently doesn't say anything about how things are between them, just talks mainly about the kids, which Maryanne takes to mean things are not good. That's all I know, which as you can see isn't much. As I said, Sydney, I don't want to know anything. Sonny is who he is and will never change. The less I know about his life the better off I am."

"I often feel the same way, but ultimately we both know that is not how being brothers works."

"Well, it does for me, Sydney. Sonny has been trouble since high school and you know it. You've had it out with him as many times as I have."

"Yes, I have, but..."

"But nothing, Sydney. Sonny's life is a disaster or one always waiting to happen because drinking is what he does."

"But we have to hope for something better."

"I don't think about him enough to hope for anything. You shouldn't either if you know what's good for you. Worrying about Sonny is self-defeating. But I get it. You're a minister so you're supposed to care."

"Being a minister has nothing to do with it, really. He's my brother, our brother. That's why I care. It's why you care whether you admit it or not."

"Yes, I do care, but I also know caring doesn't do him or me any good."

"I know, but I can't give up. I just can't. But listen, it's good to see you. Tell Maryanne hi. We hope to get over soon, all of us."

"Good to see you, bro." Harrison said as they both stood. Harrison gave Sydney a hug and said, "Take care of yourself, Sydney. Don't let this thing with Sonny eat you alive."

"I won't," he responded. "Let's do better at staying in touch."

"I will, Sydney. I will. Tell McKenzie hello."

Sydney turned and opened the door and step into the common area, waving to Mrs. Smith as he left the building.

His mother was sitting on the front porch reading a novel by a woman named Jan Karon. As Sydney greeted her with a kiss on the cheek, she said the main character in the book is an Episcopal priest named Father Timothy Kavanagh who serves a church in a town that sounds a lot like Castle Cove. She then told him that Father Tim, as he is called in the book, reminds her of him. Sydney smiled as he sat down in the rocking chair next to hers, but didn't respond to that comment, lost as he suddenly was remembering the first time he and Bailey Farmer sat there together when he was twelve years old. He hadn't thought about Bailey in a long time and wondered where she was, what she'd done with her life. She was so smart. Did she go to college like she planned? Does she have a career of some kind, married with children, perhaps a stay-at-home mom?

"I fixed some coffee," his mother said, interrupting his thoughts. "Harrison called and said you were on your way."

"Thanks, Mother. That would taste good right now."

"How are McKenzie and Leslie?" She asked.

"Good, real good, in fact. McKenzie likes teaching again and Leslie seems to like school and has made a lot of friends."

"And you? How are you, Sydney?"

"Fine, Mother. Things seem to be going well at the parish. And I had some interesting experiences meeting young people on the boardwalk at the beach last summer. A couple of them still stay in touch. I'm working with one girl whose father is abusive to her mother and would be with her, but she manages to stay away from him or get out of the room quickly before he gets to her. It's a bad scene and there's a policewoman who is staying in touch with her. It's surprising how many local kids stay at the beach during the summer just to get away from home. They often sleep on the beach or in the storage room of the business or store where they work. In the winter they hang out with friends and stay away from home as much as possible. It's very disturbing, but there is hardly anything I can do except to assure them I am available to talk whenever they need to."

"I'm sure that means a lot to them. Sometimes knowing you have someone in your corner is a big help to kids trying to get through to adulthood."

"I suppose, but I want to do more. I'm talking to the session about using a large room off our fellowship hall as a shelter for a few of them during the school year. Not sure how that would work, but a Sergeant Derby is working with me on it so we might be able to pull it off. The session is not against it, though not really for it either, but the door is open, so that's good."

"I think what you want to do sounds very good, sweetheart."

"Thank you, Mother. I will let you know if it works out."

They sat for a minute drinking their tea and enjoying the scenery.

"How is father?" said Sydney, breaking the silence.

"Honestly, Sydney, I don't think very well, though he says he is doing great. I can't tell you anything specific. I just know he is not himself. He doesn't have the endurance he had and has pains in his chest and right arm that worry me. He has been checked, but they haven't found any reason for any of it. That doesn't leave us with many options so we're kind of coasting along."

She paused to drink some tea, then continued. "I know he's worried about Sonny."

"Well, it doesn't surprise me to hear you say that. In fact, that's kind of why I made a special effort to come today. I'm worried about Sonny, too. I had a few phone calls from him that raised my concerns, but I don't know exactly why. Maybe brotherly intuition."

"I'm afraid your intuition was right," his mother said. "He's drinking again. He's showed up here a couple of times in the last few weeks smelling of alcohol. He wasn't drunk, but he was drinking for sure. One night he stayed over when he hadn't planned to. I'm worried he may end up losing that good job he has. Your father tried to talk to him, but it didn't go well. Sonny got mad and told his father he was fine and didn't like him trying to tell him how to live his life."

"How did father handle that?"

"He got mad, of course, told Sonny he was throwing his life away. All it accomplished was to widen the rift between them and that upset your father even more."

"I hate what Sonny is doing to this family, Mother," Sydney confessed. "I don't think there has ever been a time when Sonny was not a problem. He keeps all of us in turmoil waiting for the other shoe to drop, especially you and father. It's got to stop. He's killing both of you and will eventually lose his family. That's where I think this is all headed."

She sat quietly with her hands folded in her lap. Sydney could see he had only added to her anguish and worry and was mad at himself for doing so.

"I'm sorry, Mother. I don't mean to upset you. I should have just listened and not said anything. I can't seem to stop letting Sonny's behavior, his whole life, to be honest, get the best of me."

"I understand, Sydney, more than you know. It is upsetting to all of us, especially your father. At the moment he's the one I'm worried about. He doesn't show his emotions much, and he seldom talks about Sonny. He does say enough that I know he thinks about it more than he says. He's a fixer so he wants to 'fix' your brother when, of course, that's not possible."

"No, it's not, but for some reason we keep trying. But the important question is father's health. How is it, really?"

"I've already told you. He seems fine, says nothing, but is tired a lot. His blood pressure has been erratic the last few months. Sometimes it's good when he checks it and other times it's pretty high. That worries me, but he doesn't seem to pay any attention to it. That also bothers me."

"What does his doctor say?"

"I have no idea. I don't go with him for his check-ups so all I know is what he tells me. I'm sure I get all the good news and none of the bad."

"Harrison told me he doesn't think he looks good at all."

"I'm sure he's right, but I've lived with your father long enough to know he's going to do what he's going to do and nobody is going to change any of it, just like with Sonny. When I try I end up talking to myself. He doesn't listen to a word I say."

"I think I'll stop by to see him at the mill as I head out of town. I need to see him anyway and maybe he will bring up Sonny and get some of his feelings out in the open."

He stood to leave.

"As always, I love you, Mother."

"I love you, too, my dear Sydney. You make life so much better by being you." He waved as he got in his jeep.

It only took five minutes to get to the mill. Neither Mrs. Smith nor Harrison were in their offices, but he saw his father sitting at his desk.

"Father."

He looked up, smiled, and said. "Sydney, this is a surprise. Harrison told me you stopped by earlier while I was at the Lion's Club. Given the time I thought maybe you had seen your mother and had already left town."

"Not without tracking you down," Sydney responded. "I do have to head out, but I wanted to say hi and visit with you a minute."

He sat down in one of the hard chairs in front of his desk. The old comfortable ones wore out and his father didn't see much need in spending money to replace them with equal quality!

"So how are you feeling, Father?"

"Good, good, better than I have in a while."

"And your blood pressure?"

"I see you've been talking to your mother about me."

"A little. She says it is good sometimes and not good at other times."

"Well, it is what it is, Sydney. I've lived with it long enough to know that up and down is the way it's going to be these days."

"Any stress you're under that could make it go up?" Sydney asked, fishing about Sonny.

"You mean other than your brother throwing his life away?"

"Yes, that too."

"Well, he is. Makes no sense. He's got a good job, beautiful family, and seems willing to risk it all for a bottle of beer. Makes no sense."

"I'm sure you've told him so, haven't you?"

"Of course, I have, Sydney. Somebody needs to get through to him before it's too late."

"What if it already is?" he asked his father quite seriously.

"I don't believe that, at least not yet. He's gotten sober before. He's not out of control at the moment. But it's your mother, too. She is determined to help with whatever he needs until he straightens out."

"I wish that were in the cards, but both of you will keep doing what you're doing, I'm sure."

"Because we're his parents. You should know that by now, Sydney, what with that special little girl you and McKenzie brought into this world."

That hit home.

"I understand what you're saying, Father, but I've seen too many parents making things worse by bailing out children who need to know there are consequences to their behavior. You and mother have to know that."

"Of course, we do, Sydney, but it feels like we're damned if we do and damned if we don't help him. Carrie, Annie, and Anthony are affected, too."

"I know, and I also know there's no easy answer with him. I do, but enabling an alcoholic is a real thing and it never turns out good. Why don't you let Harrison and me help you and mother deal with Sonny?"

"You obviously haven't talked to Harrison much about this. He's washed his hands of Sonny. Can't say I blame him. He won't even talk to me about him. He told me last week that as far as he's concern Sonny is dead."

"Well, he's not to me and I'm not willing to leave it all to you and mother. I want to help in whatever way I can."

"I knew that already, Sydney. So does your mother. We'll keep you up to date on what's going on and ask for help when we need it."

"No, you won't, and you know it, but I will be more involved from here on. To be honest, this is why I came to Castle Cove today. I've talked to Sonny a few times lately and I knew something wasn't right, but he can hide it on the phone. I figured y'all would know more than he was willing to tell me. I got what I came for in that sense, and got to see you in the process."

Sydney thought his father looked small sitting in his chair. He had lost weight and his shoulders were slumped. His once broad arms looked almost shrunken. It was obvious his father was not the man he once was physically.

"Well, I need to get started home," said Sydney as he stood up." I love you, Father. Please don't keep things from me about Sonny. I want to help."

"Good to see you, Sydney. Tell McKenzie hello and give that Leslie a big hug for me and tell her that her grandpa misses seeing her."

# 11

Marian Beach slows down in the fall as the summer crowds leave and the beach empties. Weekends can still get busy, but nothing like they are in the summer. A few food kiosks stay open through the end of October, but the rest close up. After working with beach kids as he has for the last few years, Sydney felt himself actually missing them. Getting to know who they really are, their struggles, their fears, their dreams, their pain and suffering has become a special experience in his ministry, something he could not have anticipated when he and McKenzie moved to Marian Beach almost ten years ago. The biggest reward had been seeing how open teenagers become when someone builds trust with them. It surprised him that most of them feel judged by their elders. That had made building trust with them much harder. They not only feel unaccepted, but unacceptable.

Sydney wasn't sure why he was thinking about his beach kids as he sat in his office trying to get started on a sermon. Maybe it was the feeling of fall he felt when he came to the office this morning. The air was beginning to have a coolness to it that happens every year as summer gives way to autumn. Most people in Marian Beach love summer, but fall was Sydney's favorite time of the year. That's the mountain boy in him, he supposed. Seeing the mountains blazing with their incredible colors of red and yellow and brown was the one thing he missed most about Castle Cove. Lost in the blissful joy of those thoughts, his cell phone ringing startled him. It was his mother.

"Sydney, your father is in the hospital," she blurted out as soon as he said hello. "He's had a heart attack. It's serious."

"Is anyone with you, Mother?"

"Not at the moment. I'm at the hospital. I came in the ambulance with your father. I called Harrison as soon as I could. He's on his way. I tried to call Sonny, but he didn't answer. I haven't tried Carrie. Maybe you could do that for me. I don't want to ask Harrison. You know how he is about Sonny."

"Yes, of course. I'll call until I reach one of them, and I'll also get to Castle Cove as soon as I can. Since you and Harrison will be at the hospital I'll come straight there."

"Be careful driving, Sydney."

Always the mother, he thought.

"I'll see you soon, Mother, I love you."

He felt numb after he hung up. His father seemed okay the last time he saw him and had been sounding fine on the phone. He immediately picked up his jacket and went into Madelyn's office and told her about the call. He started to say he didn't know how long he would be gone when she recognized the situation for what it was and said, "Go, Sydney, just go. I'll take care of things here. Your family needs you. You need them. Go."

Madelyn was Sydney's version of Mrs. Smith, old enough to be his mother, and as watchful over him as if she were. She was the best. He knew she could handle things while he was gone so he didn't put up any resistance and left. On the way home he called McKenzie's school and left word at the office that he needed her to call him as soon as possible, that it was an emergency, adding that it did not involve her daughter. His cell rang a few minutes later.

"Sydney, what's wrong?"

"It's father," he replied. "He's had a heart attack and mother says its serious. I'm packing a few things and heading to Castle Cove immediately."

"Oh, my God. Do you want to wait long enough for me to pick up Leslie and meet you at home?"

"No, I think it would be better if I go now and see how bad it is. I'll call you once I know and we can decide what to do then."

"Okay. Please call as soon as you can. And tell that tough old man I love him."

"I will, but he already knows you do."

"And I love you, too."

"And I love you. I'll call you the minute I know something."

Before he left home he tried calling Sonny. No luck, but Carrie answered when he called her.

"Hello, Sydney. What's wrong?"

"Why'd you ask that?"

"Because you never call, so something has to be."

"Yes, well, there is. Father's had a heart attack. I tried to call Sonny. He didn't pick up."

"Oh, no, Sydney. I'm so sorry. How bad is it?

"I'm not sure. Mother thought it was bad, but that was only her opinion, nothing official. I'm headed that way."

"Well, I'll try to get hold of Sonny. I'm not surprised you couldn't get him. He's drinking pretty bad these days and when he does I never know where he is or what he's doing and he seldom answers my calls unless he needs me to come pick him up at some bar."

"I was afraid of that when mother said she tried and didn't get him," Sydney told her.

"Yes, well, never mind Sonny right now. Sam is the concern. I'll keep calling him until he answers. You want me to tell him to come to Castle Cove when I get hold of him? Not sure that's a good idea, to be honest."

"You're probably right. Mother, of course, would want him there, but she's never realistic about the way he is when he's drinking. I don't think she or father need to go through that right now. Why don't you tell him to stay in Halifax and that I will call him and you once I get to the hospital and find out for sure what's going on."

"Sounds good, and Sydney, I hope Sam is going to be okay. He was hard man to get to know, but I love him now like my own father. He is always there for me and the kids whenever we need him."

"Well, he loves you, too, Carrie. You and the kids have a special place in his heart."

"I know," Carrie said, her voice breaking as she started crying. "Just say a special prayer for him, Sydney. Sonny and I are not in a good place right now. I don't think I can handle losing Sam."

"You won't, Carrie. I have a strong feeling that he's going to be okay. I really do. I will call you as soon as I know anything for sure."

"Thank you, Sydney. Please do."

Sydney called Mrs. Smith about an hour away from Castle Cove and she said there was no news to report, although she did know his father was talking when they took him to the hospital.

Sydney drove directly to Castle Cove Community Hospital, parked the Jeep, and rushed into the emergency entrance. One of his high school classmates was working the desk.

"Hi, Sydney," Betty Cole said before he even reached the counter. "I'm so sorry about your dad. Let me call back to see if he is still in the ER or already in a room."

He waited. Betty was off the phone in a matter of minutes.

"He's been taken to Cardiac Care Unit. I'm sure you know where that is."

"Actually I don't, Betty. Never had any reason to know until now."

"Of course, you haven't," she said. "I guess knowing you are a minister made me assume you knew something you would know only if your church was here."

Betty gave Sydney directions to the CCU. Sarah and Harrison were sitting in the room where his father would be brought after his tests.

"Hey, bro," Harrison said as he stood up. "Glad you're here."

"So am I," he responded.

Sydney hugged his mother as she stood and held on to her as if he was afraid to let her go. She sensed how anxious he was.

"I think he's going to be all right, Sydney. He was fussing about having to have all the tests they told him he needed before they took him out of the emergency area. We just don't know how bad the attack was."

"Sounds like father," he said. "I guess this time we can all be glad he's complaining about something."

They heard noise outside the room and saw hospital staff turning Sam's bed perpendicular to the door entrance and pushing it into the room. It took a few minutes for them to connect all the lines. Just as the two men were finishing, a nurse came in and told Sam her name was Linda and she would be his nurse for the day. She took his blood pressure, placed the call button inside the right side of his bed and told him not to hesitate to use it. Sydney introduced himself to her. Harrison smiled and did the same. She assumed who Sarah was and told her to feel free to ask any questions she may have anytime. She then said the doctor would stop by in a few minutes.

As soon as Linda was gone, mother leaned over and ran her hand though his father's hair and said, "How are you feeling, Samuel?" She always called him "Samuel" when she was in a serious mood.

"Ah, Sarah, I'm fine. I don't feel like running any races at the moment, but I'm fine. Just a warning to pay better attention to pains in my chest.

I let them go for a day or so. If I hadn't I probably wouldn't be here right now."

"So why didn't you?" she retorted.

"You know me," he answered back.

"Sometimes I don't know whether I know you at all," she shot back in a tone of voice that drew Harrison's and Sydney's attention, "except that I know you can be stubborn as a mule. I hope you know you scared me to death."

"No, love, I think it's me that was scared to death," he quipped.

"I'm serious, Samuel. This is not a joke. You had a heart attack and that's always serious."

Before father could say anything else the doctor walked in.

"Hello, I'm Dr. Holston," speaking to all of us. He then walked over to Sam and introduced himself again and said, "Well, Mr. Strange, you're a lucky man. You have two blockages in separate arteries that need to be removed right away, which shouldn't be any problem, but is something that needs correcting or you may not be so lucky next time. And without surgery I can assure you there will be a next time."

That stunned all three of them. Dr. Holston was one of those doctors who didn't mince words.

"You will do the surgery?" Sarah asked.

"Yes," Dr. Holston answered. "In about an hour. No one else is in line so we may as well get it done now."

"Sound good to you, Mr. Strange?" Dr. Holston asked Sam.

Sam hesitated as if he were in shock.

"Uh, yeah, of course, doc. You're the boss."

"No, not the boss, just your doctor, but I'm glad you're willing to proceed as I am advising. We'll do it this afternoon. One of my colleagues is finishing up a knee surgery so the nurses will start prepping you soon."

"Thank you, Doctor Holston," Sarah said. "Can we stay here until then?"

"Yes, of course, and when they come to get your husband someone will take you to the surgery waiting room."

She nodded. Sydney thanked the Doctor as he turned to leave. Harrison nodded and Dr. Holston smiled back and left. Sydney also went into the hallway and dialed McKenzie, hoping she might have her cell on. She never does when she is in class. He couldn't remember her schedule, but thought she might be finished for the day. Sure enough, she answered.

"Hi, babe. What's the story?"

"Two blockages in different arteries. He will need stents, but the surgeon seems to think that should not be a problem. He told father he was a lucky man. Not sure that made an impression on him, but maybe more than I think. Anyway, they're doing the surgery right away, this afternoon in fact. I'm going to stay the night and come home tomorrow if he's doing okay. That will also allow me to keep mother from camping out here at the hospital."

"That's wise. It's too far to drive tonight. Do you want me and Leslie to drive over tomorrow?"

"No, no, there's no need for that. He is going to be fine. He would rather see both of you when he is back on his feet. I'll call you if anything changes."

"Okay. I love you."

"Love you, too."

As soon as he clicked off Carrie called.

"I was just about to call you, Carrie. Good timing."

"So what's going on?" she asked.

"He needs two stents in separate arteries. They're doing that this afternoon. The doctor seems confident it will go well and father will be fine."

"Oh, thank goodness. I've been so worried."

"Any news from Sonny?"

"Yes, he finally answered his cell. He sounded sober, but admitted he had messed up. That's the line he uses when he's trying to persuade me that he knows what he's done and will do better. Anyway, I told him about his dad. He got very quiet. I told him I didn't know any details, but that you would call him and me once you got to Castle Cove and found out how bad the situation is."

"Thank you, Carrie. I know that wasn't easy, but thank you for doing that. I'll call him after we hang up and then I will call you back as soon as father is out of surgery."

"Sounds good, Sydney. Thank you, and give Sarah a hug for me."

"I will."

"That was Carrie," he told his mother as she came out of the room and said she needed the restroom. "She talked to Sonny. I told her to tell him to stay put until I called him with an update on father's condition. I'll do that now."

"Oh, good. He should know what is happening."

Sydney punched in Sonny's number. No answer. He hung up and called right back thinking Sonny might answer if he did. He didn't, so he called again with the same results. Not the best way to have to deal with your brother, but desperate times call for desperate measures. Then his phone rang.

"Sydney, what's happening?" No hello, how are you, just the facts.

"Father is having surgery to put in two stents this afternoon. He seems okay with that. The doctor said it should go without any problems, that father is strong and should be fine."

"I was considering driving over there, maybe tomorrow."

"No need, really. I can keep updating you on him."

"What, you and Harrison don't want me there?" It was more of a statement than a question.

"Well, I won't lie to you, Sonny. Carrie said you were drinking again. Mother doesn't need to see that right now so, no, I don't think you should come."

"Oh, that's right," Sonny said harshly, "you're the good son and I'm the bad one you don't want around."

"I'm not going there with you, Sonny. Too much is going on. This is not about you. It's about father."

"It's about 'father,'" Sonny said, mimicking Sydney. "Why do you call him that? Why don't you call him 'dad' like the rest of us, and mom 'mom' instead of 'mother'."

"What's that got to do with anything?" Sydney shot back. "It's what I have called them all my life. You're just noticing that. Boy, you sure do pay attention."

"Yeah, well I pay attention plenty, enough to know when I'm not wanted around the family."

"I told you I'm not getting into this with you, Sonny. Do what you want to. I don't care. I will call Carrie with updates and you can find out from her what's going on. If you want to know anything directly you can call me. Just don't call Mother."

"Yes, sir, Captain," he snarled. "Yes, sir," and then he hung up.

"Sounds like that went well," Harrison said, standing just outside father's room. "I didn't hear it all, but all I needed. I don't know why you bother with him, Sydney. He's never going to do better and he's headed toward a bad end. Every binge gets worse and longer."

Sydney gave a big sigh and said, "I'm sure you're right. I just can't seem to cut him off. I wish I could. I keep thinking he will be one of those two out of ten alcoholics who join AA and make it."

"Not going to happen, bro. Not going to happen."

About that time Sarah came back from the restroom and the aids arrived to take Sam to be prepped for surgery. One of them told Sarah she could follow her to the waiting room. Sarah went in and gave Sam a kiss. Harrison and Sydney took a hand on each side as they wheeled his bed toward the door.

"Don't give them a hard time, dad," Harrison said to him. "Just let them do their job."

"As long as they do it my way," he replied. Harrison was sure he meant it.

The surgical waiting room was just like all the family waiting rooms in any hospital just about anywhere. A rectangular room with doors at either end and chairs in the middle creating two sides within the one room. No one was there when the Strange family arrived except a mother and three adult children who were picking up their stuff to leave. They weren't crying which suggested surgery for their loved one must have gone okay. Harrison said he needed to go to the sawmill to check on things. Mrs. Smith said everything was fine the last time he talked to her, but he wanted to make sure for himself. Besides, he said, he needed to get out of the hospital. He kissed Sarah on the cheek and mouthed to Sydney, "Call me if anything changes." Sydney nodded okay.

It was less than two hours after Sam went into surgery when the doctor walked into the waiting room.

"The surgery went fine," he said. "I was able to put the stents in with little trouble. He came through fine and is being taken to recovery now. I imagine you can see him in about a half hour, though he will still be groggy. If he has a good night, he should be ready to go home tomorrow."

"Thank you, Doctor Holsten," Sarah said. "Thank you."

"It's what I do," he said, "and this time it went as well as I had hoped.

I'm sure I will see you tomorrow before he is released. There are some dietary restrictions you will need to know about."

"Yes, anything," Sarah said.

"Thank you, doctor," Sydney said as the doctor was leaving.

Sydney made the calls he needed to, first to Harrison, then Carrie, and then McKenzie. He also called Sonny, but got no answer. He left a voice mail saying that everything went well and their father was going to be fine and would probably go home tomorrow. It was near dinner time before Sam left recovery and got settled in his own room. By then he was wide awake and said yes to a small dish of Jello when the nurse asked him if he wanted some. Sarah and Sydney stayed for another hour and then Sydney suggested they go home. Sarah resisted, but not a lot. He could tell she was emotionally spent and very tired. She finally agreed and Sam helped by telling her he was fine and didn't want her hovering over him.

On the way home Sarah surprised Sydney by talking openly about how angry she was at Sam for not taking care of himself. She hated his smoking to the point of finally forbidding it in the house. He had tried to stop about a year ago by smoking cigars to cut down on the cigarettes. She said he finally confessed that all he had accomplished was to add a few cigars to his cigarette habit, making matters worse. It also upset her that he ate everything he wasn't supposed to, making his high blood pressure worse.

Sydney listened as his mother vented. It was so unlike her so he just listened. Once they got home she went straight to bed without eating anything. Sydney made himself some peanut butter crackers, found some iced tea in the refrigerator, sat down at the counter, and punched in McKenzie's number.

"How are things?" she asked.

"Okay. I just got mother home. She was exhausted and went to bed. I'm eating some peanut butter crackers. On the drive from the hospital she was very open about her anger at father for not taking care of himself. Mad, in fact."

"What do you expect, Sydney?" McKenzie asked without it being a real question. "She's lived with the man forty years and probably never been able to influence his behavior, only this time it is a matter of life and death, at least as far as she's concerned. On top of that, your father isn't the easiest man to live with. I love him dearly, you know that, but loving Sam Strange takes work."

"I know it does, McKenzie, but he's a good man, couldn't have been a more attentive father while running a growing business. Harrison and Sonny would say the same thing. No matter what was going on at the sawmill, he hardly ever missed our little league games in any sport. That was true in high school for football. He came to my tennis matches my senior year when he realized I was serious about it."

"Of course, he's a good man, Sydney, and a good father. That's not the issue. He's set in his ways and that has made things hard for your mother. You know what I'm saying. He loves her and you and your brothers more than life. I guess all I'm saying is that he's not a perfect man."

"Of course, he's not. Who is?"

"I'm sorry, Sydney. I'm not saying very clearly what I'm trying to say. I think I'm really talking more about your mother than your dad. She doesn't know how to show anger, and when she does she is more apologetic than honest about her feelings. This sounds like it's different so I would pay close attention to her. Give her support. That's what she needs. I'm sure she will be fine. She always is."

"You're right, of course. I will try to be attentive to her while I'm here, which won't be long, without trying to fix anything, being the clergy 'fixer' I am."

"Just be you, Sydney, that's what she needs right now. I'm sure of it. Take as long as she needs you to be there. We're fine here."

Sarah was up early the next morning. Sydney had been up for about an hour when she came into the kitchen. He had always been an early riser. It's when he gets most of his reading and writing done, a habit he developed in graduate school and has stuck with it.

"You're up early, Sydney. Didn't you sleep well?"

"I slept fine, Mother. I'm always up early. It's the way I get my day off to a good start."

"Well, how about some breakfast, biscuits and gravy in fact."

"You know my weakness, Mother. I shouldn't eat the gravy, but don't want the biscuits without it, so guess I'll have to have both."

He took his coffee over to the island dividing the kitchen from the dining room and sat on a stool to face the sink and stove where his mother was working.

"So how are you, Mother? Did you get any sleep?"

"Actually, I did, sweetheart. I slept like a log. I went out the minute my head hit the pillow and I didn't awaken until six-thirty. I called the hospital immediately. They said your dad had a good night and was in the shower. They expect him to be released today. After hearing that I got up and took my own shower and got dressed for the day."

"Good, that means I will stay long enough today to help you get father home."

"You don't have to do that, Sydney," Sarah said as she stirred the gravy on the stove and checked the biscuits in the oven. "I can get your father home. I'm sure you've got plenty of things waiting on you at Saint Alban."

"I have my own version of Mrs. Smith, so you don't need to worry about anything on my end."

Sarah took the biscuits out of the oven, put them on a plate and sat them in front of Sydney.

"Put them on the table in the sunroom, please, and have a seat. It's more pleasant out there. I'll join you in a minute."

Sydney picked up the plate and did as his mother asked. She soon appeared with a bowl of gravy. He went back to the kitchen and poured his mother a cup of hot tea and refilled his coffee. He sat down and took two huge biscuits on his plate and covered then with the sausage gravy only his mother knew how to make.

They exchanged small talk. He told her about his ministry with the beach kids in more detail than he ever had before, how much he enjoyed the work, and how hard life had been for many of them. Parents drinking, doing drugs, fighting physically, inflicting emotional damage on their children. This is a common theme among them, he said. Others have the opposite kind of life, the kind he had growing up. He even thanked her for the life she and Sam had given him, Harrison, and Sonny.

"Speaking of Sonny," she said.

"I wasn't, Mother, but you know that. You were just waiting for the right moment to bring him up."

"Okay, yes, I was," she admitted. "I'm so worried about him, Sydney. He's drinking again and I know he's going to lose that good job he has if he keeps on."

"It's his responsibility, Mother, and there's nothing any of us can do.

How many years has it been? Ten, no at least fifteen, and it's the same old story."

"I know what you're saying, Sydney, but he is still my child, my wonderful, troubled prodigal who is wasting his life living in a bottle."

She got quiet and Sydney let it be. Then she said, "I need to tell you something. I haven't told anyone else about it, not even your father, so you have to promise me you won't either."

Sydney became uneasy, almost alarmed by what she had said.

"Okay, I can make you that promise," he said, "but you're making my blood pressure go up now."

"No, it's not that kind of news. I'm fine. It's just that I need to tell you about my personal financial situation that only your father knows about. I had a distant aunt who was my father's only sister, you never knew her, who moved from Castle Cove when I was quite young. She loved me like her own. My father said when I was a toddler people thought I was her daughter, not his. Aunt Clara did marry, more than once I think, but she never had any children. Her last husband was quite wealthy, an oil man of some sort. She was the love of his life and when he died he left everything to her. Soon thereafter she started putting money in the letters she wrote to me, sometimes as much as fifty dollars, which at the time was a lot of money. One Christmas she sent me a hundred dollars. Daddy decided I needed to have a savings account so he helped me get one at the Castle Cove State Bank."

"I wish I remembered more about her. Daddy and mamma did take me to see her once in New York where she lived. We took the train. It was a long trip, but I have fond memories of that weekend we spent there. To a small-town North Carolina girl New York was another world back then. A few years after our trip Aunt Clara said something strange in one of her letters, that for reasons daddy would someday explain she would likely not be writing as often as she had been. Some months later her letters stopped altogether. I asked daddy why she stopped writing and he sat me down and told me she was sick, that she had what was called Huntington's Disease, a gradual deterioration of cells in the brain that affect a person's ability to walk, talk, and move."

"I know about Huntington's, Mother. It is an awful and tragic disease."

"Well, then, you know it's hereditary which is why Aunt Clara never had any children of her own. Daddy said she was afraid of passing on the gene. I was too young to understand what he was really talking about at the time or what Aunt Clara was going through. I don't remember how long it was, a few years, I'm sure, when daddy was gone for a few days and when he came home he sat me down again and told me that he had just returned from New York, that Aunt Clara had died. I asked him if we could go to her funeral. He said that's why he was gone, that her friends there had a memorial service for her. She was cremated and he had her ashes in a box he had brought home."

Mother looked at Sydney and said, "I know this is getting long, Sydney, but there is a point to it all that I will get to in a minute."

"Take your time, Mother," he said. "we have plenty of time before we need to go to the hospital."

"Well, time moved on, as they say. I grew up and your father and I got married and had a family of our own. Your grandfather Hargis would tell me from time to time that someday I might want to sit down with him to talk about some business that was related to Aunt Clara. I never thought much about it and the years went by. About two years ago, a few months before your grandfather died, he asked me to come to see him, that it was time to settle the matter of Aunt Clara's money. I went the next day."

"'Thank you for coming so quickly, my dear,' daddy said. I had seen him only a few days before, but he was anxious about the matter and didn't want to wait until I came back on my own. 'It's about your Aunt Clara. No, she didn't die again,' he said with a sly smile. "If you remember, your grandfather had a wry sense of humor.

"'But before she died,' he continued, 'she told me she had set up a trust fund for you. You were the daughter she never had. She asked me to manage the account until I thought you should know about it. I've waited much too long to tell you about it, but you and Sam seemed to be doing well financially and I didn't want to upset anything. No matter, though, now is the time and that is why you are here. The fund has matured and is worth quite a bit of money. This may shock you, my dear, but you are now in possession of a little over five hundred thousand dollars."

"Oh, my God," Sydney exclaimed. "I had no idea my mother was a rich woman."

"Well, I suppose I am, come to think of it. But there's more to the story than your inheritance." She hesitated and then continued. "Now hear me out, Sydney, before you react to what I am going to tell you. Since Sonny will receive his portion of the inheritance at some point, I have been giving him a small amount to help him out right now, deducting it, of course, from the total he will get."

"Oh no, Mother, surely you're not doing that. Surely you're not giving him money so he can drink."

"Of course I'm not, Sydney. I'm just paying a few of his bills and some debts he has gotten himself into. He said one of them was to a loan shark who threatened him if he didn't pay up."

"How much was that?" he asked.

"Five-hundred dollars."

"Oh, Mother, Mother. You know that's not true. He just told you that so you would give him the money. There's no loan shark."

"You don't know that, Sydney."

"Of course I know that, Mother, and you do too. You know what's going on. You're enabling Sonny to drink by paying his bills and his debts."

"I didn't know what else to do," she said, her eyes filling with tears. "I can't let him go to jail, which he might if he writes a bad check again."

"What? He's writing bad checks?"

"Only a couple that I paid. He promised he wouldn't again."

"And you believed him, of course."

"The checks were small and the money I am using is really his, at least will be someday, just as it will with you and Harrison."

"Oh, for crying out loud. Mother. That's years down the road. He'll be gone long before you will."

"Don't say that, Sydney."

"I'm sorry, Mother, but it's the truth, and we both know it is. The way he's going he'll be lucky to live another year, drinking and driving the way he does. I worry all the time he's going to end up killing himself, and maybe somebody else. But that's not the point. You may as well buy him drinks yourself. Sonny is a pit with no bottom."

"Whatever he is, Sydney, he's my son before anything else. I can't abandon him. I know all about 'enabling', but how do you not help your own child? I've even been to Al Anon meetings and nobody has ever explained that one to me. I've also read that people can inherit a tendency for alcoholism. I wonder if Sonny is one of them. The truth is, Sydney, we have it on both sides of our family. Your grandfather Strange had a serious drinking problem for years until he got sober, and so did my father. What if Sonny is like them? I'm not saying he's not responsible for what he is doing, only that other factors may be contributing to his problem."

What his mother said caused Sydney to feel the full weight of being the brother of a prodigal. The pain he could see in her face was breaking his heart just as hers was breaking over Sonny. The years he has spent hoping Sonny would straighten up have turned to anger. Finding out about the money he is taking from his mother was like throwing fuel on it. And yet, he knew deep down he didn't know what he would be doing if his own child was the one they were talking about.

"No, Mother, I can't explain to you how you can refuse to help your own son, but I'm pretty sure giving him money is not helping him."

"I know that. But I don't think doing nothing is the answer either. Your father feels the same way. The bad checks really upset him because that crossed the line into potential legal problems."

"So father is in on this, too?"

"No, no, of course not. He knows about the money Aunt Clara left me, but nothing else. No one knows what I'm doing and I want to keep it that way. The money isn't important. Your father and I will never need it. So it's just there."

"Listen to me, Mother. You have to stop. The more you give him, the more he will expect you to bail him out. Isn't that true?"

She didn't respond. "Isn't it?" he repeated.

"Yes."

"Then you have to stop. It's not doing him or anybody any good, including Carrie and the kids."

She went silent again, then finally said in almost a whisper, "I know. I know."

"Will you promise me you will stop bailing him out, stop paying his debts, and for goodness sakes stop giving him cash? Will you?"

"Sydney, I cannot make you that promise. The best I can do is to tell you I will try, but he's my son, and he is your brother. Always will be. You can't change that, and neither can I. We're family, with all the good and bad that comes with it. You can understand that can't you, Sydney."

Just then the home phone rang. His mother got up and answered it, came back and said, "That was your father asking where we were, only he didn't exactly ask."

"Okay, we can go, but I'm glad we talked, Mother. We don't see Sonny through the same lens, but I really do understand what you're saying. I want you to know that."

"Thank you, Sydney, and I do listen to what you say as well, even if I don't always do what you want me to do."

They got up from the table, took the dishes into the kitchen, change clothes, and headed to the hospital.

# 12

"I was about to call a cab," Sam told Sarah and Sydney as they walked into his hospital room.

"Oh, don't be so impatient," she snapped back at him. "You know that's not true. You can't leave until your doctor comes in and releases you, and I know that hasn't happened because I asked the nurse before we came in."

"Well, if he doesn't come soon, I'm leaving without seeing him."

"You must be talking about me, Mr. Strange," Dr. Holston said as he walked through the door."

"Sorry, doc. I'm just anxious to get home."

"I'm glad to hear it, Mr. Strange, but I need to run over a few 'dos and don'ts' before you go. Nothing unusual, but two of them are very important and very difficult to follow. First, the cigarettes have to go. They are literally hastening your death so you must stop now. If you don't, you will probably see me sooner than you want to. I've written a prescription for something that will help you do that. The second thing is diet so I'm giving a menu to Mrs. Strange. Eating better is as important as giving up smoking."

"In other words," father said, "you want to take away two of the most important things I do for pleasure. Not much of a life left, if you ask me."

"I'm sorry about that, Mr. Strange, "but at least it's a life and I'm sure your family thinks it's worth having."

Sarah and Sydney both thanked Dr. Holston and assured him Sam would take his "prescriptions" seriously. The next point of contention was getting Sam to agree to be wheeled to the front door.

"I'm not a damn invalid," were his exact words as Sydney recalled later.

When the choice was staying or getting into the wheelchair because of hospital insurance requirements, Sam sat down in the wheelchair. Sydney finally got both of them home and settled in. He assured them he would stay in touch and said his good-byes. He called Harrison on the way out of town and gave him the blow-by-blow details of getting father home. Harrison promised Sydney he would stop by after work to see how they were and keep him updated.

Sydney figured his mother wouldn't stop helping Sonny and he was right. Carrie called him a week after Sam got out of the hospital to ask him to try to get her to stop giving Sonny money.

"I already have, Carrie. Believe me. We had a long talk about it when I was there. You know her, so you know what I said didn't do any good."

"Yes, I do. I know she means well. She's the most loving, gentle person I know. The trouble is, Sonny knows it, too. He knows exactly what he's doing. He tells her what he knows she wants to hear, that if she will help him one last time he will do better. She believes him because she wants to. I know he's the problem, but she's not helping him or me. I don't know what else to do."

"How bad is it, Carrie? If you don't mind me asking."

"It's bad, Sydney. The kids and I don't see Sonny much anymore. I have no idea where he's staying, but he's not here very often. I don't know for sure, but I would guess he's lost his job with C and S. My new job is a big help. There was an opening for the assistant personnel director at a huge law firm here in Halifax. My boss at Allegheny County District Schools understood why I wanted to apply and gave me a good recommendation. A month later the personnel director left and they gave me the position. It pays well and I like the people I work with. It's a good thing because it's what's keeping us going."

"I'm glad to hear that, Carrie. McKenzie and I have wondered how you were doing financially."

"Thankfully, that part is stable at the moment, but the emotional roller-coaster is what's so hard, for me and the children."

"I can't imagine," he responded.

"I've had to let him go without knowing whether he is gone for good or not. My problem is, I still love him. That's on me, but it's why I haven't done anything legally to move on with my life as my parents want me to. I like being back in Halifax and the children are doing okay. A divorce would be a mess and upend them even more. For now I've decided to ride out this storm and see where our marriage ends up. In the meantime, what Sarah is doing is not helping, but as I said, I don't know how to stop her."

"I agree, but she means well."

"Of course she does. I don't doubt her intentions. I just wish she had the strength to let him suffer the consequences of his drinking. I've wondered about calling her myself. What do you think, Sydney? Should I?"

"That may not be a bad idea, Carrie, if you're willing to do it. Maybe it will make a difference to hear directly from you that she is making things harder while she's not helping Sonny."

"Okay, I will. Wish me luck."

"You'll need more than luck, I'm afraid. But mother loves you dearly, Carrie. Who knows? If anybody can have an effect on her, it's you."

"Thank you, Sydney. Tell McKenzie hello."

"I will, Carrie."

"And thank you for being there."

"I always will be, you know that. Our whole family will, too, because you're one of us as much as Sonny is."

Sydney clicked off his cell and felt his anger rising fast. He wanted to punch Sonny or at least scream at him. He wanted to let him know he had reached a new low by playing on his mother's love and ditching his family in the process. Instead, he did something impulsive, as unlike himself as anything he had ever done. He got in his car and made the long trip to Halifax to see him in person. All the way he kept telling himself to turn around, that he was wasting his time and probably wouldn't be able to find Sonny in the first place.

Sydney actually did find Sonny, though, at the Anytime Bar where he thought he might be. He saw Sonny as soon as he walked in. It wasn't as big a bar as Sydney expected. There were three tables on his left and four booths against the wall on his right. The bar counter itself wrapped around the serving area like a half moon. It probably seated twenty-five people max. Sonny was at that far end on the second stool from the wall.

Sonny didn't see Sydney until he was ten feet away from him. It startled him when he finally did.

"Well, what do you know. My preacher brother has come into my bar."

"Didn't know it was yours," Sydney said, "just a place you spend all your time."

"Ah, testy right off the bat, I see."

"We need to talk Sonny."

"I can't wait to hear what about. I'm all ears."

"Not here. We need to talk in private, Let's go outside. My Jeep is quiet."

"Now why would I do that, brother? I got a nice beer sitting in front of me and I'm surrounded by friends."

"I don't care what you've got or how many friends." Sydney said, "We need to talk, and if I have to drag you out of this place, I will do that, and you know I can."

"Mr. tough guy are you, reverend?" He said it loud enough to draw the bartender's attention who walked toward them.

"No games. Sonny."

The bartender came over to them and said to Sydney, "I don't know who you are, though I assume from the collar that you are a reverend. I don't mean any disrespect, but Sonny doesn't seem to want to move, so maybe you should leave him alone."

He was a skinny twenty-something maybe six feet tall at most. Sydney leaned all of his six-foot two, two hundred-ten-pound frame forward, got within six inches of the kid's face, and whispered in a tone that let him know how serious he was, "I'm his brother, Mr. bartender, and this is family business. I am a reverend, as you said, but that won't stop me from picking you up and throwing you across the room, so I suggest you take a step back and let me talk to my brother."

"No problem," he quickly said as he backed up. "I just didn't know who you were. Please don't cause any trouble in here."

"Don't plan to," Sydney replied. "That's why I'm trying to persuade Sonny to go outside where we can talk in private."

"And I ain't going anywhere," Sonny chimed in.

To Sydney's surprise the bartender helped to diffuse the situation. "Go with him, Sonny. I can't have any trouble in the bar. My boss will fire me. Just go outside like he wants you to."

Without saying a word Sonny got up and walked toward the door, clipping a chair or two and moving them slightly as he did. They got into Sydney's Jeep as soon as they were outside.

"I drove all the way to Halifax, Sonny, because we need to talk about your drinking. I'm probably wasting my time, but at this point it's worth it just knowing I said what I needed to say to you. If you're determined to throw your family away and end up killing yourself, there's nothing I can say that will make you stop. But I can and will make you stop stealing money from mother."

"You're a liar, Sydney, if you say I stole money from her."

"Yes you did, Sonny, only you asked her for it by making up some tale about being in trouble over big debts you owed some bad people. Every time you run out of money you call her and give her one sob story after another, and then she sends you a check or you drive over and get it while father is at work. I'm sure you would've asked her for money while he was in the hospital if you thought you could get her alone."

"You must think I'm some kind of sorry-ass son if you think I would steal from my own mother."

"No, I think you're an alcoholic son desperate for money who knows his mother will give it to him."

"She wants to help me. I'm not taking her money. She's giving it to me."

"Oh, please, you can do better than that. You're using your own mother and it's got to stop. Can you imagine what father would do if he found out?"

"He already knows."

"What?"

"Oh, so you don't know everything after all, do you?"

"I don't believe you. He would never let you take mother's money. You know that."

"He knows, Sydney, I told him the last time I saw him. He came home unexpectedly at lunch when I was leaving, forced me to tell him what I was doing there."

"It's a wonder he didn't forbid you ever to come home again," Sydney said. "So, what did he say?"

"Nothing. Not one word. In fact, he got back in his truck and left before I did. Haven't seen him since."

Sydney sat there utterly stunned by what Sonny had just said.

"Get out," Sydney said abruptly.

"What?" Sonny asked, confused by Sydney's demand.

"Just get out," Sydney repeated. "I've said what I came to say. I want to say a lot more, but I can't right now. So just get out. Good luck with your life, whatever happens."

"Look, Sydney..." Sonny started to say when Sydney held up his hand.

"Just get out, Sonny, please."

Sonny stared at his brother for a moment, opened the door and got out. Sydney didn't bother to see which way he went. He started his Jeep and drove off.

"Is father in his office right now," Sydney asked Mrs. Smith before he got to Castle Cove. He had driven from Halifax without even thinking about whether his father would be working on a Thursday afternoon. Since his heart attack he had been taking time off, once in a while a whole day. Harrison was pretty much running the business, giving Sam time to focus on finding new customers for the sawmill lumber. Sam was his own boss and worked as much or as little as he wanted to. Business, Harrison had told Sydney at the hospital, was really good, so what father did was more gravy than meat and potatoes.

"Yes, he is, Sydney. Do you want to talk to him?"

"No, I'll be there in about ten minutes and I'll talk to him then."

"Okay, sweetie. See you in a few minutes."

Sam saw Sydney as he was giving Mrs. Smith a hug and came to the door of his office.

"Well, this is a surprise. What brings you to town, Sydney?"

"You do, father. You and mother," Sydney answered in a voice that made it clear he was not in the mood for small talk.

"Hmmm," his father said. "Sounds like we're in trouble, or probably just me. Come on in."

Sam turned to go back to his desk and Sydney followed.

"So, what's this about?" Sam asked.

"Money," Sydney answered.

"Money?"

"Yes money, money you and mother are giving Sonny. I found out when you were in the hospital that mother was giving him money from some kind of inheritance she has, but I had no idea you knew about it.

Apparently, she doesn't either, that is, unless she was being deceptive when she told me not to say anything to you about it."

"No, she doesn't know I know, Sydney, and I want to keep it that way. I caught Sonny just as he was leaving the house one day, and he told me why he had been there. I got in my truck and left. She never knew I was there."

"So why are you letting her do it?"

"Sydney, you may think you know your mother, but not like I do. You couldn't. So let me assure you, I don't tell her what she can and cannot do any more than you do. Your mother is gentle and loving, but she is also stubborn, especially when it comes to her sons. She and I have spent hours talking about Sonny. I don't need to tell you nothing we have come up with has worked. But the one thing your mother has made clear she will not allow is for your brother to get into trouble over money, especially if it might mean he would go to jail."

"So she has been paying off bad debts and even checks he's written?"

"Yes, she has and still is, but to be fair I started it."

"How?"

"It was a long time ago. I got a call from Barbara Wade at the bank asking me about a check written to Sonny that had come through on my account. She wanted to verify it because the signature didn't look quite right. I asked her what the check number was. When she gave it to me, I figured I had written the check in a hurry which is why the signature looked strange and why I hadn't remembered it. So I told her the check was okay."

"Why?"

"Because I had discovered a check missing from my checkbook a few days before Barbara called. It was pure chance that I did. I was getting low on checks and was counting how many I had left when I noticed the last check in the book was an odd number. I knew that wasn't right, that it's always an even number. The last one had been torn out. I asked Mrs. Smith if she could remember me giving her a check I hadn't written down in my ledger. She said no, but maybe I had written one to Sonny when he came in the week before. When she said that I thought I was confused since I hadn't seen Sonny for a month or more. Turns out I wasn't in my office at the time. She told him she wasn't sure when I would be back. He said he would just wait for me for a few minutes in my office, which is what he did.

I must have had the check book laying on my desk. He saw it and tore out the last one hoping I wouldn't notice. I didn't until Barbara Wade called and I put two and two together and it added up to Sonny. It almost made me sick at the stomach when I realized my own son had stolen a check from me, my own son."

"So how did that get mother involved?"

"I told her what happened. It was obvious she was more worried about him getting into trouble with the bank than about him stealing the check. My guess is he knew he couldn't keep stealing checks, so he decided to go to her for help."

"This is unbelievable, Father. It's like a soap opera. Carrie called to ask me to try to get mother to stop giving Sonny money. It's enabling him to be more irresponsible."

"I know, Sydney. I know, but I can tell you, I can talk until I'm blue in the face and she will keep giving him money until she decides not to."

"I don't think that is ever going to happen."

"You may be right, Sydney, but it is what it is. What can I do about it?"

"I don't know, father. I don't know."

"I don't either," Sam responded. "I wish I did, but I don't."

"It all makes me so angry I can't think straight," Sydney confessed, "especially when I found out you knew about the money mother is giving him."

"How did you find out?"

"Carrie called me this morning asking if I could stop mother from giving Sonny money. I told her I tried when you had your heart attack. When we hung up, I got in my Jeep and drove to Halifax to confront Sonny. I did and that's when he told me you knew what mother was doing after she told me you didn't."

"Well, at least you got some answers you needed by coming here."

"Yeah, I guess I did, but nothing that helps with the problem."

At that Sam stood up, came around his desk and did something he seldom does. He gave Sydney a hug.

"Take care, Sydney. Tell McKenzie and Leslie hello."

"I will."

Sydney left the mill office about four in the afternoon. That meant he would get to Marian Beach sometime after seven o'clock if traffic was good.

Once out of town he called Carrie as he had promised.

When she answered I said, "Carrie, I talked to Sonny."

"You mean he actually answered his phone?"

"No, he didn't. I talked to him in person. After we hung up, I got in the car and drove straight to Halifax."

"I didn't expect you to do that, Sydney."

"I know you didn't, Carrie. It was an impulse, something I had to do. Anyway, I did manage to find him, but it didn't do any good. He was defensive, said mother wanted to help him. He doesn't believe he's doing anything wrong. Then he said father knew what was going on. That upset me even more. I didn't know whether to believe him or not, so I drove to Castle Cove to find out the truth."

"And?"

"He was right. Father does know. He came home unexpectedly during the day a few weeks ago and ran into Sonny as he drove-up. Sonny told him mother had "loaned" him some money to get him through a tough patch. It upset him enough that he just got back into his truck and drove off."

"Oh, Sydney, I am so sorry you've been through all of that today."

"That's on me, Carrie. I thought I could get Sonny to stop taking the money. I knew trying to get mother to stop would fail, so I decided to go to the source of the problem. That failed as well, but at least I'm not leaving this mess all up to you. I think both of us need to accept the fact that there's not much chance we will get mother to stop what she's doing."

"I did call her as you suggested," Carrie said, "but she didn't answer the home phone and I didn't leave a message. I'll leave it alone for now."

"Probably the best thing. If I learn anything new I will let you know."

"Thank you, Sydney. I really appreciate your support."

"Always Carrie, you always have it. Take care."

"You too."

They had hardly ended the call when his cell rang. His first thought was "now what?" He wasn't in the mood to talk to anyone. He saw the call was from his secretary.

"Hello, Madelyn. Is something wrong?"

"Actually it is, Sydney. I'm sorry to bother you when you're dealing with family matters." He had told her he was going to see Sonny when he left the office this morning.

"No, that's fine. I'm on my way back now. What's going on."

"Well, it's a little bit complicated. You know William Taylor, the town jailor?"

"Yes, I know William."

"He just called a few minutes ago wanting to talk to you. I told him you were out of town and I wasn't sure when you'd be back. He asked me if there was any way he could call you. I wasn't sure you'd want me to give him your cell number so I told him no, but I could try to track you down and get you to call him."

"Did he say what he wanted?"

"Only that it involved somebody in the parish. I didn't push him for details. Sorry."

"No, that's fine, Madelyn. Give me his number and I'll call him. It's time for you to call it a day. I'll see you in the morning."

"Okay, Sydney. Be careful driving. Don't talk until you've stopped somewhere. People talking on the phone while driving is how a lot of accidents happen."

"I'll be careful, Madelyn. Thank you for your concern. Stop worrying and go home and relax."

Sydney decided to do what Madelyn suggested. Besides, he needed some peace and quiet. He decided to drive for a while knowing that he would reach the truck stop at the bottom of Murphy's Ridge by a little before five-thirty. He guessed William Taylor would likely be at the jail until six. When he reached the truck stop, he got a cup of mixed coffee and hot chocolate, went back to his Jeep, sat down, took a few sips, then dialed the jail's number.

"Marian Beach jail, William Taylor speaking," the voice on the other end said.

"Mr. Taylor, Sydney Strange. My secretary said you called my office looking for me."

"Yes, Reverend Strange. Thank you for calling me. The reason I called is that I have one of your church members in jail, a woman named Sally Barrett."

"I don't know any Sally Barrett," Sydney responded, "so I doubt she's a member of Saint Alban."

"All I know is that she says she is, joined as a child. Her family wasn't much into church, but then started attending with a neighbor family. She said she finally joined, even went through all those classes you have to take."

"Baptism/Confirmation classes," you mean.

"Yes, that's what she called them."

"Why is she there?" he asked Taylor. "Do you know what happened?"

"Apparently her family called Jack Brown, the County Sheriff, and told him she threatened to kill her father. She lives with her parents, something about being on Social Security disability for emotional problems. Her mother died this week and all her siblings and their families came home. That caused a lot of commotion that upset her. Arguments started and they said while she was screaming at all of them her father tried to calm her down and she threatened him. They wanted the sheriff to keep her in jail until Monday when they want to petition the district court to commit her to the psychiatric hospital in Shelby."

"Oh, my, this sounds like a royal family mess."

"Yeah, well, it's a family mess all right, but they are not royal by a long shot. But I got a more pressing problem. It ain't right for her to be here. This is a small jail, with three cells, two across from the other. A couple of jerks in the two cells are making sexual comments to her."

"So what exactly do you want me to do?"

"Find a place for her until Monday when she appears before Judge Penny. He's the district judge for this area, I can release her into your custody."

"But I don't have any idea where to put her. Even if I put her in the Town Inn, she may not stay there if I leave her alone and I certainly can't stay with her."

"I don't know what to tell you, Reverend Strange. I just know I can't keep her here and she says she belongs to your church."

"Listen, Mr. Taylor, I'm not in town, but should be there by seven or so. I'll at least come by and talk to her. You leave about that time, don't you.?"

"Not tonight. I'm working a double shift so I'll be here late."

"Okay, then, I'll be there before then."

As soon as he hung up Sydney called McKenzie. She answered immediately, not sounding real happy with him.

"Where are you?" were the first words out of her mouth.

"It's a long story and I will tell you when I get home. I should be there in about forty-five minutes. I just wanted to let you know I was alive."

"Yeah, well that may change once you get here. I cannot believe you didn't bother to call to let me know where you were. That's not acceptable, Sydney, and you know it."

"I do, and I'm sorry. I don't know why I didn't call earlier. I just got caught up in what was going on with Sonny, and then got a crazy call from the town jailer. That's part of the story I have to tell you. Right now, just let me wind down a little before I get there. Again, I'm really sorry."

"Okay, well, I'll see you when you get here."

# 13

Who in the world is Sally Barrett?

That was the question Sydney kept asking himself after talking to McKenzie, as if his day hadn't been bad enough as it was. He had never heard her name before now, but claiming to be a member of his parish would now obligate him to help her. His head felt like it was about to explode. He needed to stop thinking so he turned the radio on and managed to find a station playing soft, instrumental music. Given where he was geographically, he was surprised to find any station at all. It faded in and out until he got closer to Marian Beach and the reception got better. Eventually he felt himself relax as his emotions calmed down.

He drove into the driveway, sat in the Jeep for a minute more, and then got out feeling like his legs weren't fully under him. Leslie was sitting at the kitchen island doing homework when he walked in. McKenzie was stirring something on the stove. He gave Leslie a kiss and asked her what she was doing.

"Homework," she said as she kept writing.

"In the fifth grade?"

"Well, yeah," she said as if she couldn't believe he would even ask such a silly question. "But I'm finished," she added, picking up her book and paper. "I'll be in my room reading, Mommy, until supper." She gave Sydney a hug as she spun off her stool and was gone. He looked at McKenzie and hesitantly walked around the island to the stove where she was standing. She stopped whatever she was stirring, picked up a dish towel on the counter to wipe her hands, turned toward him, put her arms around his neck as he stood in front of her and gave him a kiss, a long, passionate kiss.

"Wow, that's a surprise," he said, "given our conversation an hour ago."

"Carrie called," McKenzie responded. "She told me she called you about Sonny and all about what you have been through today. I'm sorry I was so impatient with you."

At that Sydney's eyes filled with tears. He pulled her close and started sobbing on her shoulder. All the pent-up emotions of the day flowed out of him. He couldn't stop. He must have held her and cried for several minutes. It felt like hours. McKenzie didn't say anything. She just held him as if she knew that was all he needed, which it was. Finally, he managed to speak.

"I am so upset with Sonny. I can't even begin to put words to what I'm feeling."

He started to say more, but stopped. McKenzie continued to be silent, but her face said everything he needed from her.

"I wish I could be like Harrison and let him go, but I can't. I don't know why, but I just can't. There's not one thing I can do about Sonny, yet there I was spending my whole day trying to fix him. Sounds as foolish as it is when I say it out loud."

"Sounds like a good man who loves his prodigal brother," she said gently.

He just looked at her.

"I know better. We studied addiction in pastoral counseling classes. I know the philosophy and steps of AA and Al-Anon, but I keep letting my feelings control my thinking. Honestly, I'm no different than mother and father. Mother can't turn Sonny away because she's his mother, and father can't push her to stop giving him money because he's her husband as well as Sonny's father. It's all crazy, and it's driving me crazy. On top of all of that I now have this woman named Sally Barrett."

"Who is that, by the way?" McKenzie asked.

"It's a story all its own. The town jailor, William Taylor, called the office looking for me and Madelyn called while I was driving home to tell me. I called Taylor and he said this woman, Sally Barrett, was in his jail, said she was a member of our parish. I don't know if that's true or not. She told him she joined when she was a young girl, but I've never seen her. Anyway, her family had her arrested, said she was out of control at home because her mother had died, all the family was there, and she got emotional and threatened to kill her father. They want her committed to the mental hospital in Shelby. The county sheriff arrested her and took her to the jail. She is scheduled to appear before Judge Penny on Monday.

"Taylor says it's not a place for women and wants me to put her up somewhere else until Monday. I told him I would come there before he leaves at eleven o'clock and talk to her. Apparently, she has some mental or emotional problems because the family claims she is on Social Security psychological disability. She's been living with her parents for some time now, but I don't really know how long or why."

"Obviously," McKenzie responded, "Carrie didn't know anything about any of this. I thought the family was more than enough to have on your mind, but this, it's way too much overload." She paused and then said, "You need to sit down. I'll make some coffee."

"Thanks," he said with a sigh. "That would be great."

He sat at the counter where Leslie had been doing her homework. Her asked McKenzie about her day. She said it was all right, nothing but the "same old, same old." It had been five years since she went back to teaching. She still seems glad she made that decision, but the sheen, so to speak, has worn off. The best part is that it hasn't seemed to have any negative impact on Leslie. Just the opposite. She's told McKenzie several times she doesn't mind taking the bus to the high school, likes it, in fact. A couple of the high school girls have taken a liking to Leslie and she is enjoying the attention she is getting from "the big girls," as she calls them.

McKenzie hesitated and then said, "I'm not sure I want to keep teaching. To be honest, down deep I want to write, but I just don't have the time or energy while I'm teaching."

"You don't have to teach, McKenzie. We are fine financially if you don't. You have my support either way, but I hope you will do what you really want to do."

"Thank you" said McKenzie as she sat down beside him. "But what do you plan to do about Sally Barrett?"

"I wish I knew. I don't know that there is anything I can or even should try to do. I have no idea where to start. I guess I need to check the parish records to see if her name is listed on the membership role. I don't even know how old she is."

"So why not go see her first, then make some decisions after that?"

"That's your problem, McKenzie, you're just too logical. You start with the obvious." He took a sip of his coffee. "Of course that's what I should do. After supper I'll go see her."

"No, we'll go see her. I think maybe this might need another pair of eyes, specifically a woman's eye. Why don't you call Madelyn and ask her if she can come over to stay with Leslie while we're gone. She would probably be fine by herself, but I would feel better if someone were here."

"It's kind of late, but if she's home I'm sure Madelyn would be glad to. You know how she dotes on Leslie."

He pulled McKenzie close and said, "I really love you. I really, really do."

"Back at you, preacher man. You know that. It's us, always and forever."

Sydney went to get Leslie when McKenzie said the chicken casserole had about another five minutes. Their home was a ranch style home typical of North Carolina, only the inside arrangement of rooms has some unique features. The hallway runs from the front door to the dining room at the back of the house. The kitchen is to the left of the dining room. The sunken living room with a fireplace is immediately to the left when you come in the front door. Behind the fireplace is a huge master bedroom with a large private bath. Halfway down the straight hall that leads to the dining room is another section of the house with three bedrooms and two baths. Leslie's is at the end of the hallway to the right with a big, full bath across the hall.

She was lying on her bed reading when Sydney knocked and pushed open the already slightly opened door.

"Hey, sweetie, your mother has supper ready," Sydney said. She didn't budge, engrossed in whatever she was reading.

"Okay," she said behind the book. He watched her as she put her book aside and swung her long legs over the side of the bed to get up. She's getting so tall, he thought.

"Must be a good book," he commented.

"A Wrinkle in Time," she said. "I love it."

"I'm sure your mother loves the fact that you like to read. I do too."

"Daddy," she said, changing the subject, "Can I ask you something personal?"

"Of course you can. What's on your mind?"

Leslie paused for a second and hesitantly asked, "Why were you crying a while ago. I've never seen you cry before. Has something bad happened?"

The question caught him off guard. He looked at her and didn't know what to say. He stood in the doorway for a few seconds and then walked over and sat down on her bed.

"Please don't be mad at me for asking that, daddy. I'm sorry," she said looking up at him.

He wrapped his arm around her and pulled her to his side, and said, "Listen to me, sweetie, you have nothing to be sorry for, and I am not mad at you. Just the opposite. I couldn't be prouder of you than I am for being honest with me. Your question just surprised me because I thought you had left the room before that happened."

"Well, I did, but then when I got to my room, I remembered I needed you or mommy to sign a permission slip so I can go on a field trip on Friday. When I got to the kitchen door I heard you crying. You were kind of loud."

"It's a long and complicated story, Leslie, but yes, I was upset. Sometimes a person, usually an adult, holds a lot of emotions inside to keep from crying and then all of a sudden you can't hold them back anymore and you start crying without wanting to. That's what happened to me. I can't get into everything about why, but I can tell you that I am very worried and upset about your uncle Sonny."

"Why?"

"Well, do you know what the word addiction means?"

"I think so," Leslie answered. "It's when you can't stop doing something even if it's bad for you to do it. We talked about it in social studies class last month. My teacher was telling us about the problems people are having today that affect all of us, and she said drug addiction was one of them. That's when she explained what addiction meant."

"Well, she was right. It's a little more complicated than that, but your uncle Sonny is addicted to alcohol, and it's really bad for him, for your aunt Carrie, and for your cousins Annie and Anthony. I was trying to help uncle Sonny today and it didn't go very well. I also talked to grandma and grandpa and they are very upset about uncle Sonny as well. I had all these feelings inside me when I got home, and to be honest, I thought your mother was going to be mad at me for being gone all day without letting her know where I was. Instead, she gave me a hug and a big kiss. When she did, a lot of pent-up feelings inside me kind of exploded and I started crying in spite of trying not to. It happens to us sometimes like we have to release what we're feeling or we'll explode. Does that help?"

"Hmm huh," she whispered. "I'm sorry about uncle Sonny. It's fun when he's around."

"Yes, it is, sweetheart. People like your uncle Sonny. I've never known anybody who didn't like him."

"Do you like him, daddy?"

"Well, Leslie, I love him. He's my brother, but I don't always like what he does. It's very hard watching your brother do things that are really bad for him and are hurting everybody who loves him. But he is my brother and I care a lot about what happens to him.

"But how about we get to supper before mommy thinks we're not hungry. Aren't you hungry?"

"Starving," she replied.

"So am I," he responded.

They both got up and headed out the bedroom door. He stopped to call Madelyn, who said she would be delighted to come over. He told her they should be ready to go to the jail by eight o'clock or so.

The Marian Beach jail left a lot to be desired. You entered through a basement door on a side street off of Main. Five steps down with a heavy metal door on your left. The hallway was long and dimly lit with a room at the end and a sign beside the door-jam that said MARIAN BEACH JAIL.

McKenzie and Sydney walked hand in hand down the hall and through the door to the jail. The room was probably twenty-five feet long with the door in the middle and some fifteen feet wide. A single desk was on the right as you walked in. The nameplate sitting on the desk said "William Taylor, Jailor." A sign behind the desk read, "Push buzzer for help." Sydney walked over and pushed it. They heard a buzz behind the door that was next to the desk. They waited. It took at least five minutes for the door to open.

Sydney guessed it was William Taylor by stereotyping him as he imagined someone in his position would look. Short, fat, with a big mustache and mostly bald head. He was also unshaven, like someone who had a rough night and hadn't quite recovered.

"Father Strange?" Taylor asked.

"Yes, that's me. Mr. Taylor, I presume," Sydney responded.

"Yep," he said as he stuck out his hand. As he shook it Sydney introduced McKenzie. "This is my wife, McKenzie. Under the circumstances, we thought it might be a good idea for her to come with me to meet Sally Barrett."

"Sure, sure, glad you're here, Mrs. Strange."

"So," Sydney said, "what's the process here?"

"Nothing complicated. I'll take you to a room where you can meet with Sally. Unfortunately, we have to go by the two cells to get to it at the end of the cell block. I'll let you in and then bring Sally to you."

Taylor opened the door into the cell block. The room was smaller than you would think a jail would be, but then again Sydney had never been in a jail before. Two cells, one on each side of the hall, each about fifteen by fifteen, and the meeting room about fifteen feet beyond them.

"Well, would you look at that beauty," one of the two men in the cell across from Sally yelled out as he whistled at McKenzie. "I ain't seen a body like that in long time, honey babe. How 'bout you come closer and let me get a real good look at you."

"Shut your mouth, Jake," Taylor told the prisoner and apologized to McKenzie.

"Excuse me, Mr. Jailor. You can't blame a man for looking at that purdy thing," Jake replied. "And that long, blonde hair. I hope you know how to take care of a woman like that," he continued, directing his comment at Sydney.

"I said shut your mouth, Jake," Taylor responded as they quickly moved past the cells. Taylor unlocked the door and they went into the meeting room that looked exactly like what you see on television: a dim florescent light hanging over a table with two chairs on either side, and no windows. The door did have a window running from the top half-way down with what looked to be metal mesh in-between the panes.

"I feel like I'm in an episode of NYPD," McKenzie said as Taylor closed the door.

"Does kind of feel like that, doesn't it," Sydney replied. "At least we're visitors."

"I cannot imagine what Sally Barrett must be feeling," she said. "That creep in the cell so distracted me I didn't even look in the other cell to see her."

"Neither did I," he confessed. "Not sure what that says about me. Didn't even bother to try to see her. That feels awful now that I think about it."

"Don't," McKenzie answered. "The jerk kind of filled up the room with his cat calls."

The door opened and Taylor stepped aside as a woman who looked to be in her forties walked passed him. She was dressed in street clothes, a pink blouse and stretch pants, and white sneakers. Her fingernails were polished bright red. Her brown hair was disheveled like it hadn't been combed in days. She was fidgeting with her hands and barely made eye contact. When she took the chair across from them, she kept her head down.

"I'll be outside when you're finished," Taylor said, "Just knock on the door."

"Thank you," Sydney responded.

He left and the three of them just sat still for a minute or so, then Sydney spoke.

"Sally, my name is Sydney Strange. I'm the Rector at Saint Alban."

"I know who you are," Sally said without looking up. "I've seen you around town when I've been riding my bicycle."

"So you're the biker," he said. "Now I recognize you. I see you a lot during the summer. I spend time at the beach talking to the kids who are there. I've seen you riding to and from and sitting on the boardwalk benches that look out onto the ocean. You must like the water."

"Who doesn't?" she said. "No point living at the beach if you don't."

He chuckled. "Guess that's true."

"Sally, I'm McKenzie Strange."

"I know who you are, too," Sally said unexpectedly.

"You do? How's that?" McKenzie asked in a surprise tone.

"I've listened to your book talks at the library. I hide in the stacks to read, and when there is a book talk I find a way to get close enough to hear who's talking."

McKenzie turned to Sydney with a puzzled look on her face.

"Did you like any book in particular, Sally?"

"Annie Dillard's Pilgrim at Tinker's Creek."

"Why that one?"

"I don't know. I guess because I live to myself most of the time like she did at Pilgrim's Creek. After you talked about the book I read it myself. Then I started paying more attention to everything around me in nature like she did. It helps me not to feel so alone. I like to watch the squirrels play, and sometimes I bring some bread to feed them. One in particular comes right up next to me now to get the bread I put on the ground. It's like we've become friends. That probably sounds crazy, that I'm crazy like my family says I am, but I don't have any friends so I like thinking about squirrels being my friends."

"Speaking of your family, Sally," Sydney said, interrupting the conversation she and McKenzie were having. "Can you tell us what happened to make them have you arrested?"

"I don't remember."

"What do you mean, you don't remember?"

"Just that, I don't remember."

"Can you tell us anything, like the last thing you remember before the Sheriff showed up?"

"My mama died. Papa and I were with her. It was at home. She had cancer. The three of us lived together. All my brothers and sisters came to the house right after it happened. They were drinking and there was a lot of noise and laughing. It was like they were having a party instead of thinking about mama. The only thing any of them said about her was what kind of funeral to have. They wanted to do everything at her grave, no church service. I remember saying no, I wanted something at the church, your church cause that's where she went many years ago. They told me to shut up. I didn't and a big argument started. Then they started talking about selling the house and putting papa in a nursing home. They said I would have to find somewhere else to live, that I should've been on my own a long time ago anyway. I know I really got mad then. Papa told me to calm down, let them take care of everything, that they knew what was best. I guess I yelled at him when he said that. The next thing I knew the Sheriff showed up and took me away."

"Did you threaten to kill you father, Sally?"

"What? Of course not. I would never do that." Tears started running down her face. "I don't know what to do, where to go. I don't understand why papa and me can't stay at home together."

"What did the Sheriff say when he brought you here?"

"I'm not sure. I think he said my family said I was acting crazy, that he didn't want to, but he had to lock me up until a judge could decide what to do."

"Do you have any other family, Sally? Anyone you can call?"

"Not here, just someone in Greenville."

"Greenville, South Carolina?" McKenzie asked.

"Yes."

"How come Greenville? Did you live there sometime?"

"Yes, when I was married."

"Can you tell us about that?"

"Nothing much to tell, nothing good anyway. The man I married didn't like being married. He liked other girls as much as me. I told him to stop, but he never did. Then one time we had an argument and he hit me with his fist and broke my jaw. I went to the hospital and they called the police. He was arrested. When the police found out he had been hitting me a lot, they charged him with assault and battery. He finally pleaded guilty and only got probation, but the judge, a woman judge, didn't accept what the lawyers worked out, said she's had enough of men abusing their wives and sentenced Luke to a year in jail. She told him if he ever came near me after he got out, she would make him serve the rest of his time—three years. I asked the city lawyer to help me file divorce papers. He got me an attorney who didn't charge me anything. As soon as all the papers were filed, I moved back here."

"That's when you moved back in with your parents?" Sydney asked.

"Yes, but I get Social Security disability, so I help pay for food and things. I never let mama and papa pay for me. I pay for them."

"If you don't mind me asking, how did you get on Social Security disability?"

"When I came back home, I tried to work, but I kept getting nervous around people and I would leave the office where I worked. I was a good typist. The lawyer, Mr. Martin, a real nice man, told me he was going to have to let me go because I was leaving the office so often that my work was behind. He said he thought I should try to get Social Security disability for emotional trauma reasons and that he would help me. He did and I finally got it. It's not much, but I get by."

"Enough to live on your own?" asked McKenzie.

"No, enough to buy food, but not pay rent. Papa owns our house. If they put papa in a home and sell the house, I don't know what I will do."

"Well," Sydney said to her, "that's not the most pressing problem. Your family wants the county judge to commit you to Shelby."

"The mental hospital?" Sally asked.

"Yes."

"Oh no, no," she said as she raised her head for the first time. "Why do they want to do that?"

"Well, they said you threatened to kill your father."

She looked at us in disbelief. "I never did that. I told you. I love papa. I would never hurt him."

"Do you know why they would say you did?"

"No. I don't understand. I am not crazy or mean. I just get nervous when a lot of people are around." Tears began to stream down her face again. "I lost my mama. I can't lose papa, too. I don't know why my brother and sisters want to do that to me."

The three of them sat there for a moment, then Sally asked, "Can you help me?"

"Yes, we can," McKenzie said firmly. "The first thing we need to do is to get you out of here. Are you willing to go to our home to stay until we can find you somewhere more permanent?"

Sydney wasn't expecting that. He must have shown it in his face, prompting McKenzie to say, "There's no other way I can see right now. Having Sally in our home is the only way to get her out of here, so that is what we have to do. Don't you agree?"

"Well, I guess so," he said weakly.

"Sally," McKenzie said looking at her. "Are you willing?"

Sally didn't say anything, kept looking down. "Sally, please look at me." Sally raised her head and looked at McKenzie. "Are you willing to stay with us until we can work something out, or do you want to stay here?"

"If you want me to, I will go to your home. I won't be any trouble. I promise."

"Then that is what we're going to do," McKenzie said forcefully. Turning to Sydney she instructed, "Go get Mr. Taylor. Let's get out of here as fast as possible."

Sydney got up and knocked on the door. William Taylor opened the door and looked in. "So where are we?"

"We're going to take Sally home with us," McKenzie said.

"Thank you, Father Strange, thank you."

"I think you should thank her," Sydney said, pointing to McKenzie. "She's the 'lawyer' here, or the acting one."

Sally stood up as McKenzie did. McKenzie took her arm and led her out of the room into the hallway.

"Well," Jake blurted out as soon as they stepped into the cell block. "The woman of my dreams, back again."

As McKenzie, Sally, and Sydney walked by Jake's cell, McKenzie turned and looked straight at him and said, "That's all you'll ever have, dreams, because men like you don't exist in my world, or any other woman's world for that matter. So dream on because it will never be anything else."

Jake stood there looking dumbfounded, completely at loss for words.

"Guess she put you in your place," the man in the cell beside him said.

"Shut your mouth," Jake said.

Just as they left the hallway, Sydney looked back and saw the other man who was much bigger than Jake reach his arm through the bars and jerked Jake up against them in the corner where the two cells meet like he was cardboard and said, "Listen, you punk, don't ever tell me to shut up again or you will never tell anybody anything again." He then gave him a shove. Jake stumbled backwards awkwardly and quickly sat down on his bed.

Sydney smiled as if that made him feel very good.

It took Taylor about ten minutes to fix the papers to release Sally into McKenzie's and Sydney's custody. He also gave them papers with instructions for court on Monday morning at nine.

Sally didn't have anything but the clothes on her back when she was released. McKenzie told Sydney to drive to the Walmart that was still open. She took Sally in to get her a few clothes and personal items until they could get her stuff at her house. Sydney stayed in the car and let his mind run over the day that felt like a whole week. Maybe this is what he needed, he thought, to get his mind off Sonny. He could think of a better way to be distracted, but Sally Barrett was what the day had put on his plate. Sydney laid his head back, closed his eyes, and was close to being asleep when the car doors opened.

"Get what you needed?" he asked McKenzie.

"I think so, at least for now."

Sydney started the engine, moved to the exit, turned left on Auburn Road and headed home. When they arrived, Madelyn said she and Leslie talked about school and friends and had a good time together before she went to her room for the night. She looked in on her a few minutes ago she said and Leslie was already asleep. McKenzie thanked Madelyn for coming over and then headed down the hallway to show Sally the guest bedroom and the bath right across the hall. As she was getting her things together, Sydney thanked Madelyn again for her help. She said no thanks were needed when you get to do something you want to do anyway. He then reminded her of court Monday and that it would likely be in the afternoon before he got to the office.

McKenzie came into the kitchen as Sydney was getting a glass of water and said Sally was settled in so she was going to bed. He told her he would be right there. The night seemed short when he awakened at six, but McKenzie was already up so he shaved and showered and walked into the kitchen just as she got up from the counter where she was reading the paper and gave him a kiss. A little after seven, Sally stood at the doorway from the hall into the kitchen as if she wasn't sure what to do next.

"Coffee's ready if you want some," McKenzie told her, pointing to the end of the counter nearest the refrigerator. "Sugar and cream are in the bowl and pitcher."

"Thanks," Sally said. "Black is fine."

She poured herself a cup and sat down on the counter stool facing McKenzie. Sydney was at the stool at the end of the counter with coffee in hand.

"I'm scrambling some eggs and fixing toast. Will you have some with us?"

"Yes, thank you," Sally replied. "I'm not big on breakfast, but that sounds good. I haven't eaten much in a last couple of days."

It was Saturday so they knew Leslie wouldn't be up anytime soon. The three of them finished breakfast. Sydney started cleaning the table while McKenzie sat with Sally.

"We need to go to your house and get your things this morning, Sally."

"I don't want to go back there."

"Of course you don't, Sally, and I wouldn't either," McKenzie responded, "but we don't have a choice. You need some of your things. I have bags we can take. You need to get as much as you can. We don't know what the situation is going to be after we see the judge."

"What judge?" Sally asked anxiously.

"You see Judge Penny Monday morning. It's about your family trying to send you to Shelby. We'll be there with you, at least Sydney will. I have school, but I may be able to take off."

"I don't understand why I have to do that. I'm not crazy. I shouldn't be sent to a mental hospital."

"That's exactly what we plan to tell the Judge. He's a good man. He'll know what to do."

Sally got very quiet. In fact, she was quiet most of the way to her house. They drove up to a small house on the south side of Marian Beach where a lot of small bungalows were built just after WWII. Mostly veterans bought them because of the price and the VA mortgage loans being made available. They got out of the Jeep, then Sally hesitated as if she had changed her mind about picking up her stuff.

"It's okay," McKenzie assured her. "We will be right beside you. Nothing bad is going to happen."

"You don't know my brother," she said.

"Don't worry, Sally," Sydney responded. "I'll talk to your brother."

As they walked up to the porch that spanned the front of the small house a man came out of the screen door. Sally whispered that it was her brother, Buster.

"She don't need to be here," Buster said gruffly before they even got to the porch.

"Hello, Mr. Barrett. I'm Father Strange from Saint Alban Church. The city jailor asked for our help with Sally, and we brought her here just to get her things."

"Don't care. She can't come here after what she did."

"And what is that, Mr. Barrett." It occurred to Sydney that this was an opening to find out what actually happened when they had Sally put in jail.

"She was threatening our father like she was crazy."

Sydney could see Sally looking down at the sidewalk and McKenzie having to hold on to her tight to keep her from turning around.

"How's that?" Sydney asked. "I mean, did she do anything that might have hurt him?"

"Well, no, but I could tell she wanted to."

"Did she say she wanted to hurt him?"

"No, she didn't say anything directly, but she didn't have to."

"Why was that?"

"You can tell when someone is ready to do something bad. You know what I mean, Reverend."

"So Sally never said anything about hurting your father and didn't actually try to, but you knew she was going to hurt your father anyway. Is that what you're saying?"

"I know what I saw and I could tell what she was thinking, what she wanted to do if we let her."

"Why would you think Sally would hurt her own father?"

"Cause she nuts, crazy, got a loose screw somewhere. Always has."

"That's a very harsh thing to say about your sister, Mr. Barrett, don't you think?"

"Well, yeah, maybe, but it's true. Did she tell you she's on Social Security disability, mental problems is what we think?"

"Actually, she did tell us that, Mr. Barrett."

"Then you know what I'm telling you is straight."

"No, no I don't know that. What you're telling me is what you thought Sally was going to do based on how upset she was, but you're also saying she didn't actually do anything to cause you to call the sheriff and have her locked up."

"What else could we do?" Barrett asked, almost as if he was sincere with the question.

"Well, maybe everyone could have taken a step back and calmed down before doing anything. Who knows. Maybe this whole thing would have turned out different."

"Don't see how. Anyway, what's done is done."

"I agree with you there. So let my wife and Sally go in the house to get her things and we'll be gone."

"All right then, but don't take long."

McKenzie and Sally were in and out of the house in less than ten minutes.

"Thank you, Mr. Barrett," Sydney said as they were leaving. "We will see you in court Monday morning."

"What do you mean, in court?"

"In court," Sydney repeated, "where you have to testify to why you had Sally taken to jail. Then Sally will tell her side of the story and the judge will decide what to do next."

"I ain't heard nothing about going to court. I haven't talked to the sheriff since he was here last night."

"Well, I'm sure he will stop by at some point to inform you of what you have to do to have your sister taken to Shelby."

The three of them got in the car and as they drove away Sydney said to Sally, "You're not going to Shelby, Sally. I'm thinking your brother won't even show up in court Monday, or anybody else in the family. You didn't do anything to your father and they know it. I'll talk to Sheriff Brown before then."

"Thank you," she said softly.

It was obvious she was upset by being at her home and what her brother said in front of her. Sydney apologized for getting into a conversation that gave Buster the chance to say the things about her he said.

"But let me say it again, Sally. No one in your family is going to come to court. You didn't do anything that justified their actions, and they are not going to risk saying things about you that are untrue under oath."

"Thank you," she responded. I hope you're right."

# 14

Sally went to her room and they didn't see her for most of the day. McKenzie knocked on her door to ask what she wanted for lunch. She said she wasn't hungry. Leslie had finally gotten up and was eating a bowl of cereal for her lunch. Sydney explained to her why Sally was in their home and would be there for the weekend. She didn't seem all that interested so he let it go. As McKenzie put sandwiches on the counter for herself and Sydney, Sydney told her he was thinking about going to see Wanda Bolivar about giving Sally a place to stay for a while. Wanda owned Wanda's Restaurant & Bar on the boardwalk and helps the beach kids whenever one of them needed a place to stay. She also gave them food rather than having them scrounge for it in dumpsters.

"Besides," he offered, "she likes me."

"Oh, yeah," McKenzie said taking the bait, "and why is that?"

"Because I am such a nice guy, you know that."

"Yes, I do, but tell me more about this woman I've heard about, but have never met."

"Well, I eat at the restaurant sometimes when I'm working the beach, sometimes with one or two of the kids. But our relationship became a real friendship when I helped her out with the two runaways from Greenwood I told you about a year or so ago."

"The brother and sister."

"Yes, Bobby and Ruth. I never told you the whole story about them, about what happened when I took them back home, did I?"

"Don't think so, but we've got time now. I'd like to hear it."

"Okay. Well, you remember their stepfather, a guy named Louis Trent, was physically abusing them. Bobby finally stood up to him. That's when the two of them ran away. After I convinced them they needed to go home because of the dangers of living on the street, they agreed only after I promised them I would make sure the physical abuse stopped. I even told them I already had a plan for how to do it, only I didn't. At least, not exactly. I did know a good friend from high school, Darrell Martin, who lived in Greenwood. He was a heck of defensive end for Castle Cove. You were older than we were, so you probably didn't know him back then."

"Stick to the story, Strange," retorted McKenzie.

"My emerging plan was to ask Darrell to go with me to talk to the stepfather and the kids' mother. I'm decent size, but I figured having someone six feet five and two hundred and forty pounds couldn't hurt."

"You see," McKenzie inserted, "you're as smart as I've been telling you."

"I appreciate the vote of confidence, but let me finish my story. As soon as I walked in Farm Bureau in Greenwood where Darrell is the store manager, he saw me, came out of his office and gave me a bear hug. We exchanged pleasantries and he asked why I was in town. I told him about Bobby and Ruth and that I needed his help. He didn't hesitate a second before saying he was in.

"The kids directed us to the trailer park where they lived. It was decent, well maintained for such places, especially in North Carolina. Their yard didn't have junk laying around on the ground and the trailer had a nice front porch. The stepfather came to the door, saw Bobby and Ruth, and called out to their mother. She appeared, ran out the door and hugged her kids like she truly missed them. She did a mama fuss about them running away, telling them she had been worried sick about where they were. I explained how I met them and was candid about why they had run away. She ignored what I said and took them inside. That's when things got interesting with the stepfather.

"'I guess we should thank you for bringing the kids home,' Trent said without much sincerity.

"Without hesitation I came right back at him. 'You need to know that Bobby told me everything about the physical abuse he and Ruth have suffered.'

"'That's a damn lie,' he responded as he stepped down off the porch and then toward me. He stopped when Darrell came up beside me. Then he said, 'You need to get off my property.'

"'Actually, Mr. Trent, I don't think this is your property. You and the kids' mother live together, but you're not married. This is hers, not yours. But we're leaving anyway. Just understand that Bobby knows how to get in touch with me, and I had better not hear anything more about the abuse or I'll come back next time with the county sheriff.'

"As we walked away, Darrell turned around, went back to Trent, leaned over and whispered something to him. When we got into the Jeep I asked him what he said.

"'Nothing much, only that I had a little girl, too, just like Ruth, and that I couldn't stand the thought of anything happening to kids like them.'

"I looked at Darrell to let him know I knew that was not the whole story.

"'Okay,' Darrell admitted, 'I also told him that because I wasn't a minister, if I had to come back I wouldn't be nearly as nice as you had been.'

"I gave him a fist bump and started the Jeep.

"It was so good to see Darrell again," he told McKenzie. "It's easy to forget what a good friend someone once was when you don't see them for a long time. We both said we would keep in touch. I plan to do that. I want you to meet him. I told Wanda that story and she thanked me profusely for helping Bobby and Ruth. She has told me since that they are doing okay. Bobby calls her occasionally so she's keeping up with them. He graduated from high school, has a part-time job, and has even managed to finish a year of community college. He also assured Wanda that Ruth was doing okay, too."

"That's an amazing story, Sydney. There are not many people who would go as far as you did to help those kids. I'm so glad I married you, even if I am an older woman. Now let's go see Wanda. I want to meet her after all this time."

Fifteen minutes later we walked into Wanda's place. She was coming out of the back area when she saw us.

"Well, well, I don't see you very often Reverend Sydney when the summer season has gone. And who is this beautiful woman with you?"

"I told Sydney I would like you," McKenzie replied with a big smile. "I'm his sidekick, even if he doesn't like it. My name is McKenzie."

"You couldn't have picked a better one to pal around with, Miss McKenzie. This man of yours gives better than he gets working with those beach kids. He comes in here for a break and all of us love to see him."

"Don't pile it on too deep, Wanda, I have to l live with him."

"Gotcha," she replied. "Sit down, then. What would you like to drink?"

Sydney said coffee. McKenzie ordered a light beer. Wanda sat down and Sydney told her about Sally needing a place to stay. She said all her rooms were empty so that wouldn't be a problem. When he asked how much the rent was, she asked how much she could pay. He said nothing and Wanda said nothing it was.

"What if she waited tables half a day or something," McKenzie suggested. "That way she'll feel like she's paying her own way. I think that would be good for her."

"You know," Wanda said, "I have a part-timer who just had a baby. I was planning just to hold her position open and wait for her to come back, but if it's for rent the girl you're talking about, you said her name was Sally," Sydney nodded yes, "she could fill in. That would work for everybody."

"That sounds great, Wanda," McKenzie said. "Sally's a gentle soul, has had a rough time in life, but I am sure she won't give you any trouble."

"How about we bring her by Monday afternoon to meet you and get her settled," Sydney suggested.

The three of them stood. Sydney thanked Wanda and gave her a hug, So did McKenzie. "I like this woman of yours, Sydney. You better treat her good," Wanda said, turned to McKenzie and said, "McKenzie, you come by anytime, with or without him."

"I will," McKenzie answered. "I will."

It was around noon when they got home. The rest of the weekend was quiet. Sally stayed home while the three of them went to church. Sydney dropped McKenzie and Leslie off at home and went back to the church to do some paperwork for the diocese he had been putting off. He also needed to stop by the hospital. Got all that done and decided to grab a bite at the T-Room, his favorite hole-in-the-wall place to eat. The T-Room had been a filling station in its day that was located on the downhill street where the annual Marian Beach soap box derby was run. People used to sit on the roof of the station to watch the races. Converted into a hotdog joint, the T-Room slogan is, "We serve five hundred people a day, ten at a time."

There was hardly anyone in the place when Sydney opened the door to go in. It was usually full. Macy Hammond greeted him and said, "Sit anywhere, Sydney, if you can find a seat," being sarcastic. "As you can see, we've been waiting for you." Then in a more serious tone she said, "Haven't seen you in a while."

"Thanks, Macy, it has been. Been busy with out-of-town family stuff lately."

"You want the usual?" she asked.

"Yep," he answered.

Macy turned to the cook at the other end of the room working at the huge grill. "Give me two hots with double relish and a bowl also with relish."

She turned back and asked what he wanted to drink. Sydney ordered a Dr. Pepper. She opened the glass door of the refrigerator against the wall opposite the counter and sat the can down in front of him. Then she asked, "So you're spending a lot of time out of town, if you don't mind me being a busy-body."

"No, no, you know better than that, Macy. It's just been a situation with one of my brothers, and then my father had a heart attack."

"Sorry to hear that," Macy responded."

"Thank you, Macy. He's okay. Had a couple of blocked arteries they had to take care of, but he's home and doing well. For now, though, McKenzie and I are trying to help someone here in town who seems to be all alone."

"You're talking about Sally Barrett, aren't you, Sydney."

"How would you know that, Macy?"

"You know this town. Gossip travels fast. I hear her family had her arrested and want to send her to the crazy house, said she threatened to kill her own father."

"Do you know her?"

"Grew up with her. Known her all my life."

"What kind of person is she?" he asked. "I talked to her brother, Buster Barrett. Didn't much care for him, to be honest."

"Two hots and a bowl up," the cook yelled. Macy went to get them.

"Buster brat" is what we used to call him," Macy continued as she set the food in front of Sydney. "He was a bully who picked on boys smaller than him and made fun of girls. Everybody thought he was a jerk."

"That doesn't surprise me given my encounter with him yesterday. What about Sally, though. What was she like?"

"Not much of a talker. Quiet, but nice. Never had many friends. I guess you could say she was kind of strange. Just kept to herself and had fidgety hands."

"Ever get into trouble?"

"Are you kidding? You wouldn't even know she was around if you didn't see her yourself. She read a lot and was smart as a whip. Never knew why she acted so withdrawn. I do know she was scared to death of her brother. She literally shook when he came around. I'll never forget how she acted. I know what terror looks like in a person's eyes because of the way she looked when she saw him."

"Because of what you just said, Macy, I need to ask you something that is not an easy question to ask, but I have to anyway. Did you ever hear anything about Sally's brother abusing her?"

"Physically or sexually?"

"Either," said Sydney.

"Physically," Macy answered, "as far as I know. It was no secret that he pushed her around a lot. She came to school with bruises on her arms more than once. Back then teachers didn't pay much attention to that kind of stuff. Guess they thought it was a family issue. I never heard anything about sexual abuse, but it wouldn't have surprised me. He was an ugly kid in every way."

"Thank you for being so honest, Macy. This is more helpful than you can know."

"Always glad to help you, Sydney. Good to see you and don't wait so long to come back."

He handed her a twenty and told her to keep the change.

"Thanks, hon."

Sydney couldn't wait to get home to tell McKenzie what Macy had said. Unfortunately, she was watching the Green Bay Packers game. She was an avid Packers fan. Her dad got her hooked on them when she was growing up. McKenzie was an athlete in her own right, having been a starter for the women's high school softball team four years in a row at center field. She had some offers to play in college, but choose not to go that route.

"I've got something important to tell you," Sydney said, as he sat down beside her on the sofa. She leaned over and gave him a kiss without taking her eyes off the game.

"Unless it's an emergency it will have to wait 'till half-time," McKenzie told him. "It's a tight game. The Packers are up by a touchdown, but Mike Singletary is making plays all over the field. He's one heck of a player."

"The best linebacker ever, maybe," Sydney responded. I'd hate to have to try to block him."

"The Packers can't seem to block him at all. Favre is having a pretty good day, but Singletary has gotten to him a couple of times. The Bears were moving the ball in the first quarter, but haven't done much in the second quarter."

"Day ain't over yet," Sydney quipped. McKenzie gave him a loving smirk, then laid her head on his shoulder. The score stayed the same the rest of the half. Just before the second quarter ended, Sydney decided to get a cup of coffee. He asked McKenzie if she wanted anything. She said she could use a refill on her sweetened tea. By the time he was back on the couch half-time had started.

"Where is Sally?" he asked.

"In her room, been there all day unless she came out while we were at church. I'm guessing you're asking because the news you're busting to tell me has to do with her."

"It does. I stopped by the T-Room for a late lunch."

"I figured that when you didn't come home for lunch. Why you go there I will never know. The food is awful."

"Now that's a debate we'll have to have another time. I need to tell you what Macy Hammond told me while I was there. The place was virtually empty, something that is rarely the case, but it was fortuitous that it was. First of all, she already knew about what happened Friday night with Sally and her family. Apparently, everybody in Marian Beach does. Then she said she grew up with Sally. Described her as being quiet, gentle, a loner, nervous as a kid the way she is now. But she also said Sally was scared to death of her brother who was a bully and abused her physically, if not sexually."

"That explains a lot," said McKenzie. "She was scared of him yesterday when we went by the house, and he acted like the bully he apparently still is. Her hands were shaking when I took one of them to go in the house with her."

"She had real fear in her eyes as she walked past him. I saw it myself, but I didn't think too much about it until I heard what Macy told me."

"You've got to tell the judge about all of this, at least that she is afraid of her brother for good reason. He can't send her to Shelby under those circumstances."

"I don't even think we'll have to worry about that. I don't know if you heard everything Buster said, but Sally didn't threaten anyone, especially her father. He admitted that he thought she would hurt him, but that Sally didn't actually say or do anything to indicate she would. I'm willing to bet he won't even show-up in court, and neither will anybody else in the family.

"You're serious?" McKenzie asked.

"Yes, I am. He won't show."

"I hope you're right."

"I'm sure of it. Buster Barrett is like all bullies, tough when not challenged, but cowards when they face push back. I made it clear to him that we are helping Sally and would be in court with her. He's not going to show, I'll bet you."

"I won't bet you on that, Reverend Strange," McKenzie said, "but I will bet you Green Bay is going to beat the Bears."

"You're on," he replied.

# 15

Monday morning came soon enough. They got Leslie off to school and then settled on the bench outside the court room about an hour before Sally's ten o'clock hearing. That turned out to be a good thing. Sheriff Brown unexpectedly walked up the stairs and came over to where they were sitting.

"Looks like this thing is over before it got started," he said. "I was informed by your family, Miss Barrett, that they don't plan to come to court. Didn't say why, just that they wouldn't be here. I told them the case would be dropped if they didn't appear. The woman I was talking to who she said was your sister made it clear they didn't care and weren't coming."

Sydney looked at McKenzie and they both looked at Sally, who had a blank look on her face that made them wonder if she understood what the sheriff had just said. "Did you hear what he said?" McKenzie asked her softly.

"Yes, I heard, but I still don't have anywhere to go. They put me out of papa's house."

"We'll talk about that in a minute," McKenzie said. "First, let's see what comes next."

"I suggest you sit in the back of the courtroom," Sheriff Brown said. "Otherwise, the judge might carry the case over to another time if neither party is present. It's unlikely he would, but being there is the safe way to go. The town attorney will tell the judge the plaintiff is a no show and doesn't want to pursue the charges. The judge will officially dismiss the case and it's all done."

"Thank you, sheriff," Sydney said.

"I'm real sorry all this happened," he said. "I hated doing what I did Friday night, but the family wanted her charged and that didn't give me much choice. Good luck to you, Miss Barrett. They'll call you in when the judge is ready."

"Thank you," Sally mumbled.

Everything went as Sheriff Brown said it would and Sydney and McKenzie took Sally home with them afterwards. On the way McKenzie explained to her about Wanda's. She was okay with staying there, but when McKenzie mentioned waiting tables she started shaking her head.

"I can't. I just can't," she repeated. "People make me nervous. I can't stay there if I have to do that."

McKenzie looked at Sydney and he knew she was asking what they were going to do. He suddenly had an idea. "Sally, what if Wanda let you clean the restaurant at night after it closes, and also any room upstairs during the day. There are only four of them. How about that?"

"I could do that," she answered. "I could do that."

"Once we get home I'll give her a call and see what she says," Sydney told Sally.

Wanda didn't hesitate when he called and asked her about changing plans. She said she was hoping to get the help for waiting tables, but it was a slow time and so she said she would make it work somehow.

"It's the least I can do," said Wanda, given how you helped with my two runaways, Bobby and Ruth. No telling where they would be today if you hadn't done what you did."

"Sometimes kids just need a little help and they do the rest. But listen, we'll see you in a few minutes."

Sally got the few things she had, mostly what McKenzie had bought her, and the three of them headed to Wanda's and got her settled in a room facing the street. It was kind of noisy, but cozy too. Sally seemed to like it fine. The best part was the bathroom was right next to it. Sydney told Wanda to call either of them if there was a problem and that he would stop by once in a while to see how things were going.

When they got into the Jeep, McKenzie said she would work from home for the rest of the day. Sydney dropped her off and went to the church.

"How did it go?" Madelyn asked when he walked in.

"Good, the family didn't show up and the case was dismissed. Sally is staying at Wanda's for the time being. We'll see how that goes, but all in all the situation turned out better than it looked on Friday night."

"Glad to hear that," she said. "I put your mail on your desk. No calls. Things have been quiet."

"Just what the doctor ordered," he responded. "It was a long weekend.

I feel tired already and the week has hardly started. I need some time just to unwind, so hold my calls unless you think I really need to take them."

"Will do."

Sydney sat down in his chair, turned to face the window looking out on the freshly cut back lawn of the church yard, and just stared at nothing. It felt good to have nothing demanding his attention. He thought about writing in his journal, something he had done for many years. But he decided not to today. He didn't want to write or think. Just wanted to be. Saying that to himself got him thinking about what he was feeling and why he didn't want to write. Next thing he knew he had pulled out his journal and was writing about not wanting to write.

Five minutes into it he stopped writing and picked up the phone. Darrell Martin answered on the first ring. Sydney immediately apologized for not staying in touch. Darrell assured him that was not a problem. They talked for about ten minutes. Sydney told him he would drive down his way soon and would let him know when he was coming. Darrell said that should work both ways, so he would plan to get up to Marian Beach for lunch. When they hung up Sydney laughed to himself over the strange effect journaling sometimes has. He hadn't thought about Darrell in a while and then he calls him and has a good visit on the phone simply because Darrell's name appeared unexpectedly on the journal page. Mystery really is part of life, he thought to himself.

He turned back around to face his desk and decided to read the stack of mail Madelyn had put there. The last envelope in the pile had the return address: Saint Patrick Episcopal Church, 1717 First Avenue, Castle Cove, North Carolina. Sydney couldn't imagine what that was about. He cut through the top of the envelope, took the letter out and was caught off guard when he read the first words: "Dear Sydney, On behalf of the Vestry of Saint Patrick Episcopal Parish, I am writing to ask if you would be willing to meet with us to discuss your becoming our parish priest."

He finished reading the letter, put it in his briefcase, told Madelyn he was going to make a visit at the hospital. Mary Staple is an eighty-one-year-old member of Saint Alban who has the energy of someone much younger, but suddenly ended up in the hospital. She is one of his favorite people in the whole world. She smiled as he walked into the room and held out her arms as he approached her bedside. He leaned down and she kissed him on the cheek.

"How are you, Mary?" Sydney asked as he sat down.

"Going home tomorrow," she said with delight. "My lungs checked out fine. I have a little congestion, but they said I didn't have pneumonia like they thought. With medicine I will be fine."

"That's a relief," said Sydney.

"It definitely is. I'm on the committee to plan my sixtieth Elon College reunion that's next year. We meet next week and I have some research on class members to do before then."

"It can't be your sixtieth, can it? You look too young for that to be true."

"I'm afraid the hundreds and hundreds of first graders I had over forty-five years of teaching would say it is. I've had a good life, Sydney. I still remember the joy of witnessing the moment a student of mine would read out loud for the first time, a moment that changed that child's life forever. It was a privilege I never took for granted."

"I know you didn't, Mary, and how fortunate those kids were to have you as their teacher. But how are your girls doing?"

"Fine, Ellie is still teaching first grade in Raleigh, just like her mother. Both her boys are in college. Emory is a lawyer for a big firm in Charlotte. She does corporate law. I don't know much about it. Based on a few comments she's made I wonder if she really likes it or is staying because the money is too good to quit right now, especially with her twins going to UNC Chapel Hill next year. But both girls seem to be happy and that is what matters most to me."

"You did an amazing job raising them by yourself. You have to be very proud."

"I am. I feel very fortunate to have the daughters I have."

"You have a right to be, but may I ask you a personal question?"

"Sydney, I think we know each well enough by now that you can ask me anything you want."

"Thank you, Mary, it is very personal, but here goes. I know losing Robert to a heart attack the way you did was devastating, but with two growing girls, and you being who you are and as beautiful as I know you were—and still are—how come you never remarried?"

"Well, for starters, I had those two adolescent girls. They were involved in everything and were good students and kept me running. I didn't have time to be lonely. They were also very attentive to me and wanted me to go with them places when most teenager girls would have been embarrassed to have their mother with them. At the same time, I wanted to scream at God, at life, and the unfairness of what had happened. And I did. I took some days off and while the girls were at school I cried my eyes out. I slept during the day which I had never done. I sat for hours staring into space. And then I started thinking about Robert and the life we had together, twenty happy years of marriage. That made me cry more, but it also made me smile and even laugh.

"Then I got to thinking about several friends of mine who let me know in various ways that their marriages were not happy at all. They stayed because of children or financial constraints or just plain fear of going it alone. For some reason that brought me up short. I asked myself why I was letting anger and sadness control my days when I had twenty wonderful years with a man I loved dearly and who loved me the same way while my closest friends were missing out on all of that. I know the misery of someone else is a poor excuse for finally seeing the blessings in your own life, but I guess that's what happened. From then until now I have lived as fully as I can. I would still have some bad days, but they got fewer and fewer. The biggest blessing is that I have two wonderful young women as daughters and four grandchildren between them. Not everybody is so lucky."

Sydney reminded Mary that she was one of the first people to stop by to greet him when he first came to Saint Alban. He told her that after she left he thought if everyone in the church was like her he knew he had made a great decision to come there to serve. Mary then turned the tables and asked Sydney how he was doing. He told her about Sally Barrett's ordeal. She knew Sally's parents, she said, not well, but enough to feel like they were nice people who mostly kept to themselves. Mr. Barrett had been a barber all his life, she said, something Sydney didn't know, and retired only a year or so ago when his eyes really began to fail him and his hands were getting shaky. They had four children, three girls and a boy who was constantly in trouble in the elementary school where Mary taught. She knew from things Robert had said about him that he didn't change much when he went to high school. Sydney told her he had met him briefly and surmised that he hadn't changed much.

As he got ready to leave, Sydney told Mary that ordinarily he would have a prayer with her, but he could honestly say that he felt like their conversation was all the prayer they needed.

"Mary," he added, "you make the world a better place just by being in it."

She smiled and blew him a kiss.

Sydney walked down the hallway knowing that he had just experienced one of those special moments that makes you feel like what you are doing is worth something after all. Feeling better than he had all day, he decided to go home rather than go back to the church. He found a note from McKenzie on the kitchen counter telling him she was at the beach and asking him to join her if he got home in time.

She was sitting on her favorite bench about fifty yards up the way from the several kiosks that are busy during the summer, but mostly closed now. She saw Sydney and waved. He waved back, and when he got to her he gave her a kiss. His mind was still filled with the conversation he had had with Mary Staples which made him feel an overwhelming sense of love for this woman he had been married to for sixteen years.

"Sydney, this is as good as it gets," she said as they sat quietly looking out on the ocean.

"You mean my kisses," he responded playfully.

"I mean this," as she pushed her arms out toward the water. "It's easy to take this for granted. I'm sure I do all the time, but I don't want to ever again."

"What's brought this on?" he asked, knowing something was on her mind beyond enjoying the magic of ocean waves crashing.

"Well, I keep thinking about Sally Barrett, how sad a person she is, how sad her life has been. She could have been me and I could be her except for the accident of our births. Life really isn't fair. I guess getting to know her and her situation made me realize how easy I get caught up in what's happening in our lives and forget about how wonderful our life really is. I am married to the man I love dearly and we have a daughter who brings me more joy than I even knew existed. It's all made me see that our ordinary life is really pretty extraordinary."

He didn't know what to say so he didn't say anything. Then she added, "and I've decided to quit teaching at the end of the year."

"What?" he exclaimed.

"That's right. We don't need the money."

"And why do you say that?"

"You said so, for one thing."

"Ah, that's right. How could I forget? I married a rich girl, and I am now the son of a rich mother, though neither of us knew that when we fell in love."

"And because we have everything we need and many things we don't, another thing that I easily take for granted when I shouldn't. I stopped teaching once when Leslie was born and we got along fine. We certainly didn't need for me to go back to work and even disagreed about it. My point is, I don't feel fully engaged in my teaching right now, and I am ready to try my hand at writing. I've taught literature for years, now it's time for me to produce some. Or at least try."

"This wasn't what I was expecting to talk about today, but I think it is fantastic that you're willing to start writing. I can't wait to be known as the husband of the famous writer, McKenzie Strange! But," he paused, "I have something you need to read."

He pulled the letter from Saint Patrick out of his pocket and handed it to her. She looked at the envelop and looked at him obviously intrigued. She took the letter out of the envelope and started reading out loud:

Dear Sydney:

On behalf of the Vestry of Saint Patrick Episcopal Parish I am writing to ask if you would be willing to meet with us to discuss your becoming our parish priest. Our situation over the last several years has been unsettled, to say the least. We lost Father Cyrus Haynes due to some personal issues we did not know about until he shared them with us at the time of his resignation. We went more than a year without a settled priest, and then called an older man, Carl Reagan, who after four years has announced he is taking early retirement to care for his wife who has been diagnosed with Alzheimer's. She's a lovely woman and we are all deeply saddened to learn of her condition.

Your name immediately came up in our recent vestry meeting. Before we contact Bishop Stewart, we wanted to ask you directly if you would be interested in coming back home to Castle Cove to lead our parish. Please give this your prayerful consideration. I look forward to hearing from you are at your earliest convenience.

Sincerely,
Dan Mitchell


McKenzie held the letter and looked out at the ocean for a moment, then looked at Sydney.

"Well, that's a surprise."

"Yes, and now I know what to do about it. Your writing comes first this time."

"That's not what I'm thinking," McKenzie said.

"I don't understand," he replied. "I mean, it's not that I'm not flattered that they want me to come back home. It means a lot to know the people who've known you all your life have that kind of confidence in your leadership. But I like it here in Marian Beach. We've been here eleven years..."

"Almost twelve, actually," said McKenzie, interrupting him.

"Yes, well, all three of us like it here. It's a great place to live and Saint Alban is an easy parish to serve."

"Maybe too easy," McKenzie said,

"I don't know what you mean."

"Well," she said, "I believe you are the best there is in ministry, the people here love you to death, and you could probably stay here until you retire, but is that what you really want? Sydney, you are a leader. You're incredibly smart, and I think it's possible that staying in a place that is 'easy' might not be the best thing for you to do."

"Are you unhappy here?" he asked her.

"No, no I'm not. In fact, I love it here, as you said, but that is not the issue. I think we are the kind of people who would be happy just about anywhere. The question I'm raising is whether Marian Beach stretches you enough to call out the best that is in you as a minister. I'm not saying it doesn't, only that this letter may be God's way of nudging you to give it some thought."

"You think I'm coasting?"

"No, because that's not you. You work hard at anything you do. It's more a matter of having more opportunities to use your mind and your skills to make a difference in the world. I know that sounds pious and too general, but I believe talented people rise to whatever challenge they face, and I'm just wondering if you stay here will those challenges still come your way."

"I think what I do with the beach kids every summer is important. I might even make a difference in the world through them. Who knows? But I do make a difference to them. I have connected with several of them, really connected and that matters to them and to me. We both know how hard being a teenager is. I think I'm helping them get through this period in their lives, especially when so many of them come from bad home situations. They trust me. I've earned that with them. They tell each other about me, that I'm someone who isn't going to judge them and will listen to them."

"Please don't hear me as minimizing that ministry. I agree it is important, even life-saving. I'm just saying that a place that can put you in a position to help even more people might be something for you to consider."

"And you think Saint Patrick is such a place?"

"Yes, I do. For one thing it's twice as big as Marian Beach, and my parents say Castle Cove is growing a lot. I guess I'm rambling without saying what I want to say, Sydney. Staying here may be fine, moving may be. It's all fine. For me it doesn't matter because I am ready to do something new in my own life and I can do that anywhere. I just don't want you to settle."

"I have to admit this was not how I thought this conversation would go. I was ready to decline the invitation on its face, but I guess I need to give it more thought than that."

He looked at McKenzie, kissed her lightly on the lips and pulled her close as they sat quietly looking out at the ocean. After a while he said, "You don't find a scene like this just anywhere, certainly not in Castle Cove. But you do have the mountains there and they have incredible beauty of their own. I've always loved the two extremes of Carolina, the mountains on one end and the ocean on the other."

"Me, too," McKenzie said as she cuddled against him tighter.

They stayed at the beach until it was time for Leslie's bus to drop her off from school. Sydney planned to cook salmon on the grill for supper. Leslie was talkative doing her homework at the kitchen counter but wasted no time going to her room afterwards. They allowed her to have a cell phone for her twelfth birthday back in September. She could text freely but had only fifteen minutes a day for calls. They thought limiting her time on the phone could help her learn some time management. She was already complaining that fifteen minutes a day was just not enough time. They promised to review it in three months. Sydney got the salmon ready and put them in the refrigerator until it was time to cook. He refilled his coffee and went out on the back porch to relax. His phone rang. It was Carrie.

"Sydney, it's Carrie. Sonny's in the hospital. He fell last night and hit his head. He was drinking. I didn't find out until this morning because he was in Castle Cove. That's where he's spending most of his time these days. I hardly ever see him. I don't have any more information than that. I talked to Harrison. He didn't know anything, but said he would try to find out and would let me know. Honestly, though, I would feel better if you were there. I love him and want to kill him all at the same time."

Sydney could tell she was trying to hold back tears so he quickly said, "I'm on my way. Do you know if mother and father know about it?"

"Harrison said once he found out anything he would go by and see them. I'm worried they might find out before he can do that, but as far as I know they don't know anything yet."

He clicked off and had just stood up when McKenzie came out the door.

"That was Carrie. I have to go to Castle Cove. Sonny's fallen and hit his head. Drinking, of course. He's there more than in Halifax these days. He knows people in Castle Cove who will give him a place to stay, but that's an assumption. I felt like she was indirectly asking me to go, so I told her I would. She is very upset."

"You need to pack a few things. I'll make you a sandwich to eat on the way. Don't try to come back tonight. Call me once you know anything."

He was on the road in less than thirty minutes. Daylight saving time meant he would get to Castle Cove only a short while after sundown. He called Harrison as he was leaving Marian Beach and left a message for him to call as soon as possible. He had not heard back when he pulled into the emergency room parking lot. He told the person at the desk he was Sonny Strange's brother and needed to know where he was. She looked on her chart and then said he had been admitted and was on the third floor. Sydney hopped on the elevator to the third floor, exited and made his way to the main nurse's station. Room three-fourteen the nurse said when he asked about Sonny.

Sonny was alone when Sydney opened the door and walked into the room.

"Here to see the family's problem son?" Sonny quipped.

"Guess so," Sydney responded. "At least the one who seems determined to kill himself. Is that you?"

"I plead the fifth."

"No need. Intent is not the issue. Impact—no pun intended—is. You were drunk, you fell, you hit your head and could have killed yourself."

"Well, I didn't so you don't need to worry about it. Nobody does. It's my business."

"You can keep telling yourself that, but you know it's not true. It's Carrie's business. It's your childrens' business. It's the business of every member of the family. You don't live in a world all by yourself, something you've never bothered to understand. I'm not here because I heard a man fell and hit his head and decided to pay him a visit. I'm here because we're brothers. That means what you do is my business whether you like it or not. Frankly, I wish it weren't. But it is."

"Well, let me absolve you of all responsibility. I'm the one responsible and so you don't have any. You are free to leave. In fact, I wish you would."

Sydney had nothing else to say so he did what Sonny asked him to do. He left. As he got into his Jeep his cell rang. It was McKenzie.

"I'm sorry I didn't call," he said as soon as he clicked on. "I went straight to the ER reception desk when I got here and got focused on that and forget to. I found Sonny alone in a room. The nurse said he was being kept for observation and would be released in the morning if he has a good night."

"Did you talk to him about what happened?"

"Not really. He gave me his usual 'I'm the bad son' routine and finally told me to leave and I did. It was a waste of time for me to come so I'm coming home tonight. I'll talk to Harrison when he calls me back and see if he has talked to mother and father."

"I wish you wouldn't. It's getting late. Just stay there for the night."

"Well, I'll see. It's around eight now. Maybe I'll just go by Harrison's and see how that goes."

"Good. Just let me know what you decide, but I really think you should wait until tomorrow. Love you."

"Love you, too." Sydney clicked off and then called Carrie.

"It's me, Carrie. I just saw him. He's in the hospital for observation, but it looks like he is going to be all right."

"Did he say anything specific about what happened, where it happened, who he was with, where he's staying?'

"No, because we didn't really talk. He made it clear what happened was none of my business. I didn't want to get into an argument with him so I left. Maybe I should have stayed and pushed to find out more, but I didn't. I'm sorry, Carrie."

"It's not your fault, Sydney, you know that. It's Sonny. I don't know what's going to happen now, but I know it won't be good whatever it is."

"How are you managing?" he asked.

"Okay, I guess. I don't know what I would do without my job, even though my parents have been offering help for a long time. I'm trying to keep things stable for the kids. I even try to talk about their dad's problem, but they don't seem interested. I did manage to get them into Alateen. So we're okay. At least I'm staying sane so I guess that's as good as I can do right now."

"I am so sorry, Carrie. I feel so bad about what you and the kids are going through."

"Thank you, Sydney, but we can't control him and I'm trying to learn how not to even want to. Got a long way to go with that, but at least I have Al-Anon to help."

"I know that's good for you. All of us should probably be in it."

"Probably," she said. "It might get us all on the same page, but I know your mom and dad won't go, for sure your dad, and neither will Harrison. I try not to focus on that either."

"Well, just know we're here whenever you need us, just like tonight."

"I do, Sydney. Thank you."

He said goodbye just as he drove into Harrison's driveway. His car was there so Sydney figured he must be home. Maryanne answered the door.

"I wondered if you would come," she said as she gave him a hug. "Come in. Harrison is in the den."

"Good to see you, Maryanne."

"Let me get you something to drink and then I will join you. We have wine, beer, water, tea, and coffee."

"Coffee will be good," he answered.

"Hey bro," Harrison said as he looked up from his easy chair. "I'm pretty sure I know why you're here in Castle Cove. Figured I'd hear from you."

"I called your cell, but you never picked up."

"I came home after I checked on him at the hospital," Harrison explained. "I didn't actually see him. He was in tests at the time, but I was told his injuries were not life threatening so I left. I guess I turned the volume off on my phone when I went in and forget to turn it back on."

Maryanne came into the room with a tray of coffee, cups, sugar, cream, and a few cookies. Sydney took a cup, put sugar in, and picked up a cookie. Maryanne did the same while Harrison took nothing.

"I did see Sonny while I was there. It was not a good visit. He was defensive, argumentative, and then told me to leave. That was it, probably no more than fifteen minutes. I did find out that the tests didn't show anything bad. He is staying overnight for observation. That's all I know."

Sydney sipped his coffee and then asked them if they knew Sonny was staying in town. Harrison said he didn't, but work had been very busy and he hadn't had time even to take a lunch break for a week or so. Maryanne didn't say anything and so Sydney asked her directly.

"Carrie called me," she answered, "and asked me if I had seen him. That was about a week ago. She said she hadn't seen him for at least two weeks, then a friend told her she had heard Sonny was in Castle Cove staying with friends. When Carrie told me that it was the first I knew about him losing his job. I told Harrison."

"What a mess," Sydney said as he sighed.

"Has been for a long time, Sydney, years in fact," Harrison said. "We all know this is not going to end well. I can't tell you how many times when my phone rings that I think it's somebody calling to tell me he's dead."

That silenced the three of them.

"I guess I do the same thing," Sydney admitted. "A lot, in fact, and it makes me mad. It's so selfish of him. He's sucking up all the oxygen in this family, and he acts like it's nobody's business but his. That's essentially what he said tonight when I saw him."

"Sydney, I told you a long time ago that he was never going to change.

That's why I dropped out mentally and emotionally. Do I ever think about him? Of course I do. He's my brother. I even worry about him in my weak moments. He's got so much going for him. It's hard to watch it all go to hell. But mom and dad are my main concern."

"Do they know about his fall?" Sydney asked, realizing he hadn't thought about it until just now.

"I don't think so," Maryanne said. Harrison agreed and then said, "I hope we can keep it that way, at least this time."

"I agree," said Sydney. "No need since it looks like he's going to be okay."

They managed to switch the subject to other things, mostly family and work. Sydney finished his coffee and said he thought he would head back to Marian Beach. They insisted he stay the night, but he wanted to get home. Besides, he said, he could use some alone time. It was not quite nine o'clock so he wouldn't be very late getting back. He gave both of them a hug and left.

Sydney was no more than ten minutes outside of Castle Cove when his cell rang. He saw it was Harrison and immediately clicked on.

"What didn't you understand about my needing some alone time?" Sydney said jokingly.

"Where are you?" Harrison asked and Sydney knew immediately something was wrong.

"About ten minutes from town."

"Turn around. Mom just called and the ambulance just took dad to the hospital. He's had another heart attack. She rode in the ambulance. I'll meet you there."

"I'm on my way."

It took Sydney five minutes to travel back over the miles that just took him ten minutes to drive. He jumped out of his Jeep and ran into the emergency room entrance. His mother and Harrison were sitting on a bench across from the desk. He quickly went to them. As he approached his mother, she stood and he gave her a hug.

"You know anything?"

"No, not yet, but I think it was really bad this time," she managed to say before choking up. She sat back down on the bench as Sydney sat on the opposite side from Harrison.

"He's been very tired lately and hasn't looked well. I asked him how he was feeling so much it made him mad, but I knew something wasn't right."

Just then they saw the doctor emerge from behind a curtain, look down the hall and start their way. It was obvious something was wrong. By the time he got to them the look on his face told them all they needed to know."

"Mrs. Strange," he said, "I am so sorry. We did everything we could, but the damage was too severe. He never regained consciousness."

Sarah burst into tears. Harrison put his arm around her and turned his head to her back. Sydney could hardly see the doctor's face for the tears, but he managed to ask him when they could see him. He said it would be only a few minutes and the nurse would come and get them.

"I am very sorry about your dad," the doctor said with sincerity.

Sydney thanked him and then knelt down in front of his mother. Her head was in her hands. He looked at Harrison. His eyes were filled with tears as he shook his head at Sydney as if to say he couldn't say anything. About that time the nurse walked up and said they could see Mr. Strange now. Sydney took his mother's hand and the three of them walked back to the curtained area.

When they looked at Sam he looked like he was sleeping. Sarah walked over to him, gently touched his forehead, leaned down and kissed him. Overcome with emotion, Sydney turned away to try to get control of himself while Harrison stood quietly with his arms gently around his mother.

"I just can't believe he's gone," she finally said as she looked at Sydney and then Harrison. I knew he was not well. I knew it. He wouldn't listen, just kept on as if nothing was wrong. He didn't eat hardly anything for supper, but he seemed okay until out of the blue while we were watching television he told me he wasn't feeling good and thought I should call for an ambulance. They were there in a matter of minutes, put oxygen on him first thing, helped him onto the gurney and took him out. I told them I wanted to ride with them. I don't know how long we've been here, but it can't be long."

Looking at Harrison she said, "I must have called you when they first brought him in and asked me to have a seat on the bench. What time was that, Harrison?"

"I think around nine. I called Sydney immediately as he was leaving town."

"I didn't know you were here," she said looking at me. "Why were you?"

It was then that Sydney thought about Sonny for the first time. He didn't want his mother to know he was there in the hospital recovering from a fall because of his drinking.

"I had a last-minute meeting at Saint Patrick and didn't have time to call you to tell you I was coming to town. I had to go back tonight anyway, so I hadn't planned to see y'all this trip. Harrison knew I was here because I called him to ask him a question about one of our classmates who was going to be in the meeting at Saint Patrick. That's how he knew to call me after you called him."

None of what he was saying was true, but he had good intentions. The main thing at the moment was to keep her from knowing about Sonny.

"Mother, Harrison is right here. I need to step out and call McKenzie.

It was like she didn't hear him. He punched in McKenzie's cell number. As soon as she answered he said, "McKenzie, I have some terrible news. Father just died," He almost didn't get the words out.

"What?" she exclaimed. "What happened?"

"Heart attack," he managed to say. "I had decided to drive home tonight after all and was just outside of town when Harrison called to say mother had just called from the hospital. I turned around and came right to the hospital. That's where I am now."

"Oh my God, Sydney," she said as she started crying. "I don't know what to say, I just can't believe it."

"Neither can I. I'm still trying to process all that has happened. I wanted you to know right away, but I need to get mother home and then I will call you back. Okay?"

"Yes, of course. Talk to you later."

Sydney came back to his father's bedside. Harrison was standing beside his mother as she sat on the bed holding Sam's hand. He waited a minute and then asked her if she was ready to go.

"Yes, I'm ready." She turned back to Sam, leaned forward and kissed him on the forehead and whispered, "Goodbye, my sweet man, I'll see you in heaven."

# 16

Whatever he expected to feel when he first walked into his parent's home knowing his father would never be there again, Sydney couldn't have possibly anticipated the degree of sadness that overwhelmed him when they came in the door.

"Oh, my," said his mother as she walked in the house. Looking at Sydney she added, "I hadn't thought about what it would be like to come home without your father."

"I'm feeling the same way," he told her, "I don't know how to describe it. I'm half-way expecting to find out that what happened didn't, that father is still alive. I've talked to so many people who've lost somebody. Now I know what they were feeling. I thought I did, but I had no idea."

Sarah started toward the kitchen at the back of the house saying she needed some hot tea and asked Sydney if he would drink some coffee. He told her yes, but that he first needed to call McKenzie.

"Hi, it's me. I just got her home. Mother is fixing tea and coffee."

"Can you tell me more about what happened?" asked McKenzie, "or is this not a good time?'

"No, it's fine. Mother said she had thought for a while that he didn't look well, but as usual he denied anything was wrong. They were watching TV when he told her he wasn't feeling good and to call an ambulance. At some point he must have passed out. The doctor said he never regained consciousness."

"So what do you need me to do? Should Leslie and I come there tomorrow?"

"I don't know what to tell you. Maybe it would be better if you waited until I find out more. I called Dunning's Funeral Home right after I talked with you at the hospital. We will go there in the morning to make the arrangements, and I will know more after that. I'm thinking I may need to come there myself to bring Madelyn up to speed on some things she will need to take care of while I spend some time here. A lot will depend on what arrangements we make tomorrow. What do you think of waiting until then?"

"That's fine. I think I'll wait to tell Leslie in the morning before she goes to school tomorrow. She probably won't want to go. We'll see."

"Okay. We'll talk tomorrow. I love you."

"I love you, too, and wish I were there."

He went into the kitchen after he clicked off and sat down at the table in the alcove that was surrounded with windows and white curtains that looked out on the side yard of their house where he grew up. Sarah placed a cup of the vanilla flavored coffee she knew he loved in front of him and sat down on the opposite side of the small table with her tea.

"Thanks, Mother."

She smiled and took a sip and then asked, "What kind of meeting did you have at Saint Patrick that brought you here today, Sydney?"

He didn't want to compound not telling her the truth earlier so he told her about Sonny's fall and being in the hospital. He was fine, but they kept him there just to make sure.

"I knew he was in town," Sarah told Sydney, catching him off-guard.

"How do you know that, Mother?"

"He's been back a while. He came by to see me a few weeks ago. He lost his job in Halifax and I guess he and Carrie are living apart. I think he can go home if he wants to but is spending more time here than there."

"And I suppose you are giving him money," Sydney said and quickly regretted it.

"Not a lot, just enough to eat. He didn't ask, I offered."

"He would have had you not, of course."

"I suppose, but as I've told you I have the money and I'm not giving him much."

"Any is too much, Mother, you know that, but this is not the time to get into that again."

She agreed.

"But I need to tell him about what has happened. I need to call Carrie and then I will call him."

"Please do, Sydney. He needs to know right away."

"I will, I promise."

As she got up to go to bed, he refilled his coffee and went to the cupboard to get the peanut butter jar and saltine crackers."

"I should have gotten them out already," Sarah said as she saw him. "Your favorite meal," smiling as she left the kitchen.

"I know it won't be easy," he called out to her, "but try to calm your mind so you can get some sleep. You look very tired."

"I'll do my best," she hollered back, "but sometimes you just can't control your thoughts when your heart is broken."

He sat back down, put peanut butter on a couple of crackers, and dialed Carrie.

"It's me, Carrie."

"Well, hi Sydney. Didn't expect to hear from you again tonight."

"I'm afraid I have some bad news, Carrie. Father died suddenly tonight, a heart attack."

"Oh, no, no." she repeated as she started crying. "I loved him so much, Sydney, everything about him. I know he had his rough edges, but he was as good to me and the children as my own father. He treated me as if I mattered to him as much as Sonny did. He never took his side and always assured me that if there was anything I needed, all I had to do was ask, and I believed him."

"You could because I know for a fact he meant everything he told you. You were like the daughter he and mother never had."

"What are we going to do without him, Sydney?"

"I don't know, Carrie, the best we can is all I can say right now. It'll have to be enough."

"Does Sonny know?" she asked.

"No, I will call him after we hang up."

"He isn't picking up," she said. "I called him twice in the last hour and he didn't answer."

"He may have his phone turned off or it may be with his stuff they took when they checked him in. If I can't get him, I'll call the phone in his room and then call you back if I think there is anything you need to know. Otherwise, I will call you tomorrow to let you know about the funeral arrangements. We're going to the funeral home in the morning."

"Just hearing you say that sounds so unreal. I'll wait to hear from you."

Sydney said good-bye and dialed Sonny's cell. He didn't answer. He called the switch board and asked to be connected to his room. He didn't remember the number. He was told they didn't have a Sonny Strange listed as still in the hospital. He then asked to be connected to the nurse's station on the third floor.

"Third floor nurse's station," said the woman on the other end.

"Hello, my name is Sydney Strange,"

"Hi Sydney, this is Molly Ferguson. We went to school together. Listen, I heard about your dad. I am so sorry."

"Thank you, Molly. I am still in shock. That's kind of why I was calling. My brother Sonny was in for overnight observation, but I can't get him to answer his cell, and for some reason the switch board doesn't have him listed. Do you know what the story is?"

"He checked himself out," Molly immediately answered. "I tried to get him to stay, but he said he was feeling fine. We couldn't force him to stay so I signed him out."

"Was that before you heard about my father?"

"Yes, maybe thirty minutes or so."

'Molly, thank you for your help."

"If I can do anything else, please call. And, again, I am sorry about your dad."

Sydney thanked her and closed his phone. He wasn't sure what to do next. News travels fast in Castle Cove, and he didn't want to take the chance that someone would say something to Sonny before he talked to him. He decided to go looking for him in some of the places he knew he frequented. He couldn't think of anything else to do. The air was getting cool when he brought his mother home so he grabbed his jacket and left to go find Sonny.

Looking for his brother to tell him his father died made Sydney mad just to think about it. The first place he went was Blue's Bar, one of the oldest in town. It was small, a long bar with a few tables directly across from it against the wall. Each table had room for two people on either end. It looked like about half the seats at the bar were taken. Sydney went to the end where several seats were empty and leaned on the counter without sitting down. The bartender asked him what he wanted. He told him he was looking for his brother, Sonny Strange, and asked if he knew him. He said he did, but that he hadn't seen Sonny in a couple of days. Sydney thanked him and left.

His next stop was the Tap Room, an old bar he knew Sonny liked.

It was built in the fifties and looked the part. Ugly stools covered in red plastic lined up at an old Formica bar. Red plastic also covered the seats in the booths that ran from one end of the room to the other on the wall opposite the bar. J. C. Maddox was the original owner and now his son, J.C., Jr. did. He was several years older than Sydney, but they knew each other pretty well. Castle Cove's size made it easy for different generations to know each other. Junior was tending bar as usual. Sydney took a seat. Junior came over, looked at him hard and said, "Well, Sydney Strange, what a surprise to see you here. How in the world are you?"

"I'm okay, Junior. How are you?"

"Good, actually. Business is real good, though I guess that's not something you're glad to hear."

"Man's got to make a living," Sydney said.

"Yes, we do, Sydney, and right now I'm doing well. But I hear you are over in Marian Beach. What's living at the beach like?"

"You know, Junior, it's actually pretty nice. McKenzie and I have been there several years now and it feels like home. Our daughter Leslie is twelve and she likes it, too."

"Tell me, if you don't mind me asking," Junior said, and be straight with me. "Is McKenzie still as hot as she used to be? That woman was the love of every boy in Castle Cove when she was in high school."

"She sure is," Sydney said without blinking an eye. "Even more now that she's matured. I'm a lucky man, Junior, to have such a beautiful woman take up with a guy like me."

"Must be the clergy part that appeals to her, Sydney, cause otherwise she has no standards at all when it comes to men."

They both laughed, and then he asked Sydney what he wanted to drink. He told him he could use a cup of coffee. Junior looked at him curiously, went to get the coffee and was back in a couple of minutes.

"So what's with the coffee?" he asked Sydney. "I know you're a minister, but you've never been shy about having a beer with an old friend."

"My father died tonight, Junior."

"Oh, man," said Junior. "Man, I am so sorry to hear that, Sydney. I really am. This town won't be the same without him. Your dad is as respected a man as anyone who ever lived here. My father had nothing but good things to say about him. What happened?"

"Heart attack earlier tonight. Took him almost instantly."

"He had one before, didn't he?" Junior asked.

"Yeah, a few years ago."

"I remember he did. So how is your mom taking it?" Then he said, "I guess that sounds like a stupid question, but I didn't mean it to sound that way."

"It didn't, Junior," said Sydney. "She's a trooper so she is okay. I happened to be in town when it happened. Providential, I suppose. I'm spending the night so she's not alone."

"Well, I am glad you felt comfortable coming here on a night like this," he said.

"Actually, I have a reason to be here. I'm looking for Sonny."

"Does he know?"

"Nope, that's why I'm looking for him. He was in the hospital himself. Fell earlier in the day and hit his head. They wanted him to stay the night for observation, but he checked himself out just before father was brought in. I don't think he knows anything yet. I wanted him to hear it from me rather than somebody else."

"I heard about his fall. Hit his head pretty good from what somebody said. He's been in here a lot the last couple of weeks. I thought he lived in Halifax, so I asked him when he first came in what brought him to town. He told me he was here more because of work, but then I heard that was not true, that he had lost his last job where he was making some big money."

"Was he here tonight?"

"Not yet. He usually gets here pretty late, but after hearing about the fall I haven't been expecting him."

"Do you have any idea where he might be staying?"

"I think with Billy Hughes. You remember him?"

"Yeah, I do."

"Well, I can't remember who told me that he was letting Sonny stay at his house right now. Even has him answering the phone at his garage in exchange for rent. Whether or not any of that is true I have no idea. Just telling you what I've heard."

"Where does Billy live?" Sydney asked Junior.

"On a side street off of Saw Mill Lane, not far from your dad's mill. You can't miss it. He keeps several junk cars in the yard that gets him more than a few complaints to the city from neighbors. They make him clean them out and then six months later his yard is filled again. Billy's a decent guy, just a slob of sorts."

"Thank you, Junior," Sydney said as he laid five dollars on the bar. Junior pushed his hand back and said good friends don't pay.

"Good to see you, Junior. I'll stop in again sometime under better circumstances."

"You do that, Sydney. I'll be looking for you."

Junior was right about not missing Billy's house. There were at least five vehicles or parts of them strewn across his front and side yards. Sydney parked on the street. The house was a small wood frame ranch with a covered stoop-like porch for the front entrance. Lights were on in what he figured was his living room. Sydney hadn't seen Billy in years, but when he opened the door he looked pretty much the way he did in high school.

"Sydney Strange," Billy blurted out. "I could have tried for days to guess who would knock on my door on a Tuesday night, but I would have never come up with your name."

"Good to see you, too, Billy. Is Sonny here by any chance?"

"As a matter of fact, he is, but he ain't feeling or looking too good. Just got out of the hospital, but I told him when he showed up that from the looks of it he should've stayed there."

"Could I see him?"

"Sure, come on in. He's downstairs, through that door," he said, pointing to a doorway off the hall just behind where he was standing. Sydney went down about fifteen steps that ended facing a wall. He turned to the right and saw Sonny lying on a sofa with his back to him facing a television that was on with the volume turned down low. Sydney could tell he was sleeping so he nudged him on the arm. When he opened his eyes, he was so startled he almost fell off the couch.

"What, you didn't finish your sermon at the hospital so you made a house call," Sonny said sarcastically.

"I tried to call you, but you didn't pick up," Sydney shot back.

"Yeah, I told my secretary to hold my calls."

"Well, you should've taken mine."

"Why, what have I done now?"

"Because father died of a heart attack tonight."

"What?"

Sydney knew as soon as he saw Sonny's face that he shouldn't have blurted it out like that.

"I'm sorry, Sonny. I shouldn't have told you like that. I wasn't trying to be mean. I'm sorry. It was sudden. He and mother were watching T.V. when it hit. He told her to call nine-one-one and then he must have passed out. The ambulance got there fast and they took him to the hospital right away. He never regained consciousness."

Sonny's eyes filled up with tears. He sat still staring into space. Then he said, "I killed him, Sydney, I killed him. We had a big argument two days ago. I had seen mother, but she doesn't know I went to see him after I saw her. I don't even know why I did, but he started telling me I had to get myself straight or I was going to lose my family. I can't remember what I said, only that we argued and I left mad without saying good-bye. I killed him."

Sonny started sobbing.

"For one time in your life don't make this about you, Sonny. This is about father dying, about mother now being alone, about our family never being the same, about what all of us are going to do without him. It's not about you, what you did or didn't do. You didn't kill him. Father had a bad heart and it finally took his life. End of story. I didn't come here to blame you, I came to tell you before you heard it from somebody else and wondered why we didn't call you."

Sonny didn't say anything, put his head in his hands and covered his face.

"I came by to let you know what happened, that's all," Sydney told Sonny. "We're going to the funeral home in the morning. I'm not sure what time, but if you turn your phone on I'll call to let you know"

He still didn't say anything. Sydney turned and headed toward the stairs.

"Can I go home with you now?"

The question stopped Sydney in his tracks. He didn't respond immediately.

"Never mind," Sonny mumbled as if talking to himself.

"If that's what you want to do," Sydney answered. "I'm sure mother would want you to be there with her, with all of us. We probably need to go now if you're going."

"Let me get a few things together. It won't take but a minute."

It didn't. Sonny put some clothes, a pair of shoes, and some toiletries in a gym bag, put on his sport coat and they headed upstairs.

"My dad died," Sonny told Billy as he and Sydney walked through the living room.

"Oh, my God, Sonny...Sydney. That's awful."

"I'm going to mom's house for the night. I may not be at work in the morning, but I should be there by afternoon."

"Yes, of course, no problem. Take all the time you need. I liked your dad. He was always good to me, to any of us who weren't from the best side of town. We never forgot that."

"Thanks, Billy," Sydney said. "We'll see you later."

Sonny and Sydney both seemed lost in their own thoughts on the drive to their mother's house until Sonny said, "You remember the time we were washing and waxing the car like dad made us do every year just before going on vacation and I was cleaning the inside and decided to start the car."

"Nobody will ever forget that," Sydney said and laughed out loud.

"The keys in the ignition pulled my hand to them like a magnet and the next thing I knew dad was screaming, 'Turn it off, turn it off'. Scared me so bad it took me a second to know what to do." Both of them were laughing now. "I got out of the car and went around to the front and there he stood with his shirt half ripped off and oil spewed all over his face and chest. I started to run, but my legs wouldn't move. He had just pulled the dip stick out to check the oil when I started the engine. Oil blew everywhere and the end of his unbuttoned shirt got caught in the radiator fan and ripped most of it off him in a second."

"I thought you were dead, brother," Sydney added. "Father had the meanest look on his face I've ever seen and just stood there, and then he burst out laughing. I couldn't believe it. Only you could do something like that and live to tell the story."

"Yeah," Sonny replied, "but I almost didn't the day I hit him in the head with a five ounce sinker." Sonny started laughing again. "I can laugh now, but I thought I was done for when that happened. He had taken me, Donnie Butler, Johnny Martin, and Barry McFaden up to Perch's Corner upstream on Castle Cove River to fish. We had just gotten back from Hampton where Uncle Buck took us fishing off the pier. When the bunch of us got to Perch's Corner dad told us to wait until he changed the sinkers, that five-ounce ones would take the line to the bottom and would probably get hung up in something and we'd lose the line. He was changing theirs when I decided to cast out anyway. Because I knew the weight was heavy I gave a heave with all my might just as dad stood up from the tackle box with his back to me. The sinker hit him right in the back of the head and knocked him into the river."

"He didn't burst out laughing on that one?" asked Sydney sarcastically.

"Are you kidding? I thought I had killed him. You know how kids think. Luckily it didn't knock him out. He landed in shallow water and once he got his bearings he managed to climb out of the water. I know he yelled at me, but I don't remember what he said. What I do remember is that he told all of us to get our stuff together and get in the car. We put everything back in the trunk and the four of us piled in the back seat. Nobody dared get in the front and not a word was said all the way home. As soon as we got home everybody was gone in five seconds, leaving me alone. That was a day I won't forget. It took a long time for me to be able to tell that story at a family gathering and get dad to laugh about it."

"The strange thing is that for a lumber man," Sydney said, "father was never what I would call a 'handy-man.' He could cut down a tree perfectly, but couldn't fix a lawn mower. Give him a chain saw and he was in his own element. Give him a hammer and nails and he couldn't build a dog house."

"Guess he had us for that stuff."

"Us? What do you mean 'us'? You mean Harrison and me. As I recall you managed to get out of everything we had to do around the house. I don't think you ever cut the grass once. Somehow you had to go somewhere or do something that wouldn't take long except you never came back until Harrison or I, mostly me, had done it."

"That was good because you were so much better at yard work than I was."

They got to the house just as Sonny said that. The mood quickly changed. Both got out of the Jeep without saying anything else and went inside. Sarah was sleeping, or at least still in her room. Sydney told Sonny he was tired and needed to get some rest, and then headed off to his old bedroom. Sonny did the same.

# 17

"Did you get any sleep?" Sydney asked his mother as he walked over to her at the sink and put an arm around her.

"A little," she replied.

"Sonny is here," he told her.

She didn't respond.

"I tried to call him to tell him about father, but he didn't answer so I decided to go out and find him. He was staying with one of his friends. I told him the story and as I was leaving he asked if he could come here for the night. I was sure you'd want him to so I said yes. He's in his old room."

"Thank you, Sydney. That's one worry off my mind. I kept wondering during the night whether or not he knew, and if he did how he responded. Bringing him here was the best thing."

"I knew that's what you would think. It was an easy decision. I told him we would be going to the funeral home this morning. He may want to go or may not. He didn't say last night."

"I want him to go," she said. "I want all of us there, together as a family."

"That's fine, but you need to let him decide. Pressure him to and I'm sure he will not be helpful."

"No, I won't try to persuade him if he says no, but I can let him know I want him to go without doing that."

"I'm sure you can," Sydney responded with a grin.

"How about some breakfast?" she asked.

"You don't need to do that, Mother."

"Yes, I do, sweetheart. It is exactly what I need to do. Fried eggs and toast okay?"

"Sure."

Sarah took out the frying pan and was getting ready to crack the eggs when Sonny walked in the kitchen.

"Good morning," she said as she hugged him. "Sydney told me you came home with him last night. I'm so glad you're here."

"Thank you for letting me stay, Mom. I can't believe dad is gone."

She put a hand on his cheek and went back to the stove. Sydney said he had just called Dunning's to arrange a time to come in. They suggested ten o'clock. He said he called Harrison and that worked for him. What he didn't say was that Harrison wanted to know how Sydney managed to find Sonny and get him to the house. Sydney explained.

"I went looking for him last night. Didn't want him to hear about father from somebody in a bar. He was staying at Billy Hughes's. After I told him about what had happened I started to leave. Out of the blue he asked me if he could come here with me. I knew mother would have wanted me to say yes so I did."

"And?"

"And it's been okay so far, but who knows what he'll do. Mother, of course, wants him to go to the funeral home, but we won't know until we get in the car."

"Thanks for the heads-up, Sydney. I'll see you at ten."

Sonny didn't hesitate when his mother asked him to go with her to the funeral home. Sydney was surprised that Sonny's clothes weren't dirty and didn't look like he'd slept in them as the three of them got ready to leave. A few minutes later he pulled his Jeep into the funeral home parking lot right on the hour. Houston Dunning, whose father established the funeral home, was waiting for them in his office. So was Harrison. Sydney was impressed at how Houston handled the situation. He couldn't have been nicer or more professional. No pressure about casket type or vault, no special sales pitch about floral arrangements or a special (meaning expensive) guest book for posterity.

They were there less than an hour, then left to go to the cemetery to sign the papers to have the grave opened. Sarah and Sam had purchased gravesites in the Strange family plot years before. After she signed the papers, Sarah wanted to show the boys the site. Sydney drove around the car path for about a half mile and then stopped at the crest of a little hill. There was a nice view of the entire town of Castle Cove. This was the first time as adults the three of them had seen the tombstone of their paternal grandparents. Sydney immediately thought about the argument his grandfather and father had over Abe Jordan working as a lumberjack.

Sonny walked around the hill looking at several graves of distant members of the family. The Strange roots go deep in Castle Cove. The tombstone of the brother of their great grandfather had the inscription, "Marcus Strange, beloved husband and father and esteemed citizen of Saw Mill," Castle Cove's initial name that came from the family business literally written in stone. Sydney walked up as Sonny was looking at it.

"Where was Saw Mill, North Carolina?" Sonny asked.

"Right here, Sonny," said Sydney. "I thought you knew that Castle Cove's original name was Saw Mill, named after the sawmill great grandfather started."

"I'll be damn," he said. "I never knew that. Guess we were pretty famous back then."

"There weren't many people living here back then, so I don't suppose it was all that significant."

They walked back to the site where father would be buried. He didn't see Harrison. Sydney asked where he was. Sarah said he got a call from the mill and had to go back to work. He and Sonny drove her back home. Once there he told his mother and Sonny that he needed to go to Saint Patrick to see the rector about the service, so they could put the day and time in the obituary that would go in the paper.

Carl Reagan greeted Sydney graciously and spoke highly of his father as one of those "salt of the earth" kind of men. He also said Sarah was among the nicest, kindest, and supportive people in the whole parish. He seemed sincerely saddened by Sam's death. Sydney told him he had heard his wife was not in good health. Carl confessed that it was the saddest moment in his life when they found out she was in the early stages of Alzheimer's. They had been married forty-seven years and she had been the real intellect in the family and now the disease was taking everything away from her.

"Sydney, it's the most difficult thing I have had to face in my life and in my ministry. It seems that every word I have spoken to more people than I can count in situations like this brings me no comfort at all. I wonder if that was actually the case to all those people I thought I was helping? Words come cheap, I've found, something I wish I had known a long time ago. I've tried to be sensitive to others and I've resisted the unhelpful stuff we've all heard like 'God needed another angel in heaven' and 'everything happens for a reason.' I'm not sure anything I have ever said has been of any help."

"I think we all feel that way, Carl, but I was told by a mentor of mine years ago that we are among the worst judges of our own work because we either give ourselves too much or too little credit for what we have done. I try very hard to remember her words when I fall into self-assessment. I'm not saying personal reflection is not important. I believe it is, even necessary, but making final judgments on our effectiveness is best left to others. What matters is the tragedy of what is happening to your wife and the stress and sadness you are feeling. I am so sorry both of you are going through this."

"Thank you for saying that, Sydney, but you're not here to talk about my situation so let's get back to why you are. Do you or your mother have any special requests for your dad's service?"

"No, we don't. I think mother would prefer the traditional Prayer Book service, but not everything so it won't go too long. Use your own judgment about that."

"Do you want to do the eulogy?" he asked Sydney.

"I haven't had enough time to think about that, to tell you the truth. Anything I do would be in addition to yours so right now let's just keep it as an option. What about a day and time. Do you have a suggestion?"

"Today is Wednesday, so I would say Saturday, if that works for your family. That would give the people of Castle Cove more freedom to attend since it wouldn't be a workday."

"That should work, but I will check with mother and get back to you. Is eleven o'clock in the morning okay?"

"Yes, that works fine."

Sydney thanked Carl and got ready to leave when he stopped him.

"Sydney, I need to say something. I know about the letter the vestry sent you just before your father died. I just want you to know that I hope you will give it careful thought after all of this is behind you. I don't mean to be insensitive to your grief, but I can't think of anyone better to lead this parish than you. You have the mind to challenge a congregation of highly educated members and the heart to lead them to think of more than their own welfare and comfort. They are good people who can do a lot better at being Christian than they are doing right now."

"I hardly know what to say, Carl. Given who you are and the respect you have earned in this diocese, I am humbled by your confidence in me. I promise I will think seriously about the possibility at the right time."

They shook hands and Sydney left. The parking lot was empty as he got into his Jeep. For a moment he sat there trying to think about what Carl Reagan had just said, but instead his thoughts went immediately to the fact that he had just sat in a church to talk about burying his father. He started crying. Almost uncontrollably as the emotions came tumbling out of him. This was the second time he had held his feelings tight and then they exploded out of him. Talking about the service made his father's death real in a way it hadn't felt before then. A deep sadness came over him as he thought about never seeing him again. It just couldn't be true, yet he knew it was. He wanted Leslie to know him better. He wanted his father to see her become the wonderful woman he knew she was going to be. Sam Strange was not one to show his feelings openly, but he showed his love for his boys by his attentiveness. It wasn't until they were grown that Sarah told them about the extent to which their father went to in order to see them play a game or some school event they were in.

Sydney thought about what Junior Maddox said about the kind of man his father was. He knew he was a man of his word, making deliveries of lumber at a construction site that needed more than they had ordered simply because Sam had told them that if they ran short they could count on him getting them the material right away. Customers trusted him. That's why they were customers.

The permanency of death was what Sydney was feeling. You don't think about what it means to know your parents are always there until one of them isn't. How lucky he and his brothers had been to grow up in a loving home, yet he was sure he had taken it for granted until now. His father's death had changed everything. Family gatherings at Thanksgiving, Christmas, other special occasions would never be the same. Going home to see his mother would never be the same. All of it felt heavy and made him wish he had the power to go back and undo what had happened. Instead, the reality that he couldn't was overwhelming. He cried until he didn't have any more tears to cry. They finally stopped and he began to feel in control of himself again. He looked at his phone and punched in McKenzie's number and waited for her to answer.

"It's me," he said when she said hello.

"How are you?"

"Okay, I guess, at least at the moment. I am fine one minute and then I'm overwhelmed with emotions the next. It's hard to keep control of myself."

"How's your mother?"

"Better than I am, I think. She has a strength I don't seem to have right now. She did well at the funeral home. I just finished talking to Carl Reagan here at Saint Patrick about the service. I'm still in the parking lot as a matter of fact. The service will be Saturday at eleven."

"Why don't you stay in Castle Cove, Sydney. Leslie and I will come over today. I'll bring your clothes. That way you can be there with your mother."

"That makes sense," he responded. "Yeah, that makes sense. When do you think y'all can come?"

"As soon as I can get everything together. I've already taken off from school and I kept Leslie home today as well. She wants to be with you as soon as possible. I think we can be there by mid-afternoon."

"Can't wait. I love you."

"Love you, too."

Sydney then called Carrie and told her where things stood—about the funeral arrangements, about Sonny spending the night at home, about going to the cemetery with them.

"Hi Carrie, it's Sydney. I just finished making funeral arrangements. The service is Saturday at eleven o'clock. Sonny is at mother's. He went to the funeral home with me, mother, and Harrison. He's pretty quiet, but seems okay on the surface. Has he called you?"

"No, but I haven't been expecting him to. I'm trying to let go of any expectations of him. Al Anon teaches that the level of your serenity is inversely proportional to the level of your expectations of others. It's hard, but I'm working on it. So I haven't thought about him calling me."

"I understand. We're all trying to get through this as best we can. It's not easy, but we're making it so far. It will be good to have the three of you here."

"The kids and I plan to drive over Saturday morning."

"Actually, we are having visitation on Friday night. Is there any way the three of you could be here for that. I understand if you can't or don't feel up to it, but it would be great to have you here."

"Absolutely, we can be there. No reason not to. I said Saturday without thinking about a visitation. That's not a problem. I know the kids will want to be there as I do."

"Good, and I know mother will be pleased to hear that. Just come to the house and plan to stay here. There's plenty of room as you know."

"We can do that," Carrie said. "We should be there by supper."

Friday night was an experience Sydney had never had as a minister, in fact ever. He had been to more viewings than he could count, but this time he was not stopping by to pay respects, as the saying goes, he was the one to whom respects were being paid. He never knew what that felt like until then, and it was better than he could have imagined. His focus had been on his mother. When the hour arrived for the family to start receiving people he felt like he could breathe a sigh of relief.

From the number of people who kept coming it seemed as if everyone in Castle Cove was there at some point during the evening. Business associates the family didn't know, friends of the family past and present, members of Saint Patrick, a contractor from Halifax who came by to tell Sarah that Sam was the most honest and trustworthy man he had ever known in business. The surprise of the night was a guy the Strange brothers had played ball with named Sammy Austin. He was the best baseball pitcher in Allegheny County back then. Everybody thought he would make it to the pros. But "pitcher's elbow" got him. Like too many kids, he threw too hard when he was young. As soon as Sammy walked in, Harrison, Sonny, and Sydney knew exactly who he was even though they hadn't seen him in probably twenty years.

The four of them talked for a long time, as if no one else was in the room. As he was leaving Sammy said, "I remember Mr. Strange being at all our ball games and giving us a ride to away games. Afterwards he would let several of us pile in with one or both of you and take us home instead of just dropping us off back at the school. I saw the obituary in the paper and told my wife there was no way I could not come by to pay my respects."

Sydney told Sammy that words couldn't express what his taking the time to come by meant to him and the family. He seemed surprised by what Sydney said and told him it meant a lot to him to be there. They shook hands as Sammy said good-bye. When Sydney turned to walk away he saw another familiar figure he had not seen in several years standing beside his dad's casket. He walked up behind the man and stood there without saying anything. Tears were running down Abe Jordan's face. He put his arm around Abe's shoulders. Abe looked up and when he saw Sydney he turned and gave him a bear hug.

"Sydney Strange, my son, I am glad to see you and so sorry it is under these circumstances. Your father was the best, the first white man ever to treat me with respect and give me work based on my abilities, not by the color of my skin. He was a good, good man."

"You are too, Abe, and father knew that, as well as seeing how good you were at your job. I want to tell you something I don't think you ever knew about when he first put you in the woods. He had a big argument with my grandfather who was, I hate to say, a racist. I was nine years old at the time. They didn't know it but I heard every word they said. Father made it clear that he hired you because you could do the job and that was all that mattered to him and if grandfather didn't like it that was too bad because he wasn't running the mill anymore."

"You're right, Sydney, I didn't know anything about that. That speaks to the man your dad was. He treated me just like everybody else, not a common thing back them for black people. It changed my life."

"And you changed mine, Abe. Those summers I worked in the woods with you helped make me into the person I am today. That day you trusted me to cut down my first tree and then later told me, after we helped the guy that got hurt, that father let me in the woods because he also trusted me is something I have never forgotten. I think about it every time I get down on myself."

"He was proud of you, Sydney. He said it more than once."

"Thank you, Abe, and thank you for coming tonight. Please be sure to speak to mother before you leave. She will want to see you."

"I will do that, Sydney. I knew I needed to come by, just didn't know all the reasons why until now."

They hugged again and Sydney told him he hoped they would see each other before another twenty years had passed. Abe agreed it had been too long.

Later when the family got ready to leave Sydney sat down beside mother and asked how she was doing.

"Good, Sydney. Tired, but good. Your dad had so many friends. Our family does. But the thing that meant so much to me personally were the people I would never have guessed would come tonight. To a person they had a story to tell about your father and why he meant so much to them."

"I experienced the same thing. A kid we grew up with named Sammy Austin came by. He played baseball with us and remembered father taking us to and from games. That meant so much to me, to Harrison and even Sonny. We had a nice visit with him. And did you see Abe Jordan?"

"Yes, I did. That was so nice of him to come. Your father had such respect for Abe. I'm sure he is smiling down from heaven right now. But there have been so many here tonight just like Abe. It sounds strange to say it, but it's been a good night, a healing night. My heart is filled to overflowing at so many people showing your dad such respect. I don't know if he ever realized what a good man he was, but I saw the fruits of his good life tonight. The ache in my heart feels a little less suffocating right now."

Samuel John Strange was laid to rest on a cool November Saturday afternoon. To his family, friends, and even business colleagues his death felt out of season, his life cut short. It was as if death snuck in the door like a thief in the night and kidnapped him. Sam wasn't a perfect man, but he was a man of character, always true to his word. He was a faithful husband and a loving father. The crowd at the funeral home the night before made it clear he would be missed in Castle Cove.

Sydney was worried about his mother. Nothing could replace his father coming home every night for the last fifty-three years. He wished Harrison being nearby would help with her sense of loneliness, but his work ethic had picked-up where his father's had left off. He would be quick to respond to any urgent need his mother had, but otherwise he would likely see her only now and then. Sydney made a commitment to himself to call her more often. But he knew nothing could take the place of regular in-person visits the distance between Castle Cove and Marian Beach made impossible.

Those thoughts brought to mind the letter he had received before his father's heart attack asking him to be a candidate for Saint Patrick. Dan Mitchell, chair of Saint Patrick's vestry, had even asked him after the funeral if the two of them could have lunch the next day. Sydney wanted to meet with Dan, but he needed to get back to Marian Beach to prepare for Sunday. They agreed to talk at a later date. Sydney was keenly aware that his father's death had dramatically changed the circumstance surrounding coming back to Castle Cove. He wished he and McKenzie were not in separate cars driving home so they could talk further about it.

Sydney went directly to the church once they got to Marian Beach while McKenzie and Leslie went home. He needed to get things ready for tomorrow's service. McKenzie had supper ready just as he arrived home. The three of them talked about his father. Leslie was open about what she was feeling because of her Papa Sam being gone. They assured her they felt the same sadness she did and wanted her to feel free to tell them what she was feeling whenever she wanted to. Later in the evening as he and McKenzie sat in the family room reading he told her about Dan Mitchell asking him to go to lunch.

"I was actually sorry I didn't have time. Father's death has made me wonder if I should think about Saint Patrick instead of dismissing it."

"Of course, you should," McKenzie said without hesitation, as she put down the paper. "Your mother is alone now. Harrison works all the time the way your father did. As I told you before all this happened, I think you should make sure staying here is still enough of a challenge."

"I guess you're right. I think I will call Dan on Monday to see if we can arrange to meet. Mother is going to need some help next week dealing with all the paperwork related to father's death. I could meet with him while I'm there helping her."

Sydney got very quiet when he said that, as if he couldn't say anything more. McKenzie could see his grief was still close to the surface. She came over and sat down in his lap and laid her head on his chest.

"It's a tender spot, Sydney. It will be for a long time."

"I'm sure it will be."

"Are you sure you want to preach tomorrow? I know it's late, but one of the retired ministers in the congregation would certainly be willing to sub for you under the circumstances."

"I've thought about it but, no, I want to go ahead. I don't think it will be any easier next week than it will be tomorrow."

"You may be right," replied McKenzie. "Do what you need to do. You will be fine because you always are."

"I'm sure it won't be easy, but I think I can make it through okay. The liturgy may help settle me down before I have to preach. Once tomorrow is done I can focus on meeting with Dan and maybe get a sense of what to do about Castle Cove."

"I would like to go with you next week, but I think I'll stay here with Leslie so we can have some time together. We haven't talked much about your dad's death. Just plan your schedule as you need to and we will be fine here."

The Sunday service went better than Sydney expected, and the congregation embraced him emotionally and physically to an extent he didn't realize he needed. It was obvious that McKenzie was right. They did love him and he loved them. He felt guilty that he was even thinking about leaving. In spite of what he was feeling he did call Dan on Monday morning and told him he was coming back to Castle Cove to help his mother with some business concerns and would like to meet. Dan expressed gratitude to Sydney for calling. He then suggested they include the entire vestry to save time, if that was acceptable to Sydney. He agreed and they set the time for Wednesday evening at seven-thirty.

He called his mother and told her he was coming to Castle Cove to go to the bank and help her get things settled there. She said she could do it on her own, but he insisted he wanted to be there. Besides, he said, he had a meeting at Saint Patrick he would tell her about when he got there. That seemed to satisfy her that he was not making an unnecessary trip just for her sake. He told her he would not get to Castle Cove until after supper on Monday. She said she would have coffee and dessert waiting.

He gave her a hug when he walked into the house, took his bag to his room, and came back to the sunroom where she was already sitting drinking her tea. He got a cup of coffee and sat down to a large piece of cinnamon coffee cake she had made that afternoon.

"How are you, mother?'

"I'm fine, Sydney. Better than you might think. It's lonesome around here, but it's only been a few days. I will begin to fill my time and things will get better. I am not as fragile as you and Harrison think I am."

"I know you're not, Mother. Most of my worry about you stems from my own feelings of loss, and I'm sure the same is true for Harrison. We hide it by doting on you."

"And I love you for it," she said. "I just don't need it."

She took a drink of tea and he took a bite of the coffee cake.

"Delicious, as usual, Mother. It's been a long time since I've had your cinnamon coffee cake. Thank you."

"You're certainly welcome. There's plenty, too. But tell me about the meeting you have on Wednesday."

"Well, they have asked me to consider becoming their rector and the meeting is with the vestry to discuss that possibility. It's only exploratory at this point. It won't be easy to leave Saint Alban. They showed so much support at yesterday's service. It felt like I was being showered with love. It eased my aching heart immediately. It was truly remarkable. Right now it feels very unsettling to think about leaving them."

"That speaks well of you and them, my dear. That is not always the case, as you well know. But I need to keep saying what I have said several times. I can take care of myself and you need to understand that. It would be lovely to have you, McKenzie, and Leslie here in Castle Cove, of course, but that is not a reason for you to move back here."

"I understand what you're saying and I agree. I know you are going to be fine by yourself. I also know the three of us love Marian Beach and Saint Alban, so if we leave it will be on the merits of the call, not on whether or not you need us to be here. Okay?"

"Okay sweetie, I just needed for us to clear the air on this and we have."

The next morning they were at the bank right when it opened. Sarah took Sam's name off the checking and savings account. Harrison's name had been added by Sam when he had his first heart attack. Sarah checked the safety deposit box and found some stocks and sawmill papers she didn't know anything about. Sydney looked at them and told her they had to do with ownership of the land his father had purchased for the sawmill. The stocks were investments in Ford, GM, and Chrysler. Sarah said she wasn't surprised about the automobile stock. Sam always believed the automotive industry was the engine that ran the country's economy. They left everything in the deposit box as they found it.

On the way home Sydney mentioned to his mother that he had recently talked to Carrie to see how things were, especially financially. She had said everything was stable in spite of getting no help from Sonny. He suggested his mother also check in with Carrie from time to time to make sure she really was doing okay. Sarah thought that was a good idea and promised she would.

Sydney worked on a sermon at his mother's house Tuesday afternoon and Wednesday morning, then went to see how Harrison and his family were doing. Mrs. Smith greeted him with much affection as always. She tried to say something about his father, but her emotions got the best of her and she just hugged him again and walked away. Sydney turned and went into Harrison's office and sat down.

"I'm keeping my own office," Harrison told Sydney. "Can't bring myself to move into dad's so I decided I didn't need to. I've been doing fine working in here. It's less painful to stay put, for now anyway, but I miss him. Sydney. I miss him a lot."

"I do, too. I know what you're feeling. And I think you're wise to keep using your own office. You'll know if and when to make the move. But how is everybody else handling father's death?"

"Okay. The kids are fine. They've got their own lives, as you know, so they moved on quickly. Maryanne still gets teary, but otherwise she seems fine. McKenzie and Leslie okay?"

"I think so. Leslie hasn't said much, but enough to make us think she's fine. McKenzie has taken it hard. She loved father dearly, or as she called him, 'that old man'. But the reason I stopped by was to tell you we might be moving back to Castle Cove. I'm meeting with the St Patrick vestry tonight. Nothing's been decided, but if they call me, I think McKenzie and I are prepared to say yes, and we think Leslie will be fine with it as well."

"I am delighted, bro. It will be great having y'all here."

"Thank you, Harrison. I feel the same way. We'll see what happens. It's a big decision."

"Of course it is, and whatever you decide is up to you. No pressure on this end. I just want you to know having you back in Castle Cove would be great."

"Well, I'll let you know as soon as we know something."

"Sounds good. Hope the meeting goes well."

"Tell Maryanne hello."

"You do the same with McKenzie."

Once the vestry meeting started and introductions were made, the conversation focused on Sydney's ministry in Marian Beach. He answered various questions the vestry members had, but then he wanted to know what they were expecting from him if he were to come to Saint Patrick. Administering the sacraments, preaching, and pastoring were of their core expectations. The rest they would leave to him, including ways to be involved in the Castle Cove community.

Okay with the answers they were giving, Sydney still felt like something was missing in the conversation, and then it dawned on him what it was. Every member of the vestry except the two new church members had known Sydney all his life, and yet there was no way they actually knew who he was as an adult, and especially as a minister. He decided he needed to talk about that with them.

"Before we close the meeting, I need to bring up something we've talked around but not about. It has to do with who I am. Let me try to explain. I think most of you are assuming that we all know each other, and on one level that is true, but on another it isn't. I grew up here and will always be thankful for that. It is a major reason why I am in ministry. But I have matured in my thinking in ways you may not realize and consider some issues important that may surprise you or conflict with your own views. Take, for example, welcoming all people into the church. Our state has fought racial equality and racial justice every step of the way. We have made progress, but not enough. North Carolina churches were as segregated as the state was, including Saint Patrick, as late as when I was in high school.

"I know you have said you are open to everyone, a decision I applaud and take at face value. Part of what that means, though, is that I will never hesitate to address racial discrimination when it raises its ugly head here or anywhere else. I will also welcome anyone to our church regardless of the color of their skin or their sexual orientation. The latter, sexual orientation, is, I believe, the next big issue churches and our nation will be facing. We're seeing signs of that already in regard to military service. About the only time I have ever agreed with Senator Barry Goldwater was his recent article in the Washington Post where he said he supported having gay members of the military. The statement I remember in that article was something like, 'you don't have to be straight to shoot straight.'"

They all laughed, perhaps as much out of nervous tension as anything.

"I am not what you would call a crusader. I prefer working behind the scenes, but I do believe my responsibility as your rector would be to do the best I can at applying the Bible to daily life in my preaching and teaching. I will never claim to know all the answers, but I will always help you and me together know what the right questions are. I am saying this knowing that it may cause you to want to rethink wanting to call me to lead you. That would be understandable, so I thought it best to try to explain myself now than for you discover who I am later and wish you had known more about me before extending the call."

The room went silent. No one said a word. Sydney had definitely gotten their attention. Then a young woman in her mid-twenties who had not spoken since the meeting started raised her hand to indicate she had something to say.

"Reverend Strange, we just met so I will tell you my name again.

I am Rachel Yates and I have been a member of Saint Patrick for seven years, since I moved here right out of college. This is my second year on the vestry. We don't know each other, but I know your mother. I would even say I know her quite well. We have become good friends in the seven years I have been here. She is the mother I never had and as wise and kind a woman as I have ever met, She is also very proud of you, as I am sure you know. Tonight I found out why. And whatever you and we decide about your future as our rector, I just want to say that you have given me hope for the church. Saint Patrick was my last stop before leaving the church altogether.

"The people like your mother are why I am still here, but I have struggled with what relevance any church has when most of the time we ignore the problems of racism, poverty, sexism, discrimination of all kinds by saying the church shouldn't get involved in politics. In the few words you said tonight I felt myself being filled with hope, hope that the words and teachings and life of Jesus might make a real difference here in Castle Cove. So thank you not only for having the courage to say what you've said, but for what you said."

The room went quiet again, all twelve vestry members looking down except Dan Mitchell who was staring at Rachel with a smile on his face. Then he spoke.

"Rachel, I, too want to thank Sydney for his candor, but also for the views he expressed. And I want to thank you for what you said, too. The vestry knows Saint Patrick is a proud parish with a long history, but we also know that these days churches that rest on their laurels, or perceived laurels, are quickly finding themselves ignored and in decline. We don't want to be one of them. The challenge we believe Sydney will bring to us will help us avoid that fate. It will also serve to remind us of perhaps the worst days of racial discrimination in North Carolina when Reverend Chambers, our rector at the time, reminded the church that we were called to believe in and support liberty and justice for all. The majority of the parish stood with him and against a large portion of Castle Cove residents. We lost some members, but we gained some, too. Mainly, though, we did what was right. Since those days we have been coasting, at least I believe we have, and I think others on this vestry do as well. If Sydney should accept our invitation, we are confident he will lead us to new life and energy as a church. And, I might add, so will members like you."

Dan didn't stop there. He put the other members on the spot. "If I am alone in what I just said, we need to know that tonight. So let's go around the room to see if we are ready to meet the challenges just put before us."

Every single person said yes. No one even hesitated. One man said he didn't know if everyone in the church felt as he did, but he believed they would still support the vestry's decision to call Sydney.

"Then you have my answer," Sydney said firmly. "This meeting has confirmed for me that coming to Saint Patrick is a genuine call of God and I am humbled and honored to say yes to your invitation."

The room burst into applause. Dan said that the Bishop was fully aware of what was happening and that he would call him tomorrow to inform him of the decision. He then closed the meeting with prayer. Sydney stayed afterwards to speak with vestry members and to meet Rachel Yates formally. He thanked her for what she said and for her comments about his mother, and told her he looked forward to getting better acquainted and working together.

As soon as he got into the Jeep he called McKenzie.

"So, how did it go?" was the first thing she said.

"You won't believe it. Nothing like I expected. In fact, no way I could have expected anything like what happened."

"So tell me!"

"Well, it all went as these things do, but something was bothering me. I finally realized that these people didn't know me, truly know me. They only knew who they thought I was. I decided to be completely honest with them. I told them I needed them to know the kinds of things I believed in and the fact that no subject could be off limits in my preaching, that political issues were life issues, and I wouldn't hesitate to preach and teach about how the Bible helps us think about them."

"Guess we'll be staying in Marian Beach a bit longer," she said.

"Wait, I haven't told you the whole story. When I finished the room went deathly quiet, and then a young woman named Rachel Yates spoke up. She is probably in her late twenties, maybe early thirties. She's been a member of the church since moving to Castle Cove after college seven years ago. She knows mother and thanked me for what I said that helped her understand why mother was proud of me. She then told the group that what I said gave her hope for the church. I was very moved by her statement. And then Dan Mitchell thanked her and me for what we said and told the vestry I was exactly what Saint Patrick needed. Everyone in the room agreed."

"That sounds wonderful, Sydney, better than anything I was thinking while it was going on. I'm all in if you want to accept the call."

"I already did, McKenzie, right then and there."

"Oh, so it's pay-back time."

"What do you mean?" he asked, honestly not knowing.

"Five years ago, when I told superintendent Ward I accepted the teaching job he offered before talking to you again about it."

"Oh...well no, that's not what this is about. That never crossed my mind, McKenzie, I promise I..."

She interrupted. "I'm kidding, Sydney, just kidding. I'm glad you accepted. You've had a wonderful ministry here and the people love you to death as you found out last Sunday. It's not going to be easy to tell them you're leaving, that we're leaving, but I believe it is the right thing to do. And you know what, I'm willing to bet the Saint Alban people will support you even though they don't want you to leave."

"I hope you're right about that. You know I love Saint Alban, but I am excited about what just happened and the future unfolding in front of us."

"Me, too. Are you coming home tomorrow?"

"Yes, I told mother I would be leaving in the morning. She is doing okay right now. In fact, she's spent most of her time assuring me that she is much stronger than I think she is."

"And I'm guessing she's exactly right, Sydney. Just drive carefully."

"See you tomorrow. I love you."

"I love you, too, Sydney, and very thankful for our life together."

# 19

Sydney dreaded telling Madelyn he was leaving. In so many ways she had made his ministry at Saint Alban much easier than it would have been. Since McKenzie and Leslie were both in school he went directly to the church to tell her he was leaving to avoid any chance she would hear it by the grapevine.

"Well, I didn't expect to see you here today," she said as he walked in the office. "How is your mother doing?"

"Better than I expected," I answered. "Father was such a dominant figure in our family, I guess I never realized how strong mother is. I saw it plainly during the funeral last week and again this week. She was on top of all the business we needed to do. She probably could have done it without me, but I'm glad I was with her anyway. "

"As a mother I can tell you, she was glad you were there, too, even if she seemed like she would have been fine on her own"

"You're right, I'm sure. At least we got everything done that needed attending to right now. Harrison is handling everything related to the sawmill so that is taken care of. But I need to talk to you about something else."

Sydney sat down in the cushioned chair across the room from her desk, took a deep sigh and began.

"Madelyn, I don't even know how to tell you this, but..."

"You mean that you're moving to Castle Cove and Saint Patrick parish?" she interrupted to say.

He was dumbstruck.

"How do you know that?"

Her eyes were teary, but she was in complete control of her emotions, nothing new for Madelyn.

"I've been waiting for you to tell me, Sydney."

"What? Wait a minute. I am completely lost."

"Well, let me help you find your way back. I knew about Carl Reagan deciding to retire to care for his wife. The diocese sends out emails detailing such things periodically. I also saw the letter from Saint Patrick you received just before your father's heart attack. I figured it had something to do with Carl leaving. When you decided to go back to Castle Cove this week after being there all last week, I figured it was more than going to check on your mother. I know her, too, remember, and I knew she would tell you she didn't need for you to come back so soon, maybe later, but not days after you just got home. So I've been preparing myself for this news. I knew you would leave us sometime. You're too capable to stay here in Marian Beach forever. Based on what's happened and your schedule, it was easy to put two and two together. It doesn't make it any easier, but I know it is the right thing for you and your family."

"I am so relieved to hear you say that, and for you to know. All I could think about driving back today was how to tell you and how you would react. I should have known it would be fine, that you would be fine."

"Well I wouldn't go that far, but, yes, I am okay. I knew this day would come eventually. It saddens me that you are leaving, but I could not be more pleased for you, McKenzie, and Leslie and, of course, your mother. I know Sonny is a worry to her and having you there will be more help than she even realizes herself."

"He is a worry. He hasn't changed and I am sure the things I've told you he has done, especially taking money from her, will get worse. Harrison has checked out completely on him so it will be up to me to try to keep him from draining her dry. Mother is strong in so many ways but not when it comes to her children."

"That doesn't surprise me, Sydney, it's who mothers are."

"I'm sure Carrie wouldn't agree. I suspect she would say that mother was helping Sonny be irresponsible without paying a price for it, and I would agree with her. I know mother is living out of her heart and her hurt and sadness, but enabling Sonny doesn't actually help him or anyone else."

"Sydney, you know as well as anyone that Sonny is the only one who can help Sonny. I'm not saying your mother is right, but I do know she is just being a mother. Think of Leslie. You know you will always help her no matter what the circumstances. I probably shouldn't say this, but if Leslie ever got herself in trouble, McKenzie would be more likely to refuse to bail her out than you. Dare I say you are getting very close to seeing the speck in your mother's eye while missing the stick in your own?"

"Plank," Sydney said.

"What?' Madelyn replied.

"Plank, not stick. Jesus said 'plank', not 'stick'."

"Oh, right. I forgot you're the scholar, not me, but understanding the message matters more than the words, wouldn't you say?"

"Touché, Dr. Madelyn, touché."

He went into his office for a few minutes to check emails and then came back out and told Madelyn he needed to run an errand. He walked behind her desk, kissed her on the head and told her he loved her. That almost undid her. He apologized for upsetting her. She waved him off and he left to go see Wanda and Sally. He didn't want them hearing about his leaving on the grapevine either.

Sydney saw Sally cleaning one of the tables as soon as he walked in the Café. She smiled and motioned for him to sit down at the table she was cleaning. He did and asked her to join him.

"So how are you?" Sydney asked. "I was surprised to see you down here. Thought you cleaned the rooms for rent and didn't want to wait tables."

"I don't. Wanda asked me if I would be willing to bus tables as part of my cleaning chores. I said I would give it a try and so far it's been good. She also started paying me in addition to room and board."

"I am so glad to hear that."

Wanda came out of the kitchen, saw him, and blurted out, "Reverend Sydney. I haven't seen you in a month or so. The lunch special is almost ready. Today is clam stew. Can I get you a bowl?"

"No thanks, Wanda. Actually, I stopped by to see how everything was going and to talk you and Sally. Come sit down."

Wanda wiped her hands on her apron and came over and sat down. "I wanted to tell both of you something so you wouldn't hear it from anyone else first. I'm leaving Saint Alban to move back to my hometown of Castle Cove."

Sally started wringing her hands the way she does whenever she gets nervous, and then said hesitantly, "So what happens to me?"

"I'm not sure what you mean, Sally. This doesn't change anything for you. It looks like you're doing fine on your own. Just keep doing what you're doing now."

"But you're the reason I'm here."

"No, that's not true, Sally. You're the reason you're here. I brought you here and Wanda gave you a place to live, and now to work, but that's all your own doing. No one could do that but you."

"That's right, honey," Wanda said to Sally. "You're doing great. All you needed was a chance. Sydney helped you get that, but you took the next step."

"And Wanda helped you, too," he inserted, "Both of you are making this work and I am a cheerleader, not a participant. And I will continue to be. My hometown is only two hours away and McKenzie and I love Marian Beach so you'll be seeing us more than you think. I promise."

"I hope so," Sally said, tears in her eyes. "I will miss you a lot."

"I will miss you, too, Sally, and you, too, Wanda. Both of you should know that."

"You better come back here often, or I'm going to be very upset with you," Wanda told him.

"Not to worry, Wanda, not to worry."

They exchanged hugs and waved good-bye as Sydney left. He drove away feeling like helping Sally Barrett was one very good thing he had done during his twelve plus years in Marian Beach, maybe the best. It's now up to her.

Self-reflection must be a part of what happens when you are moving from one ministry to another because it seems like that was all Sydney was doing after telling the vestry and the congregation about leaving. Both were gracious, which made moving harder and easier at the same time, but his attention finally turned to getting ready for the move. He began having more and more contact with people in Castle Cove, from members of the parish, to a realtor, to his mother, to Harrison, to some old friends. It began to feel like he was living in two places. Leslie wasn't nearly as upset about moving as McKenzie and Sydney thought she might be. She even wanted to go with them when they looked at houses in Castle Cove.

One day while he was talking to his mother on the phone she asked if they would be interested in putting their furniture in storage and moving in with her while looking for a permanent place to live. McKenzie surprised him when she said she thought that was a good idea. They hadn't had any luck thus far and she was beginning to feel the pressure of the moving date. Moving in with Sarah would give her time to look once they had moved without feeling rushed. Leslie was okay with it as well. Sydney was the one who had hesitations until he realized the problem was that his father was gone. Once he understood why he was feeling the way he did he was okay with saying yes.

Sydney called Harrison to tell him the moving plans. Harrison thought moving in with his mother made sense, but he reminded Sydney that Sonny was still around.

"He'll likely show up there once in a while," he told Sydney. "He must be in town. Last I heard he was still at Billy Hughes's."

"Have you talked to him?"

"No, I haven't and I prefer to keep it that way. I'm just telling you so you won't be surprised when you wake up some morning and he's there. Mom is never going to turn him away."

"I know," Sydney acknowledged. "I've tried as much as you have to get her to at least stop giving him money but she's going to do what she wants to do no matter what either of us says."

"That's why I'm staying out of it, Sydney. It drives me crazy. I'm better off not knowing anything."

"I wish I could say the same thing, but you know I can't."

"As I've told you before, Sydney, that's why I supply building material for churches and you work for them."

"Yeah, well, thanks for the heads-up. We aren't planning to stay with her very long."

The few months before they moved went by quickly. The day they drove out of town as residents for the last time, all three of them seemed to have a good balance between feeling sad and glad, sad for leaving, glad they had spent the years they did in Marian Beach, and glad they were headed to Castle Cove, ready to continue their lives in a new place that didn't seem new at all.

McKenzie and Leslie assumed responsibility for finding a new place to live while Sydney was trying to get settled in at the church. Within three months they found a nice Colonial ranch style house they were sure Sydney would like. Leslie was elated that she would have a bathroom right across the hall from her large bedroom she could treat as her very own. They settled a month later and moved in exactly four months after they left

Marian Beach. A day later life for Leslie got exponentially better when she answered a knock at the front door.

"Hi, I'm Leslie Carrington," Sydney and McKenzie heard a voice say. "I live a block down around the corner. I saw the moving truck yesterday and caught a glimpse of you going into the house. Thought I would welcome you to the neighborhood. We just moved here, too. My father is the new minister at First Congregational Church. Where are you from?"

"Marian Beach, North Carolina. That's where I was born and lived until now. My father is also a new minister here, at Saint Patrick Episcopal Church. He and my mother were born and raised here. My name is Leslie, too. I'm thirteen."

"Oh, no, I can't believe it. We're both named Leslie and we're both thirteen," Leslie Carrington replied.

"It's weird, don't you think?" Leslie Strange asked.

"Very weird," Leslie Carrington said. "It's like we're twins."

"Not quite," Leslie Strange said. "Your skin is brown and mine is white. Actually, I like yours better. It's smooth and beautiful. Mine is freckled, rough, and sometimes so pale I'm almost invisible. My mother says I have skin so light the sun can seriously burn it if I'm not careful."

"I like your color. Being my color means some people are not very nice to me."

"That's terrible. My parents have told me people who treat others badly because of the color of their skin are just not nice people and want to hurt others to make themselves feel better."

"My parents have told me the same thing, but it still hurts when somebody calls me an ugly name, especially that 'N' word.

"I'm sorry you've been called that, Leslie said. I will never do that, I promise."

"I believe you so let's be friends from now on."

"Friends, it is."

"Great, so would you like to come over to my house so I can show you my room?" the other Leslie asked our Leslie.

"Are your parents at home?" When Leslie asked that question McKenzie and Sydney looked at each other with delightful pride, already overflowing because of what she had already said.

"Yes, my mother is."

"Then, yes, I would like that very much." Leslie asked her parents if it was okay. They said yes and the two girls were immediately gone.

It was not until the monthly meeting of the Castle Cove Ministerial Association a couple of weeks later that Sydney met Stephen Carrington for the first time.

"Let me guess," Stephen said as he approached Sydney, "you're the father of the second Leslie to move to town, right?"

"You got me," Sydney responded.

"Delighted to meet you. You're coming back home, aren't you?" Stephen asked.

"Yes, I am. My family has been here since the town was founded."

"That's what I heard, but why don't we go to lunch and we can talk more then?"

"Sounds good," Sydney answered.

"Great," Stephen said. You know where the Corner Café is."

"Yep, sure do."

"Let's meet there after the meeting."

"Sounds good," said Sydney.

Sydney and Stephen hit if off from the start. Stephen came from a family of four children, all of whom graduated from college. He did his undergraduate work at Howard University in DC worked a couple of years in business and then decided to become a minister like his father. He got his Master of Divinity at Princeton Theological Seminary, then entered its PhD program in pastoral care and counseling. He told Sydney he reached a saturation point with academics after he had finished all his classwork. Instead of staying to write his dissertation he accepted a ministry position at a large church near Princeton with primary responsibilities in pastoral care and counseling. He spent five years there before coming to Castle Cove. He has been working on his dissertation, but it's been slow going. He was reaching the deadline so he contacted his doctoral supervisor to see if he could get a two-year extension. His request was highly unusual and he thought it would be rejected, but he had just learned a couple of weeks ago that a departmental committee agreed to extend the deadline.

Sydney and Stephen started meeting for lunch once a week on the same day, at the same time and same place like clockwork. Sydney found out they had politics in common as well as religion. Stephen's father served three terms as a Democratic Representative in the Maryland state house. Now semi-retired, he is still active in the civil rights movement. Sydney told

Stephen the Strange family had always been active in Democratic politics. The majority of Castle Cove white voters were typically North Carolina conservative, though some considered themselves Democrats, a sign that southern Democrats thought more like Republicans than Democrats.

"The Strange family members are 'New Deal 'Democrats," Sydney explained to Stephen, "meaning we believe in an activist government. That's why we are not Republicans. We think their philosophy of small government means letting businesses and corporations operate in an unregulated market. The average person doesn't have a chance against their power. We believe our only ally is the government as a watchdog on corporate power. Republicans hate it. Democrats believe it is the only way to keep the playing field level."

"I agree with what you're saying, Sydney, but you do know that you're talking from a white perspective. My family has never had the chances you have simply because you're white and we are black. I know your heart, brother, so I know you don't like that anymore than I do, but it's a fact that is always there."

"You're right, Stephen. I grew up seeing it every day here in Castle Cove. It's still here. But there are white people like me who are working with you and the black community as a whole to change things. Don't you agree?"

"Yes, I do, but we have such a long way to go. Progress has been made. I know that. But attitudes are the hardest part to change and we have made far less progress there. Here's what I don't get about white people, specifically, white Christians. How is that you go to church every Sunday and believe in heaven and hell and salvation and all that stuff that keeps Christianity in power, but make no connection between your faith and the world around you? Think about it. You and I grew up in a segregated America. There was hardly a church in North Carolina, or anywhere else for that matter, that not only didn't support integration, they supported segregation, How did that happen in white churches?"

"I ask myself the same question again and again. The disconnect between the gospel and American culture is stunning and churches accept it as normal. It's enough for me sometimes to wonder why I stay in ministry given the attitudes I see in my own church members when it comes to race, sexual orientation, wealth and poverty, and just about anything and everything else. I guess I stay because I have made myself believe I can make a difference, even though I probably can't and aren't."

"Do we stay with it or throw in the towel?" Stephen said. "That's what you're asking. Both have consequences, but which one has more integrity. I honestly don't know, but what I do know is that I want white ministers like you to stay in because you're the only friends we have. Besides, you're the best friend I have, Sydney. We can talk honestly without worrying about either of us getting mad."

"I appreciate you saying that. To be honest, I've wondered if my being white makes you uncomfortable at some level."

"I've had the same thought about my being black, if that bothers you in some way. But I decided the pleasure of humiliating you on the basketball court made any risk worth it."

Sydney smiled and said. "Now that we're being honest, I confess I felt the same way the last time I wiped you out in tennis."

Tennis and basketball had become a way for both men to get a break from "thinking so much," to use their own words. For someone who had only played sandlot tennis, Sydney found that Stephen was better than a lot of the people he had played against in college. In return Sydney's size gave him a fighting chance against Stephen in basketball.

"All kidding aside," Sydney said, "here's to friendship," lifting his water glass. Stephen tapped it with his and said, "Here, here," and then added, "pretty pathetic, wouldn't you say, when you have to use water to make a toast?"

"Ah, my friend," said Sydney, "doing it with water is why we will remember it."

The next morning Sydney was at the office at his usual early hour when his office phone rang. It was Stephen.

"You're calling me at six forty-five in the morning. I didn't know you were up this early."

"I'm not usually, but after our conversation yesterday I got to thinking that we both needed to get into some good trouble."

"Well, you've got my attention. What do you have in mind?

"Do you know anything about the controversy down in the Car Line neighborhood over the construction of highway four-sixty that's underway?"

"Not much, but you won't believe the irony of you asking me about it. The first girlfriend I had, actually she was never my girlfriend, she was more than that. She was my very best friend, the same way you are. We were inseparable for a year and then she suddenly moved away and I never saw her again. Her father worked for the company that turned a single lane partly unpaved into a nice two-lane paved highway more than thirty years ago. Some coincidence, huh?"

"All the more reason you need to go with me. There's a meeting this morning at nine-thirty at the Car Line Community Center. It seems that in its infinite wisdom the state highway department has a plan to dead-end Car Line Street where the bridge of the current two-lane highway goes over it. They say it's too costly to build a new bridge to span four lanes over Car Line with the other two bridges at either end of town already under construction. Of course, Car Line being a black neighborhood and the communities on either end being white played no role in the decision. We can all believe that.

"After initial pushback the state came up with a solution that doesn't build a new bridge, but involves laying a culvert fifteen feet high and a hundred-fifty feet long under the four-lane highway that will allow residents to walk from one side to the other. In other words, they want to build a tunnel instead of a new bridge in the black community. This is exactly the kind of systemic racism we talked about. The state never thought about doing the same thing at either end of Castle Cove, both of which are predominantly white. I think you and I should attend the meeting and stand with the Car Line community."

"I'm in," Sydney said without any hesitation. "In fact, I'll pick you up, say around nine o'clock."

"Excellent," Stephen said. "See you in a little while."

They arrived at the community center early and walked in together. Sydney was the second white person in the room. Already sitting down was a woman name Catherine Penny, the wife of the district judge. Sydney knew her by reputation as a force to be reckoned with in Castle Cove on issues of racial justice. There were empty seats near the back but not two together. Stephen pointed Sydney to one on his right and he took one on the left. Sydney spoke to the black man who looked to be about his age sitting in the chair next to the one he took. He said hello back, and then Sydney noticed the man was looking at him curiously. Finally he smiled and said,

"You don't know who I am, do you Sydney?' Calling him by his first name surprised Sydney.

"No, I'm afraid I don't," he answered.

"Jesse Hutchinson," said the man, "but you knew me when we were kids as 'Sonny boy'."

Sydney was stunned, as if he had been hit over the head. The feeling of shame came over him. One summer Jesse came over to Sydney's house to play ball. That began a friendship that lasted through the summer. They became fast friends, only Sydney didn't know him as "Jesse" back then. He knew him as "Sonny Boy."

"I don't know what to say, Jesse, except that at the moment I feel so ashamed for calling you by that awful name."

"No, no Sydney. I didn't know any different back then either. We were just kids, about seven years old as I recall. It never bothered me. I don't remember thinking about you being white and me being black. We were friends that summer and I played ball with you and all the other white kids like I was one of you."

"You were, but, still, kids or not, we should have never called you that name."

"What's done is done. Sydney, but let me ask you, how is your mother?"

"She's doing okay. My father died not long ago, but she's managed well. Thank you for asking."

"I saw the news about your dad when it happened. I'm glad your mother is doing okay. I remember how nice she was to me all those years ago. She treated me just like she did you, Harrison, and Sonny. Your mother was a nice person. I have thought many times I should stop by and say hello to her, see if she would remember me."

"Oh, she would remember you, Jesse, I promise you that. You would make her day if you visited."

"I did ask Sonny the first time I saw him how she was. He said fine, but didn't mention anything about your dad dying."

"You've seen Sonny?"

"Yes, well, to be honest I ran into him at the Fifth Street Tavern. He comes in once in a while, enough in fact that nobody pays any attention to him being white. Everybody likes Sonny."

"That's part of the problem. He's the life of every party, which means every party likes to have him around."

"I know what you mean. I've got a brother with a similar problem. Sonny's one of the nicest guys around. I don't think there is a place in this town where Sonny Strange is not welcomed."

"As I said, that's part of the problem."

The meeting was being called to order. Sydney whispered to Jesse how nice it was to meet him again for the first time. He smiled and nodded. During the meeting it became quite obvious that Jesse was a leader in his community. When he stood to speak the room would get very quiet and all eyes would be on him. He made it clear to the highway officials that their plan to cut off the Car Line Community was unacceptable. If that meant seeking a court injunction claiming racial bias in the design of the highway around Castle Cove, so be it. Catherine Penny stood in support of what Jesse said. She then extolled the state officials present to do the right thing. That got her a round of applause.

That is how the meeting went for another hour or so until the officials said they had heard the community's grievances and would submit a redrawn plan that included a bridge over Car Line much like the other two at either end of town. They said they were confident it would be approved. The meeting was then adjourned. Sydney spoke to Jesse again and reminded him that his mother would be delighted to see him sometime. He also thanked Jesse for the words he spoke during the meeting. He told Sydney he was still teaching, now at the community college outside of town, and to stop by sometime. Sydney promised him he would.

As Sydney and Stephen climbed into the Jeep, Sydney paused to thank him for inviting him to the meeting.

"You were exactly right, Stephen, that was some good trouble to get into."

Sydney drove Stephen back to his church, but said very little. Stephen knew something was wrong.

"Okay, Sydney, what's bothering you?"

"I don't know what you mean," he responded.

"Sydney, it's me, the pastoral counseling expert who can see right through you. Something is on your mind. What is it?"

"Some bad memories, to be honest."

"What triggered them?"

"The man I sat next to, did you see him?"

"Yes, Jesse Hutchinson. He's one of my church members."

"Well," Sydney said as he pulled into the church parking lot, "I grew up with him, but I didn't recognize him. He saw I didn't and told me who he was. When he did I was ashamed like I have never been before."

"What do you mean?"

"You know what name I used to call Jesse when we were kids? 'Sonny Boy.' My brothers, me, every kid in the neighborhood, we all called him 'Sonny Boy', Stephen. How awful was that? And you know what makes it ten times worse. I never knew his real name until today. I am so ashamed. I apologized to him several times, but it didn't make me feel any better. I just can't believe we did that, I did that."

"What did he say?"

"He said we were kids and didn't know any better, that it was in the past and didn't matter now."

"Doesn't surprise me in the least," said Stephen. "I can assure you Jesse meant it."

"I don't question that, but it doesn't make me feel any better right now. I can't believe I called him 'Sonny Boy'. It's too awful to say out loud."

"Sydney, listen to me. I know Jesse and I am sure he doesn't want you to feel ashamed. If you think about it, he's given you a gift I think you should accept. Don't tarnish it by beating up on yourself. He was right. You were just kids. The gift he's giving you is forgiveness, and reconciliation. Take it and be thankful. You don't need to do anything else."

Sydney sat silent for a minute and then said, "I hear what you're saying, Stephen. I do. But my sense of shame is overwhelming."

"You'll have to make your way through it," said Stephen, "and you will. I'm here if you need my help."

"As I have to keep saying," Sydney said, "thank you."

Stephen got out of the car, and Sydney drove off.

Jan G. Linn     197

# 20

Hiring Lydia Henson was the first and best decision Sydney believed he had made since coming back to Castle Cove. He tried to persuade Jane Almond not to retire, but after thirty-three years she said she wanted to travel before she got too old. Stephen recommended Lydia, a member of his church, and Sydney knew as soon as the interview was over that she was who he wanted. She accepted the position and took no time proving she could run the office without any interference from Sydney. She is so professional, in fact, that Sydney has told her more than once the congregation would let him go before losing her.

He was thankful she asked for the morning off to attend her daughter's play at school. Her husband teaches and coaches at the junior high school. They have three children, a girl in third grade and twin boys in kindergarten. After the morning he had, Sydney needed some time alone. His mind was still spinning over the embarrassment and shame he had experienced seeing Jesse Hutchinson again. He realized how easy it had been and still is to live his life unconscious of the white privilege from which he benefited without ever thinking about it. It sickened him to think that his best friend had to think about it every day. Worse, he knew, was the fact that there is virtually universal blindness to it by white people who are the cause of it. The more he thought about it the more ashamed he became. He called himself a minister of the good news to the poor, the oppressed, the forgotten, the downtrodden, but was there any reason he should. Instead, was he as phony as he was feeling?

If that wasn't enough, he couldn't stop thinking about what Jesse had said about Sonny. He didn't think there was a bar in town where Sonny wasn't known, is what Jesse said. Sydney tried to work on the sermon, but just couldn't do it. He must have wasted an hour before he decided to go see his mother. He wanted to ask her what she remembered about Jesse

Hutchinson. He called to see if he could take her to lunch. She said no, which is what he expected her to say. She wanted to fix something for them there.

Sydney pulled into his mother's driveway a little before twelve-thirty and was getting out of his Jeep when Sonny came out the front door. As soon as he got close he could see his eyes were red and glassy and he smelled of alcohol.

"Don't say it, Sydney," speaking before Sydney had a chance to. "I don't need a sermon. I was having a bad day so I decided to come by to say hello to mom."

With that he was in his car and gone. When Sydney went inside his mother was in the kitchen putting the finishing touches on two salads she had prepared. She looked up and smiled. He walked over and kissed her on the cheek and sat down.

"Guess you ran into Sonny as he was leaving," she said.

"Yes, I did. He looked and smelled the way he apparently does all the time these days."

"I don't know what's going to happen to him," said Sarah. "Since your father died he has been drinking all the time, but I suppose the truth is, he was before."

"Did you give him any money?"

"No, not this time. I won't anymore because I know it doesn't help him, probably makes things worse, as you've told me many times. I see that now. It was never my intention to..."

"Mother," Sydney interrupted. "We all know that. But let's not talk about Sonny. Tell me how you are doing. I'm sorry I haven't been by recently."

"You're busy, Sydney, and I don't need looking after. I'm doing fine. I go to lunch weekly with my Bridge Club friends. I'm still active in the Women's Fellowship at church, as you know. Gregory is playing on the junior high basketball team as you also know. He is getting so tall, almost as tall as Harrison. Your father tried to go to his games as often as possible so I am trying to now. I actually enjoy them. Jillian sometimes goes with me. She has become a very pretty sixteen-year-old and very popular, but she doesn't seem to mind sitting with me. I think she's inherited a little of her mother's red hair, at least a tint of it."

"Well, I'm glad you're keeping active. Our life is settling down some.

I expect to be coming around more than I have been. In fact, I have an idea. Why don't we start having Sunday lunch as the Strange family, all of us. McKenzie and I can host it first, then go to Harrison's and Maryanne's, then here. Not every week, but at least once a month. What do you say?"

"I think that is a marvelous idea, but I want it here and I want to cook."

"Mother, that's too much on you, way too much. Let us share the work, please."

"Listen to me, Sydney, I have cooked meals for this family longer than you've been alive. It's what I do and it's what I want to do. It gives me energy just to think about it. The thing that helps me the least is my family trying to help me as if I can't do anything myself. I need to be needed, to have expectations of myself. Losing your father was like losing myself. He was the reason I did most of what I did, especially after the three of you were gone. My schedule revolved around him every day. Suddenly all of that is gone. It has left me without an anchor for my life. The prospect of fixing a family dinner for everyone thrills me. It is not only what I want to do. It's what I need to do."

"Then that is what we will do. Let's tell everybody and then leave it open for whoever can come. If they let you know by the Friday before will that give you enough time to prepare?"

"Yes, that will be fine, and if someone can come at the last minute, that will be fine, too."

"I will contact the whole family. The second Sunday in June is two weeks away so that should give them plenty of time to put it on their schedule. I will also include Carrie and the kids, and Sonny, though I doubt he will show up."

"Yes, I want Carrie and Annie and Anthony, if they can get here. If Sonny comes, fine. If he doesn't, it's his choice."

It dawned on Sydney as he was getting ready to leave that he had forgotten all about the reason he came to see her in the first place.

"Mother, I almost forgot to ask you something that was the reason I called in the first place. Do you remember a kid named Jesse Hutchinson when I was growing up who used to come over to play?"

"Yes, of course. I remember all your friends."

"I saw him this morning for the first time since we were kids. He teaches at the community college and is a leader in the black community."

"He was always polite and seemed very smart. He seemed to like coming to our home."

"Do you remember what we called him back then?"

"'Sonny Boy', I think. I always called him Jesse, but I remember the kids in the neighborhood called him 'Sonny Boy.'"

"I was ashamed when he reminded me of it."

"Why did he?"

"Because I didn't recognize who he was when he introduced himself. I was so embarrassed."

"It was a different time, Sydney. Lots of things went on back then that were wrong. I think of how black people were treated and I can hardly believe we were that bad to them."

"I know. Seeing him was a rude awakening that we still have a long way to go in overcoming racism. It's kind of ironic that my best friend now is African American, maybe the best friend I've ever had."

"Things may not be as good as they should be, Sydney, but your friendship says a lot about the progress our country has made, even in states like North Carolina. I'm not naïve about how things are today, but we have a lot to build on going forward. I'm just proud of you. I hope you know that."

"I do, Mother, but you are my mother, after all."

"I'd be proud of you if I weren't."

"Thank you, Mother. Now I need to go. I love you."

"Love you, too, sweetheart. I'm excited about our Sunday family dinner plans."

"I am, too," Sydney said as he headed for the door.

Later that evening as he and McKenzie were enjoying the evening on their patio, he told her that today he saw his mother in a way he never had before.

"You know, I thought I knew my mother, and I do, but this afternoon I saw her for the amazing woman she is. For years her questions have always been about me or you or Leslie. She has been the same way with Harrison. But what she said about why she needed to fix the Sunday family lunches and her comments about progress in race relations because of my friendship with Stephen helped me see her as someone who is more than my mother. Based on some books she mentioned, I realized that she is a voracious reader. I think she reads more than I do and is eclectic in her choices, from novels to biographies to contemporary issues and problems. I also noticed what was hiding in plain sight. Since father died she has taken up painting again and it obviously gives her a lot of pleasure. She has them sitting on the floor around the house. She also told me she has been writing poetry for the first time in many years. I think my mother is a genuine "renaissance woman.'"

"As I once told you when you were surprised by the feelings she expressed about your father when he had his first heart attack, she has lived the role her generation of women were expected to live. I don't think she minded, but it never allowed her true passions for her own life to come out."

"I think you're right, and I have not helped. I have seen her as Sonny's victim for so long I never questioned whether or not I was right. Now I see how wrong I have been. She is not only doing what she wants to do when he asks for help, she is doing it fully conscious of why the rest of us think she shouldn't. She weighs the pros and cons each time he comes to her wanting help. My agreement or disagreement with her choice is immaterial. Mother is as capable as I am in making the decisions she makes for her life. When we talked about the Sunday family dinners she could not have been more self-reflective. We didn't move back here because of her, but I guess I have thought that at some level we did. Boy, was I wrong about that. It's been more for me than her. I thought she needed my protection when all she really needs is for me to be her son. Maybe seeing that now will help me focus on my struggle to be Sonny's brother instead of always telling her how to be his mother."

"You're making progress, Reverend Strange. I'm proud of you. I'll even remind you of it whenever you forget."

"Not sure I want you to go that far," Sydney answered as she got up to go inside.

They both picked up glasses and snack trays and headed to the kitchen. Sydney's cell rang before he had gotten to sleep.

"Sydney, J.C. Maddox. Sonny's here at the bar again. I don't think he should drive."

"I'll be there in a few minutes, J. C," Sydney quickly responded, not waiting for J. C. to say anything more.

J. C. helped Sydney get Sonny in the Jeep. He was asleep almost as soon as the engine started. Once he got home, Sydney managed to get him into the house and to the bedroom downstairs.

"Bad?" McKenzie asked sitting up in bed as Sydney was undressing.

"Yep. Too drunk to walk without help. He's asleep downstairs." He sat on the side of the bed and turned to her. "I don't know what to do, McKenzie. I want to wash my hands of him like Harrison has, but I can't do it. I don't think this kind of stuff will ever stop until something bad happens."

"You'll never be like Harrison, Sydney. You have to be yourself and I trust that more than anything. You need to do the same. There's no easy solution here. Sonny is an alcoholic. That time he drove all the way to Marian Beach to make amends I thought—we both thought—he might stay sober. This is not your fault or anyone else's. Sonny is making his own choices and you can't stop him. You have no responsibility in it."

Sydney turned the light off and laid down beside her. He must have gone to sleep immediately because the next thing he remembered was looking at the clock at six-twenty the next morning. McKenzie was still sleeping. He shaved and was drying off from his shower when she came in the bathroom.

"Good morning. Sorry if I awakened you."

"You didn't," she replied. "I've been trying to sleep for the last hour, always a losing battle so I got up. It's time anyway. Leslie needs to get ready for school. And I'm substituting at the high school for one of the English teachers. I forgot to tell you."

"That's a surprise. I didn't realize that was something you wanted to do."

"I don't. I mean, I hadn't given it any thought, but the principle called and asked if I could. The teacher who's out is pregnant and is having some problems. I told her I would do sub short-term, but that's all. She said she was good with that."

Sonny was in the kitchen taking a cup of leftover coffee out of the microwave. He looked terrible, just terrible.

"Hey, Sonny," McKenzie said when she saw him. "Looks like you could use some breakfast."

"Nothing for me, McKenzie, but thanks."

"Thanks aren't necessary. I fixed some sweet rolls last night to put in the oven and I'm guessing you're not going anywhere until Sydney has one so you may as well, too."

He sat down at the counter with his back to the small kitchen table where Sydney was sitting with the paper.

"Do you remember anything about last night?" Sydney asked Sonny to break the silence.

"Not a lot. Guess J.C. called you from the Tap Room to pick me up."

"He did."

"I don't know how you can keep this up, Sonny."

"I would just as soon not get into it this morning, Sydney. I'm sorry J. C. got you involved."

"I didn't mind, Sonny. In fact, I would rather pick you up than have you driving in your condition."

"Sometimes it's amazing how well I'm able to drive."

"Yeah, until something bad happens. It's not worth the risk. It would be nice if you could see what you're doing and stop."

"I've tried several times, Sydney. You know that. I have given it an honest try. It's just not in the cards for me to give up drinking. I like it too much."

"More than Carrie? More than Annie and Anthony?"

"Of course, not, but you cannot understand the kind of hold it has on me. It's a vice-grip squeezing the life out of me."

"It may be hard to stop, Sonny, but it's not impossible. People have done it, you know."

"Yeah, but I'm not one of them. Drinking is who I am."

"You're more than that, Sonny. Maybe if you realized it you would change."

"Maybe you're right, but what I see when I look in the mirror is a drunk who's ruined his life. Pretty hopeless if you ask me."

"That's all you see, but the rest of us see more. Until you do, you're right. Nothing's going to change."

McKenzie put a sweet roll in front of him and then brought one for Sydney and herself as she sat down at the table. The conversation stopped long enough for them to eat and finish their coffee. Sydney got up and told Sonny he was ready to take him to get his car.

"Sonny, don't go in," Sydney said as Sonny got out of the Jeep at his car. "Go to an AA meeting. Go home. Just don't go get beer."

He didn't respond. Sydney drove off thinking that for more than twenty years the family has been consumed by Sonny's behavior. He punched in Stephen's number. When he answered Sydney asked if he had time for him to stop by for a few minutes. Stephen offered him coffee as he came into his office. He welcomed it and sat down.

"Last night I drove Sonny to our house after the bartender at the Tap Room called to say he was in no shape to drive. Just dropped him off back at the bar to get his car. He may still be there. I called you because I needed to talk. I wish I could let him go and be done with him, but I can't do it."

"That's pretty normal, don't you think?" Stephen asked Sydney. "Who wants to stay around someone who makes them miserable?"

"Guess you're right. It just doesn't feel right to think that way."

"Sydney, I don't need to tell you that feelings don't have any morality. We don't choose them. They just appear on their own. Thoughts are the same way. Morality kicks in when we start acting on our thoughts and feelings."

"I know what you're saying is true, but it doesn't seem to help. Lately I've been irritable and fidgety and can't sleep very well. It's like he's driving me over the edge. I hate him and worry about him at the same time."

"Well, you don't hate him. Let's clear that up. You don't wish bad things to happen to him, and you keep going to pick him up and take him to your house when he's too drunk to drive. None of that is hate behavior so put that away for good. The rest of it you need to take seriously. In fact, you need to do something to take care of yourself or your own health is going to be affected."

"What do you suggest?"

"Silence."

"You mean like a silent retreat, time away and alone?"

"That's exactly what I'm suggesting."

"I used to go on silent retreats regularly early in my ministry," Sydney said, "but I haven't been on one for several years. Most of them have been with a group. I've only done one by myself that I recall."

"That's the kind I think you need, silence alone without anyone else around."

"You know, I think you may be right. I know McKenzie will be fine with it if I explain to her why I need it."

"Then do it, and do it now. Don't wait. Make arrangements as soon as you can."

"Thanks, Stephen. I will."

Sydney sat there without getting up to leave. Stephen let the moment linger, then said, "Okay, Sydney, what else is it?"

"There you go again, Stephen," Sydney answered. "I wish you weren't so intuitive."

"Occupational hazard," he replied, "but it doesn't take an expert to see you still have something on your mind."

"You're right, of course, I do. I just don't know how to get into it."

"Say whatever is on your mind, Sydney, and trust me to understand."

"Okay, so let me ask you a question: Can you and I be friends, real friends, when I'm white and you're black?"

"Well that is certainly not what I was expecting to hear, but tell me why you're asking that question?"

"Because of Jesse Hutchinson. Not only him, though. It's everything related to the Car Line bridge and the obvious racism that was underneath the state making such a stupid decision to close off the community like they wanted to do. I mean, does being white make us, make me, incapable of understanding my own prejudice, my own privilege, my own failure to recognize the effects of historical racism that exists today? And if it does, how can you trust me as your friend? Why would you even want to?"

"Wow, Sydney, that's a heavy load you're carrying. I guess I thought you had processed your feelings about your conversation with Jesse, but I can see you haven't and it's weighing you down."

"I know. Truth be told, it feels like the whole world is on my shoulders, which sounds ridiculous when I say it out loud, but it's how I'm feeling."

"Then let's start there, with the weight of the world, and what I am confident is something you already know. The feeling you have is real, but it is coming from an illusion in your mind. You are not responsible for the world, including the history of white racism. Just because you're white you don't have to share in collective guilt. You're not responsible for your race, just for you, and only you. I think guilt about your history with Jesse has caused you to fall into the trap of what psychology calls the Atlas syndrome that comes right out of Greek mythology. In the war between the Titans and the Olympians the Olympians won and banished the Titans to Tartarus, a deep abyss that was a prison. But Zeus, the Olympian chief god, chose to punish Atlas in a different way, to make him hold the world on his shoulders for eternity. That's the origin of the phrase, "carrying the weight of the world on your shoulders."

"That's how I feel," Sydney told Stephen.

"Okay, but what you're forgetting is that Atlas was being punished, and in my experience people who feel like they have the weight of the world on their shoulders feel the same way, consciously or unconsciously. They feel like they have done something for which they should be punished or are being punished. Guilt weighs people down, and if it goes on long enough it can lead to serious problems."

"And you think I'm doing that?"

"I don't know, Sydney, but it certainly sounds like you are. You said yourself you feel ashamed about the fact that you and all the white kids in your neighborhood called Jesse 'Sonny Boy'. Making you feel worse is that you didn't know his real name until now. You may be connecting your own guilt to the guilt you think all white people should feel about systemic racism like we saw in the highway department's initial decision."

"Okay, I can see that, but why am I questioning our friendship?"

"You're not, Sydney, you're questioning why a black man wants to be friends with a white man, and specifically why I would want to be your friend. But it's not about me. It's about you. I think you don't feel worthy of my friendship with you because of guilt. That means I cannot convince you that our friendship is as genuine as it is. Only you can do that, and it doesn't look like you've been able to yet. Unless and until you forgive yourself for what you did to Jesse, you will continue to feel guilty for something you can't change, which is that you are white."

"My God, I feel so messed up inside."

"No, you're not. Well, actually you are because we all are. None of us comes into adulthood unscarred by what happens to us growing up, but most of us do okay coping with our wounds, especially the more we understand ourselves. You can't not be white, Sydney, just as I can't not be black. We are who we are, "warts and all," as the saying goes because it's true. But guilt is always the nemesis for people who want to be good. In this instance you want to do better than whites have done in the past, but what happened with Jesse makes you question whether or not you can.

"Guilt always attacks good people, not the bad ones, Bad people pay no attention to it. It's the good people who feel guilty, who wish something had not happened, who wish they could have changed something. I'm afraid you are letting it win in your struggle to put 'Sonny Boy' behind you. One way to stop doing that is to accept your own humanness. You're a good man, but not a perfect man, and sometimes you're not even a good man because of things you say and do, all because you're human. So am I. And that is why I want to be your friend, why we are friends, like brothers. The only way you can trust that is to accept Jesse's forgiveness, stop trying to be Atlas, and accept the fact that you're just as human as I am. I trust you and you have to trust me the same way."

Sydney let all that sink in without saying anything for a few minutes, then said, "It's a lot to process, but I know what you're saying is true. I just need some time and space to think about it more and I'm thinking that's exactly what a silent retreat will give me. I need it for myself. I can see now that dealing with my feelings about Sonny and Jesse is the same work. It comes down to me and no one else."

"Then go on retreat, Sydney, and do it soon."

# 21

Sydney called the Sisters of Loretto Convent about twenty-five miles from Castle Cove to see if any of their individual cottages was available for a personal retreat. All six were empty so he had his pick. He reserved the one most isolated from the others along with meals at the Convent House in the private room they have for people in silence. He would leave Sunday afternoon and stay through Wednesday. He went home for lunch to talk to McKenzie. She thought the idea was just what he needed. She was honest in telling him she thought he was obsessing over Sonny and it was beginning to worry her.

On previous silent retreats it usually took him an evening and morning to slow down his internal engine before he could begin serious solitude. This time he was already feeling inwardly calmed by Monday morning. He spent most of the day walking, reading, and sleeping. By Tuesday he was feeling relaxed enough to write in his journal. He had written only a paragraph when the thought hit him that trying to get away from Sonny was like trying to get away from himself. Their lives were bound together. Pretending otherwise was a losing battle. But it was more than that. He knew the person he needed to confront was himself, not Sonny.

For the first time in weeks, if not months, Sydney lay down and had a quiet, restful nap. He awakened about four o'clock and decided to take a walk. After a while he came to an opening and in front of him was a large pond with a bench located in a spot that allowed him to see the reflection of the trees on the water. He sat down and gazed out on the lake, being as still as he could. Not one to pray out loud, he remembered the Catholic writer Henri Nouwen once saying that he believed praying without ceasing meant thinking in the presence of God. Sydney decided to trust that and let his thoughts be his way of praying. A few minutes passed when he had a thought almost as if someone had spoken it to him: "Sydney, you need to make peace with your brother." As he sat in silence it stayed with him as if it was demanding attention.

As simple as those words were, he didn't understand what they meant. He and Sonny were not in open conflict. He was even staying at his house when he needed to. What does making peace with him mean? How do you make peace with someone when you're not in conflict with them? And then it dawned on him. It wasn't about what was going on between him and Sonny. It was about what was going on within himself whenever he thought about Sonny. He was constantly thinking about how he could get him to stop drinking, to change his behavior, to change his life. What if the key to making peace with his brother involved stopping his efforts to change him?

"Oh, my God," Sydney said to himself. "I bet Sonny sees my efforts to change him as passing judgment on him. I haven't tried to hide my frustrations and even disgust about what he is doing. It's all my way of judging him and he knows it. Changing my behavior toward him has to be what making peace with him means. I need to stop telling him how he is messing up, hurting everyone around him, telling him he needs to straighten up. I need to start being his brother again instead of his judge."

Sydney felt an intense sadness come over him. All this time he thought he was trying to help Sonny when he was only pushing him away. At least Harrison left Sonny alone while Sydney knew he spent all his time trying to change him, driving a wedge between them that was the opposite of what Sydney wanted to do.

He stayed by the lake until it was almost dark, turning his thoughts over and over in his head until he knew what he had to do. He went back to the cottage, packed his bag, and left for home. On the way he called McKenzie to tell her he was coming home early. He assured her nothing was wrong, that actually things were right and that he would explain when he got there. She was waiting for him when he walked in. She kept the chicken casserole warm that she and Leslie had eaten for supper. Sydney sat down at the counter as she put a plate of it in front of him, then sat down next him with a cup of tea.

"So tell me all about it," she said.

"Well, you can never predict what silence will bring to you, what the experience is going to be like. It seems like the experiences always have their own distinctiveness, I suppose because of whatever the circumstances are in your life at the time. It's not surprising that my relationship with Sonny was prominent in my thoughts, though not in a way I could have anticipated."

"What do you mean?"

"Well, I started having this persistent thought that I needed to make peace with him. It was as if someone said that to me out loud. But it didn't make sense, given the fact that we are not in any direct conflict. That's what confused me initially, but it didn't take long before I realized I was in conflict with him, but not in the way I usually think of conflict. The conflict is my trying to change him, to get him to straighten up, rooted in my anger about the way he is hurting everybody in the family. As I thought about it more I realized he probably feels very judged by me, something he has essentially said, but I've ignored. That's what his "you're the good son" routine is about, my passing judgment on him by telling him everything he's doing that is wrong. He hears that as me saying he's the black sheep in the family."

"Okay, I understand all of that, though I know judging him has never been your intention."

"Doesn't matter. It's how he sees it. Besides, I'm driving myself crazy trying to change him."

"That's because it never works, Sydney, you know that," McKenzie told him.

"I do, which is why I have to stop. More than that, I need to prove to him I can be his brother without trying to reform him."

She didn't say anything else, but reached over, squeezed his forearm, and asked him if he wanted anything else to eat.

"No, I'm full. It was delicious, as always, worth coming home to even if the rest hadn't happened."

McKenzie told him she would clean up. He went into the hallway, picked up his bag, and went to the bedroom to unpack. He put it on the bed, took out his cell and called Sonny. He actually answered.

"Sonny, this is Sydney."

"I didn't figure somebody stole your phone."

Sydney let that one pass.

"Listen," he said, "let's have lunch tomorrow if you're free, on me."

"What's up?" was his response.

"Why does something have to be up?" Sydney responded. "I just want to have lunch, that's all."

"Sure, okay by me," he said, "but you're buying."

"Said I would. Let's meet at Pick's Café, say around twelve-thirty."

"Okay. I'll see you there."

Pick's was a local hole-in-the wall café that has been in Castle Cove forever. Sonny drove up as Sydney was getting out of his car. He waited for him to park and they went in together. Several people spoke to them. The Strange brothers were still well known in Castle Cove. Once seated the waitress was there with menus and water.

"I already know what I want," Sonny said to her. "A hot hamburger." The menu describes a hot hamburger as a hamburger without a top bun smothered in gravy and onions.

"I can't believe you still eat that thing," Sydney commented.

"Nothing like it anywhere else," Sonny responded.

"Have you ever wondered why?"

"No," Sonny said and smiled. "As long as they have it here I know where to get it."

Sydney looked at the waitress and said, "I'll have tuna salad sandwich and a coke."

"Make that two cokes," Sonny told her.

"Guess you guys have been here before," she commented.

"You could say that," said Sonny. "Been coming since we were kids."

"My family just moved here from Virginia so it's all new to me."

"Well, welcome to Castle Cove, Bonnie," Sonny said as he leaned forward to read her name tag. "Shouldn't you be in school?"

"No, I finished last June. I'm taking classes at the community college here and hope to go back to Virginia to school next year."

"Where?"

"Madison."

"Good school," said Sydney.

"Both my parents graduated from there. Guess I'm carrying on the family tradition. But I'm going there because I want to. They didn't pressure me to."

"I'm sure you will like it," Sydney added.

"Thanks. I'll go put your order in."

Bonnie walked away and Sydney decided to plunge right in.

"Listen, I said on the phone that I just wanted to have lunch, but the truth is, I have something to talk to you about."

"I figured as much," Sonny responded.

"No. It's not what I think you're thinking. It's not about you at all. It's about me, about something I realized the last few days while I was on a personal retreat. The thought came to me that I needed and wanted to tell you something I don't think you know, or if you do, may not believe when I tell you. It's that I know we're brothers and nothing will ever change that and I don't want it to. We've stretched our relationship to its limits for sure, but at the end of the day I know you're my brother, and I'm glad you are. To prove it I'm going to stop telling you how to live your life. Doesn't mean I don't think you should stop doing what you're doing, only that I realize I'm not the one to try to get you to do it. No more advice from me. That's a promise. We're brothers and that's what matters."

Bonnie walked up at that moment with their food and sat it down. "Anything else I can get you?"

"No," said Sydney, "I think we're good."

"Well, if you need anything else, let me know," placing the ticket on the table. "Nice to meet you."

"Nice to meet you, too, Bonnie," Sonny said as Sydney smiled and nodded his head.

They both started eating without saying anything more about what Sydney had said. The rest of the conversation was about anything and nothing. When they were close to finishing Sydney asked Sonny if he wanted anything else.

"No, I'm full. I probably should be going. I need to check in with Billy to see if he's got any work for me."

"Okay," Sydney said. "I'm done, too. I'll walk out with you."

Sydney picked up the ticket and took out his wallet to leave Bonnie a tip when Sonny said, "Listen, Sydney, despite our differences I know we're family. I haven't forgotten that."

"That's why I'm done trying to get you to change," Sydney replied. "We're brothers and that's the way I will treat you. That's my promise."

The both stood. As Sydney was paying the bill Sonny went outside.

"Thanks for meeting me for lunch," Sydney told his brother when he came out the door.

"Glad we did," he replied and headed to his car.

Call me any time," Sydney yelled to him. Sonny waved back.

Sydney got in his car, started the engine, and then dialed Stephen.

"I just had lunch with Sonny. Do you have time for me to stop by to talk?" he asked Stephen.

"Sure."

"Good," Sydney responded. "I'll see you in a few minutes."

Sydney had hardly gotten seated in Stephen's office when he started talking.

"I went on retreat as you suggested and the lunch was the result. In the silence I had one thought that dominated everything else: Sydney, you need to make peace with your brother. I wasn't sure what that meant until I realized it was quite simple. Tell him the obvious, that you're his brother and you always will be. That's what I did at lunch."

"How did he respond?"

"Okay, I think. He didn't say much except when we got ready to leave he said he knew we were family. That was about it. But it didn't matter how he responded. I needed to say what I said for me. How he responds is out of my hands."

"That's a breakthrough, I'd say. A significant one, in fact. How do you feel now?"

"Good, although I'm still processing it all. The silence made me realize this whole deal with Sonny was as much about me as him. I think I have been consumed by his alcoholism almost as much as he is, just in a different way. It hasn't been easy for me to be his brother. It's taken everything I have to stay with it, but in the silence, when all the noise inside my head stopped, I came to the realization that thinking and acting like we are brothers is what matters. Everything else is secondary. In fact, I think I can deal with everything else better because I see in a different way what it means to be brothers."

"So you're giving up on trying to fix Sonny, not that you knew you were doing that. We seldom do when we've been conditioned to be the fixer. More than a few clergy have that problem, or should I say, need?"

"I would have fought you on that before my retreat, but now I understand exactly what you're saying. I've been Mr. Fixer all my adult life. It's been the source of so much frustration because I always fail at it. Sonny's been telling me for twenty years I wasn't succeeding. It's time for me to listen."

"I can tell you from personal experience it won't be easy, but it is definitely worth it."

"I believe that, too. But something else I have realized is that the problem of being the fixer can be easily hidden while Sonny's alcoholism doesn't allow him to hide his weakness. It hangs out for everyone to see, unfair if you think about it. I now know we're actually in the same boat for different reasons. Not seeing that is why I haven't resisted the opportunity to tell him what he's doing wrong. That is the first thing I have to stop doing to prove to myself that I am serious about just being his brother."

"At the same time, Sonny still has his own work to do when it comes to you," Stephen suggested. "He wants you to accept him as he is, but he's got to do the same thing with you. But that's on him, not you."

"I guess it all comes down to the fact that before we are anything else, we're human first, all of us. You wonder why it's so hard for us to see that."

A few days before the celebration of Independence Day, Sydney remembered that the fourth was always his father's favorite time of the summer. It may have been because the third was his birthday. Whatever reason, every July fourth the family would pack up and head to Big Trout Lake for a day of fishing and swimming, one of those childhood experiences that gets seared into memory. This year the fourth would be on Saturday. He suggested to McKenzie that they take a vacation weekend and go to Marian Beach. Margaret Evans, his assistant vicar, was already schedule to preach. It would be the first time in months that they had been back. Leslie had been invited to spend the weekend with Leslie Carrington. Stephen had assured Sydney that they had no special plans for the weekend and the two Leslies would be good company for each other. McKenzie was all in so he called Wanda to see if she had a room available for a couple of days. She was thrilled that we were coming. Sydney and McKenzie arrived late Thursday night, visited with Wanda and Sally as they ate breakfast together the next morning, and were out on the beach before noon. He and McKenzie agreed they missed the beach and needed to come back more often than they had.

The Sea Captain restaurant on the boardwalk about a mile from Wanda's was one of their favorite places to eat. They decided to go there for supper that night. Sydney had the stuffed flounder and no one steamed lobster the way the Sea Captain did as far as McKenzie was concerned. The evening seemed perfect. They even ordered two glasses of red wine to toast his father's birthday, sharing with each other how much both of them still missed him.

"You never know how big a hole someone will leave in your life," McKenzie said, "until they're actually gone. Each parent is special and neither can fill the void left when the other is gone. I'm just grateful both of us have been fortunate to have mothers and fathers who loved us, still love us, in fact, and have always done the best they could by us."

"I want Leslie to say the same thing about us some day," Sydney answered.

"So here's to father, a gift I sometimes took for granted, but the kind of man who showed me what being a father means."

"And the best father-in-law I ever had," McKenzie added.

As they touched glasses Sydney said, "May I remind you, Kenz, he was the only father-in-law you ever had," to which she replied, "Day ain't over yet, Sydney Strange." He leaned over and kissed her.

The light was just beginning to come through the window early the next morning when Sydney was awakened by his cell phone ringing. He immediately knew something was wrong when he saw it was Harrison.

"Harrison?"

"Sydney, Sonny is in the hospital. It looks bad. He got drunk last night, fell again, and hit his head on the concrete floor in Billy Hughes's basement. Apparently, everybody else was as drunk as he was so no one found him for hours. A classmate of mine who works in ER admissions called me after she did the paperwork on him and couldn't find anybody from the family in the waiting room."

"Where are you now?" Sydney asked.

"I'm at the hospital."

"Look, McKenzie and I are in Marian Beach for the holiday weekend. We'll leave right away, should get there before noon."

"Oh, I remember now you mentioning y'all might go there, but I wasn't sure if you actually did."

"It was a last-minute thing."

"Okay. Look, I'll call you if anything changes. Once I know more from the doctor I'll go tell mom."

"Sorry you have to do that alone," said Sydney.

"It's not a problem. Just get here when you can. As I said, it sounds pretty serious."

"We'll see you in a little while."

McKenzie was awake by then and Sydney filled her in on the details, then hurried to shave and shower. By the time he came out of the bathroom to get dressed she had finished packing everything except the clothes she laid out for them to wear. She went into the bathroom and was out again in what seemed like a matter of minutes. She dressed and they headed downstairs. Sydney told Wanda what had happened and that he needed to pay the bill quickly. No, she said, insisting they get on the road. They could settle up another time. They both gave her a hug and left.

Mother, Harrison, Maryanne, Carrie, Anthony, and Annie were sitting together in one corner of the intensive care waiting room when Sydney and McKenzie walked in. Everyone exchanged hugs and tears and then Sydney asked what the latest was on Sonny.

"Nothing good," Harrison responded in a low voice as if he didn't want anyone else to hear what he saying. "He suffered a cerebral hemorrhage. The internal bleeding is apparently massive, in part because he was unconscious on the basement floor for hours before anyone did anything. The doctor said he doesn't seem to have much brain activity. It's very bad."

"Have you seen him," Sydney asked.

"Yeah, a couple of times, the first time Maryanne and I together. Mom insisted on seeing him so the second time I went in it was to take her. She broke down, of course, but did okay considering. Carrie took the kids in once. They did okay as well."

McKenzie held on to Sydney's arm as they went in to see Sonny. They stood there looking down at a broken man with a IV in his right arm and an intubation tube coming out of his mouth. Tears rolled down her cheeks. Sydney surprised himself by being able to hold it together. After a few minutes they went back to the waiting room.

The day went pretty much that way, with different family members going in every half hour to see Sonny. Later in the evening Sydney suggested everyone go home for at least a while. They had been there since early morning. Because he and McKenzie were the last ones to the hospital, he wanted to stay the night. He promised to call immediately if anything changed. By ten o'clock everyone had gone, including McKenzie. She said she would let Leslie stay at the Carrington's for the night and then go get her in the morning. Sydney even persuaded Carrie and the kids to go back to their grandmothers while he stayed.

The nurses told Sydney it was fine for him to stay with Sonny. He pulled a chair up to the bed and sat there where he could see Sonny's face.

Sydney just sat there looking at his brother dying too young. He wasn't even fifty years old. Life seemed forever when they were young and now it seems so short. He thought about the three of them growing up in the same home and turning out so different. How does that happen? Harrison takes over the business, he become a minister, and Sonny drinks his life away. Their parents loved each of them equally. If anything, Sonny got the most attention because he was always doing stuff he wasn't supposed to do. Now this. He found himself wishing he and Sonny had more time together as brothers. He even imagined Sonny opening his eyes the way they do on television. He almost laughed at himself for the fantasy, but it was all he had at the moment.

His thoughts were so fixed on Sonny that he didn't hear Stephen's voice until he touched Sydney's arm, making him jump.

"Didn't mean to startle you, Sydney. Sorry about that. I spoke, but you were lost in thought and didn't hear me."

"No, no, I'm fine. Lost in thoughts and memories of Sonny, of growing up. You're a good friend to come here tonight. Guess this is the end of the conversation we had about my making peace with Sonny. Seems like a long time ago now."

"A couple of years, actually," Stephen said.

"It's just so sad, Stephen, so sad. I thought I felt sad when father died, but this, this is different. It's like a piece of me is dying with him. I keep thinking about how things could have been different, and what our lives would have been like if they had been. Now I'm trying to get my head around what life will be like without him. He's been in my life since I was born. But I'm rambling, as you can tell."

"No, you're talking about the price we pay for love." Stephen said. "Makes the fact that we keep doing it pretty amazing. Love is the primary source of joy and pain, but we would never give it up for a minute. Love is the basic ingredient of relationships and relationships are what give life meaning. That's why you're sitting here, Sydney. That's what we talked about that day you came by the office after having lunch with Sonny."

218    *A Brother's Peace*

"That's a day I will never forget. It was the most real moment I ever had with Sonny, and the most important one. You know, since then I have had an amazing calm about him. He's called many times drinking and not once have I gotten upset or told him he was messing up his life or hurting everybody in the family. We've talked as if everything was normal when nothing was. Other times he called sober and we talked about politics, sports, family like brothers do. All because we had lunch that day. It's the only solace I have as I sit here watching him slowly fade away."

They both sat in silence after what Sydney had said. Finally, Stephen put his hand on Sydney's shoulder and said he was going and would check in again in the morning. Sydney stood and gave Stephen a hug and thanked him for coming. After Stephen left he sat back down to wait. He lost track of time until Carrie came in.

"I thought you were at mother's," Sydney said as he looked up at her.

"I was, but I didn't sleep well and woke up early. The same with the kids. They said they wanted to come back here so we got dressed and just walked in. They're in the waiting room. But you need to go home, Sydney. You've been here all night. Take my car. The kids and I will stay. I'll call if anything changes."

Sydney hesitated, then agreed, kissed her check and left. When he walked into his mother's she and McKenzie were up and, of course, his mother was fixing breakfast. McKenzie was drinking a cup of tea. He told them there was no change when he left the hospital and that Carrie promised to call if anything did. He got himself a cup of coffee and sat down with McKenzie. Sarah put a plate of eggs and bacon in front of both of them. She joined them, but didn't eat anything. They were cleaning up the dishes when Sydney's cell rang. He answered, listened, and thanked Carrie for calling.

For a moment that felt like an eternity to McKenzie he looked down at his phone. She knew he was trying to collect himself so she didn't say anything. Finally, he turned to them and gently said, "Sonny just died," his voice breaking as he said it.

"Oh, dear God," Sarah said as she looked up from the table with tears flowing down her face. "My lovely, troubled Sonny. What could I have done different?"

McKenzie walked behind her chair, leaned over and hugged her close. "Not a thing, Sarah, not a thing. You're the best mother these boys could have ever hoped to have. You've loved them unconditionally and that is the one thing we all know Sonny knew."

Sarah reached her hand around to touch McKenzie's arm. As she did Sydney remembered he had Carrie's car.

"Oh, my goodness" he said, "Carrie told me to take her car. I need to go back to the hospital and pick her and the kids up."

"I'll go," McKenzie said. "You stay here with your mother. Talk to her. Make sure she's thinking straight. You can call Carrie and tell her I'm on the way."

After he called Carrie he got another cup of coffee and sat down with his mother.

"You okay?" Sydney asked.

"No, of course not, but I will be."

"Guess that was an unhelpful question and not even what I wanted to know."

"And what is that?"

"I want to know what you're honestly thinking and feeling. You've lost father and now you've lost Sonny. I don't have to be a minister to know how devastating those loses are. So I want to know how you are, honestly."

"My heart is broken, Sydney, not just for me, but for Carrie, Annie, and Anthony for all of us. I tried to get him to stop drinking. We used to have good talks when he would show up here drinking. I usually waited until the next morning at breakfast. He talked to me, more open than you would think. He was miserable. A mother knows when her child is hurting inside. Sonny was. I'm not sure what it was all about it, but I know he was. He was a tormented soul, and now I am worried sick for his soul."

"What do you mean?" Sydney asked.

"His soul, where he's going to spend eternity."

"Are you talking about heaven and hell, that you're afraid Sonny is in hell?"

"Yes, I am. Of course, I am. Aren't you?"

"Oh, Mother, no, no, no. You don't need to be thinking that way. It's stuff you learned as a little girl that you're still holding on to. God is not about sending people to hell. God is better than that. The church has used the fear of hell to scare people—kids, especially—to walk the straight and narrow path and it has done more harm than any good it ever did. God is not about punishment. God is about love and forgiveness. God doesn't punish people. No loving parent would punish their child to prove how powerful they are or who's the boss, and God is the best parent, if you can think in those terms. You and father loved Sonny no matter what he did and you never stopped. You never turned him away even when Harrison and I tried to get you to. That's how strong and deep a parent's love is, and it's the same with God. You're worrying about something you don't need to worry about. I don't believe that is what God wants you to do. If I believed God is punishing Sonny right now, and I mean this, I would quit the ministry today. You can release all of those thoughts. Sonny is fine."

We sat in the quiet before she said, "Sydney, I want to believe that what you're saying is right. I do, truly, but I guess I haven't come very far since I was the child who was scared of God, Sonny's sudden death caught me off guard and I reverted to what was ingrained in me all the years I was growing up. But knowing the man of faith you are, I can trust what you're saying. I can believe God is a far better parent than we humans will ever be. That is a great comfort to me and that is what I need right now more than anything else."

"Well, I will say one last thing. If God is half as good a parent as you are, Mother, Sonny is in good hands."

# 22

Sonny was buried next to his father. It was his mother's wish. The cemetery staff tried to talk her out of it, certain that she would regret not having a spot next to her husband at the time of her own death. when her time came. She listened politely, then told them she knew what she wanted and expected them to honor her wishes.

The family chose to hold a graveside service. The two-hour visitation time they had last night had to be extended for another hour to accommodate the crowd, as if everyone who lived in Castle Cove and Halifax came. Sarah and Carrie wanted Sydney to do the service. It was something he actually wanted to do, but he wasn't confident he could do it alone so he asked Stephen if he would help. He didn't hesitate in agreeing. Stephen followed the abbreviated Episcopal Prayer Book service and then Sydney stepped forward to give Sonny's eulogy.

As he did he was once again amazed at the number of people who were present. Last evening had surprised him, but so did today. It was an outpouring of love for Sonny that was truly moving. He was so glad Annie and Anthony were seeing how much people loved their dad. It was a kaleidoscope of the city of Castle Cove. Sonny's drinking friends were there. So were the mayor and several members of the city council. So were his former high school football coaches, co-workers, long-time friends of his and the family. Sydney took a deep breath and began to speak.

"I think last night was the real eulogy for Mason Dixon 'Sonny' Strange. Yes, mother and father really did give him that name. (people laughed, which helped Sydney release some of the tension he was feeling.)

The funeral home was filled with people from all walks of life, just as this gathering today is. All of those last night and those of you here today share one thing in common. Love and friendship with my brother.

Mark Twain once said he never met a person he didn't like. Sonny never met a person who didn't like him. An overstatement, perhaps, but close enough to the truth to be able to say it.

It was no secret that Sonny had a problem, a serious one, one that finally took his life. One of you said to me last night that he only had one enemy in life—the bottle. We would be less than honest if we did not acknowledge how true that was, and that his alcoholism was a source of deep pain and agony for our family. In the early years we made a lot of mistakes in trying to cope with it. We were learning about this horrible disease, and how to cope with it. We were slow learners.

The one thing I did learn, though, finally, mercifully, was to distinguish between his alcoholism and him as a person. Sonny suffered from a disease that has touched most people in some way. But alcoholism didn't make him a bad person. It made him a very sick person. And it didn't make him any less a child of God. I don't say that simply as his brother. I say it as a minister, as one whose business it is to ponder the ways of God. My faith is that the unconditional love of a merciful God holds all of us here and also holds him now. If goodness and merit are prerequisites for heaven, whatever that may be, Sonny won't be there...and neither will any of us. It's not our goodness that makes us acceptable to God. It's God's goodness that makes us acceptable. And don't let anyone tell you any different.

The most enduring lesson I learned in dealing with Sonny has been and remains the simple and profound truth that he was my brother and he always would be. Mother had, of course, told me that before I came to see it, but, then mothers are always smarter about life than their children.

There is a bond that exists between brothers that borders on mystery, a kinship that exists deep in the soul. Of the relationship between sisters I know nothing, as with the relationship between brothers and sisters. But I do know about the bond between brothers. As most of you know, I am the youngest of the three Strange brothers, which means there has never been a moment in my life when I have not been a brother. I have not always been conscious of this bond, of course. And there have been times when Harrison, Sonny, and I have pushed it to its limits, as if determined to prove that no such bond exists between us at all. But in the end the bond has always won out, a kind of victory of the soul of sorts.

It usually happens in a moment of crisis, my becoming aware of this bond. It seems important insights come to me this way, in the midst of a crisis when I see for the first time what has been there all along. I remember the moment this bond between me and my brothers first came to me. It felt as if light had dispelled any darkness that existed between us and all that mattered was that we were brothers.

That bond is why the sense of loss I feel today is unlike any I have ever experienced. I lost my father, a deep loss, but one that is a natural part of family life. Losing a brother who was only forty-nine years old is not. It feels out of season, inconsistent with the way life is supposed to be.

That is how love affects us at a time such as this. Love makes it hard to let go. We want to go back and change the events of last week, last month, last year, and many years before that because in the end all that has happened is why we are here today, and it's hard to be. We were and are Sonny's family, Sonny's friends, and holding all the memories that go with that fact.

Sonny was too young to die. And his death changes everything for us. We know that nothing will be the same now. We will heal, but we will never be the same again. But we can say that we are thankful that we had him as long as we did. Feelings of sadness and gratitude stand beside each other at times like this, mainly, I think, because we are born to love, and thus to weep. My prayer, then, is, to use the words of the Psalmist, that our weeping will linger for this night, for many nights, I am sure, but joy will come in the morning, some morning, soon."

Sarah sat quietly as people began to leave. Several came to her chair and expressed their condolences. Finally, Harrison suggested they leave. Sarah slowly got up. He took her right arm and Maryanne gently held her left. Gregory and Jillian walked ahead of them to the car. Sydney remained standing where he was when the service ended. Leslie came up, gave him a hug, and told him she loved him. McKenzie kissed him on the check and explained that Carrie, Annie, and Anthony had ridden with her and Leslie and they would see him at his mother's. Finally, everyone was gone and Sydney let the sacred silence of the cemetery fill his senses as he ran what he had said about Sonny over in his mind. Was it adequate, enough, not enough, too much?

Stephen had been quietly standing behind him the whole time. He stepped to Sydney's side, put his arm around his shoulders and said, "You did well, brother, you did well."

# Readers Guide

Chapter 1:

1. Does American society put too much pressure on young star athletes who are not mature enough to handle the attention they get and the expectations placed on them?
2. Have you known anyone who got hooked on pain medication that led to drug dependency and/or addiction?

Chapter 2:

3. What do you think was most revealing about Sonny's reaction when Sydney told him he was quitting football?
4. What does the way his father responded when Sydney told him he wanted to give up a promising football career say about their relationship?

Chapter 3:

5. What memories did stories about Sydney's two childhood friends stir up in you?
6. Do you think Sam was being stubborn or principled in what he said to his father about hiring Abe Jordan as a lumberjack?

Chapter 4:

7. What does the difference between how Sonny and Sydney responded to having to work at the sawmill say about each of them?
8. What influence do you think Sydney's relationship with Abe had in shaping his attitude as a minister?

Chapter 5:

9. Could Sam have handled Sonny drinking on the job differently? If so, how?

10. Does the relationship between siblings allow them to understand each other better than parents understand their children? Why or why not?

Chapter 6:

11. Did you find McKenzie's initial reaction to Sydney's call to ministry understandable?

12. What do you think Sydney would have done had McKenzie said she could not marry a minister?

Chapter 7:

13. Was Carrie wise in leaving Sonny and moving back to her parents' home with her children? Could she have chosen a better alternative?

14. What did Sonny telling Sydney he was his mother's favorite son say about how Sonny felt about himself. Could Sydney have responded to Sonny in a different way?

Chapter 8:

15. Do you think the relationship between McKenzie and Sydney is a genuine love story? If so, how?

16. In what ways does McKenzie know Sydney better than he knows himself?

Chapter 9:

17. How did you respond to McKenzie deciding to go back to teaching before talking to Sydney about it again?

18. What does Sydney's apparent acceptance and eventual support of her decision say about him and their relationship?

Chapter 10:

19. Was Harrison's attitude toward Sonny more helpful than Sydney's efforts to try to change him?
20. Do you find Sydney's conversations with his mother and father helpful or did they make things worse?

Chapter 11:

21. Were you sympathetic to Sarah's feelings about Sam's disregard for his health?
22. Was Sarah enabling Sonny's addiction or was she just being a mother helping her son?

Chapter 12:

23. Was Sydney trying to be "Mr. Fixer" in his relationship with Sonny? If so, was he making the problem worse?
24. When Leslie asked Sydney why he was crying, what did his response tell you about the kind of father he was trying to be? Would you have told her as much about Sonny's problem as he did?

Chapter 13:

25. Is Sally Barrett an example of people who are "invisible" in American society?
26. Were you surprised by the role McKenzie assumed in helping Sally Barrett? Why or why not?

Chapter 14:

27. Have you ever known or known about a Wanda type of person?
28. How well do you think Sydney handled the situation with Bobby and Ruth?

Chapter 15:

29. What does the way Sydney and Harrison respond to Sonny's fall caused by his drinking say about each of them, and with whom do you most identify?

30. How does Sam's sudden death change the family dynamics? Would Sydney's relationship to Sonny been different had Sam not died?

Chapter 16:

31. What did the "Sam stories" Sonny and Sydney shared on the way back to their mother's tell you about their relationship and their family?

32. What does Sonny's behavior when he is with his mother and brothers the day after Sam's death reveal about him that his alcohol addiction tended to hide?

Chapter 17:

33. What does Sydney losing control of his emotions in the church parking lot as he did with McKenzie earlier say about how he handles his emotions? Is this typical of men?

34. What experience(s) at Sam's funeral home visitation stood out to you the most? Why?

Chapter 18:

35. Do you think Sarah telling Sydney she doesn't need for him to move back to Castle Cove for her sake believable or is she just saying that?

36. What did Sydney's comments to the vestry members say about him as a person and a minister?

Chapter 19:

37. How do you think you would have responded to the experience Sydney had of meeting Jesse Hutchinson?

38. What did you think of Stephen's response to the feelings Sydney had after seeing Jesse Hutchinson again?

Chapter 20:

39. Do you think the "Atlas Syndrome" is a real thing and have you ever struggled with it?
40. Are men more likely to experience it than women?

Chapter 21:

41. What image of God did Sarah reveal when she told Sydney what was worrying her about Sonny dying?
42. Do you think Sydney's response to her was helpful? Why or why not?

Chapter 22:

43. Having read the book, what are some possible meanings the author had in mind when he titled the book, *A Brother's Peace*?

CPSIA information can be obtained
at www.ICGtesting.com
Printed in the USA
BVHW070955111022
649147BV00017B/1512

9 781632 933874